Texas, my Texas! How I love stories about my great state. Martha Rogers covers all of my favorite literary elements in *Winter Promise*—a quintessential Texas tale with a strong romantic thread, a touching family theme, and a heroine who loves books. Highly recommended!

—JANICE HANNA THOMPSON
AUTHOR OF *LOVE FINDS YOU IN GROOM, TEXAS*

Martha Rogers creates characters that live on once the last page is turned. Do not miss this endearing tale!

—KATHLEEN Y'BARBO-TURNER
AUTHOR OF *DADDY'S LITTLE MATCHMAKERS* AND
THE CONFIDENTIAL LIFE OF EUGENIA COOPER

If you enjoy romance, you'll LOVE *Winter Promise*. Martha Rogers delivers yet another excellent historical romance, full of remarkable characters and a pleasing storyline. You won't want to miss this sweet romance set in my favorite location, the Old West.

—MIRALEE FERRELL
AUTHOR OF *LOVE FINDS YOU IN SUNDANCE, WYOMING*

Winter Promise, the third installment in Martha Rogers's Seasons of the Heart series, continues the saga of frontier romance in the town of Porterfield, Texas. Rogers gives us a multifaceted heroine, but the reader's heart goes to the conflicted hero. Blaming himself for a tragic medical mistake in his past, he shuts himself off from people—and God. Rogers gently leads him to acceptance and a second chance at love.

—DARLENE FRANKLIN
AUTHOR OF *LONE STAR TRAIL* AND
CHRISTMAS AT BARNCASTLE INN

WINTER PROMISE

SEASONS
of the HEART
BOOK THREE

MARTHA ROGERS

REALMS

Most CHARISMA HOUSE BOOK GROUP products are available at special quantity discounts for bulk purchase for sales promotions, premiums, fundraising, and educational needs. For details, write Charisma House Book Group, 600 Rinehart Road, Lake Mary, Florida 32746, or telephone (407) 333-0600.

WINTER PROMISE by Martha Rogers
Published by Realms
Charisma Media/Charisma House Book Group
600 Rinehart Road
Lake Mary, Florida 32746
www.charismahouse.com

All Scripture quotations are from the King James Version of the Bible.

Cover design by Gearbox Studio
Design Director: Bill Johnson

Visit the author's website at www.marthawrogers.com.

Library of Congress Cataloging-in-Publication Data:
Rogers, Martha, 1936-
    Winter promise / Martha Rogers. -- 1st ed.
        p. cm.
    ISBN 978-1-61638-498-2 (trade pbk.) -- ISBN 978-1-61638-640-5 (e-book)
    I. Title.
    PS3618.O4655W56 2012
    813'.6--dc23
                                    2011035110

First edition

12 13 14 15 16 — 987654321
Printed in the United States of America

To Lane and Aimee Peterson
and their precious son,

Connor Allen Peterson,
January 18, 2011–February 3, 2011

*In his few short weeks on this earth, Connor touched
the lives of so many. His parents' faith during this
difficult time is a testimony of God's love
and support for His grieving children.*

*May Connor's spirit live on in the pages of
this book as Connor Allen Winston.*

Acknowledgments

To Shirley Dobson, librarian of Houston's First
Baptist Church, for her encouragement and support.

To my friends in First Place 4 Health, whose prayers,
love, and encouragement spur me on to write.

To my husband, Rex, who reads my books and
actually likes them and then tells others about them.

As always, to Debbie Marrie for her continued belief
in me and my stories.

To Deborah Moss and Lori Vanden Bosch for
their tremendous help in polishing and editing the
manuscripts. You make them rock, ladies.

To my agent, Tamela Hancock Murray,
who encourages me every step of the way.
Thanks for believing in me.

To my Lord and Savior,
without whom I could nothing.

Know ye that the Lord he is God;
it is he that hath made us and not
we ourselves; we are his people,
and the sheep of his pasture.

—Psalm 100:3

CHAPTER ONE

Porterfield, Texas, 1890

"*P*ORTERFIELD, NEXT STOP in ten minutes." The conductor's announcement sent the butterflies to dancing again in Abigail Monroe's stomach. Ever since they entered the state of Texas, her mind had flitted from one thing to the next in a series of images that blurred one into the other. What she remembered from her visit last spring had been enough to give her the desire to return as a permanent resident.

All around her passengers began gathering their belongings and preparing to leave the train. Mrs. Mabel Newton, who had accompanied her on the trip, adjusted her hat and picked up her handbag. "Well, your adventure will begin shortly."

Abigail grinned at the elderly woman. If it had not been for Rachel's aunt's desire to come west to visit her daughter, this trip may have been delayed indefinitely. "Thank you so much for coming with me, Aunt Mabel. You know how Father worried and didn't want me to travel alone." Abigail had fallen into calling the woman "Aunt Mabel" due to her close friendship with Rachel.

"And well he should have been. It isn't safe for a young woman of your standing to be crossing the country by train without an escort." She tilted her head toward Abigail, and the feathers on the black hat covering her gray hair quivered with the movement.

Her parents had at first refused to even consider such a move for their only daughter, but as they began to realize that she was almost twenty-two years of age, their objections lessened. They had been in Porterfield a few months earlier for the wedding of Daniel, Abigail's brother who came to Porterfield a year ago as the town's only attorney. Now he served as county attorney and prosecutor. When Mabel Newton had said she wanted to visit her daughter and niece, Father had finally agreed to let Abigail go.

Another factor in her decision to leave Briar Ridge had been Rachel Reed, her very best friend since childhood. Rachel's husband, Nathan, had taken Daniel's place as an attorney for the citizens of Porterfield, and now they too lived in the Texas town. As far as Abigail was concerned, God had orchestrated a great symphony of opportunities, and she had seized the score to become a part of the music.

"Aunt Mabel, do you think my plan for establishing a library is a sound one? Nathan and Daniel have found a building they think is suitable and will negotiate the purchase of it if I approve."

"Every town needs a library whether they know it or not.

Your brother and Nathan have good judgment, so the place must be about perfect."

A snicker escaped Abigail's throat. Daniel had always been her protector, and if the building suited him, it most definitely would suit her. She'd been so angry with him for leaving her behind in Briar Ridge last year. Of course he thought it was because she'd miss him, but it was really because she'd been jealous of his new adventure.

"I'm sorry things didn't work out for you and that young Wentworth. He seemed very interested in you when you and Rachel were in Boston."

Abigail had been interested too at first, but when she realized what all would be expected of her as the wife of a Wentworth, her interest cooled, and so had his. Now she had this new adventure ahead of her.

"It worked out for the best, but life became so dull in Briar Ridge without Rachel or Daniel that I could hardly bear it. I'd grown tired of entertaining with Mother and taking part on church committees. I want to do something on my own for a change."

"I see. So the fact that Porterfield has an overabundance of single men of all ages didn't have anything to do with your decision." Aunt Mabel's blue eyes sparkled with merriment.

Abigail's cheeks filled with heat. She truly wasn't interested in finding a husband anytime soon, even if other people thought so. The train whistle screeched through the early afternoon air. Abigail clutched her handbag and closed her eyes. *Please, Lord. Don't let this be a mistake. Help me to do the things I want to do for Porterfield with books and accept whatever else You have planned for me.*

The train stopped with a jolt that sent her forward with a lurch. She assisted Aunt Mabel with her bag then followed the older woman down the aisle. Dozens of people lined the platform waving as the train emptied itself of its load of passengers. As she stepped from the train car, Abigail scanned the crowd, and her heart leaped with joy when she spotted Rachel.

Rachel rushed forward and grabbed Abigail. "Oh, I'm so glad you're finally here. I thought the last three months would never end." Then she turned to hug her aunt. "I'm glad you're here too. With Seth, Sarah, Abigail, and you, I won't feel at all lonesome, not that I could the way the Muldoon clan has taken us in."

"When I met them at Daniel's wedding, I knew they would make all of you feel right at home. I'm anxious to talk with Mrs. Sullivan again." Abigail had been impressed with the boardinghouse and looked forward to living there.

"You'll get to see her soon enough. She's waiting for you and has your room all ready. The Muldoons are having us all for dinner at the ranch tonight."

That meant a quick study of the members of the Muldoon family would be in order before the trip out there. She hugged Rachel again and noted the glow in her eyes and face. "You must really be happy here with Nathan."

Before she could answer, Aunt Mabel stepped back and eyed Rachel. "My dear, are you in the family way?"

Heat flooded Rachel's cheeks, and she grinned. "Yes, I am, and so is…" She clapped her hand over her mouth. "Oh, I almost slipped. She wants to tell everyone herself at dinner."

Abigail ran through the list of possibilities. Kate? Erin?

Sarah again? Whoever it was, the baby would be welcomed by many loving aunts, uncles, and cousins.

Arms wrapped around her shoulders from the back, and she craned her neck to see who it could be. "Daniel!" She turned and hugged her brother. "Isn't this exciting? I'm here at last. We had a delightful train trip, and I can't wait to see your new house. And where's Kate?"

"Hey, slow down, little sister. No need to get it all out at once, but to answer your question, Doc Jensen and Elliot had an emergency at the infirmary, so she's there. She said she'd meet us wherever we were when she finished."

"I believe Aunt Mabel will be staying with Sarah and Donavan. At least that's what she plans on. Mrs. Sullivan said she has a room for me at the boardinghouse, so that's where I'm headed."

Daniel frowned and peered at her. "But Kate is hoping you'll live with us."

"Oh, Daniel, you two are newly married. Besides, I'd rather be closer to town so I can take care of the library." Kate and Daniel didn't live far from town, but her staying at the boardinghouse would be less of an intrusion on their new marriage.

They headed toward the cart where the baggage had been unloaded. Aunt Mabel busied herself with telling Rachel all about the trip cross-country. Abigail gazed at the town beyond the depot. Porterfield, Texas, would be her home now, and it looked just as friendly and nice as it had when she'd been here in the spring. A little more primitive than Briar Ridge, it still had all the stores and businesses one could need, including a delightful bakery.

Daniel heaved down a trunk and headed to his surrey with

it. Abigail walked along beside him and noted how the men stopped to stare. Her cheeks filled with heat. She may as well be on display in a store window.

"I didn't realize…never mind." She grinned and hop-stepped to keep up with her brother.

He pushed the trunk onto the floor behind the front seat. "By the way, the building Nathan and I have in mind for you is across the street from the infirmary. It's where the land offices were until the new courthouse opened. Now it's vacant, and it's just about the size you'll need for the library."

"I'm sure it will be fine if you and Nathan think so." She shook her head and giggled as they headed back for more of her things. "I still can't believe he and Rachel moved away from Connecticut. I always figured that when they did move, it would be to North Carolina, his home."

Another man had joined the group and helped unload Aunt Mabel's bags. She recognized him as one of Kate's older brothers she had met at the wedding. What was his name? Oh, yes, Cory, the lawman and only single male in the Muldoon family, as well as one of the most handsome men Abigail had ever met.

Daniel grabbed her arm and took her over to greet him. "You remember Cory, one of Kate's brothers."

Abigail smiled and extended her hand. "I certainly do. You and your brothers were quite the pranksters at the wedding."

Red tinged Cory's well-tanned face. His eyes, more green than blue, sparkled with humor. He pushed his white Stetson back on his head, revealing sandy red curls on his forehead, much like her brother's dark ones. "Guilty as charged, but we had to make up for not doing anything at Erin's. Didn't want to play tricks on the reverend."

Getting to know the Muldoon family would be fun, but getting to know Cory might be even more so. Perhaps she should reconsider her decision not to become involved with any of the eligible young men in Porterfield.

Elliot finished the stitches to close the wound on the balding head of Cyrus Fuller. He'd tripped coming out of the bank and fell, cutting his head on the edge of the boardwalk. Elliot used five stitches to close it. "There, now, Mr. Fuller. You'll be right as rain. Come back to see me in a few days and let me check on the stitches. Don't get it wet for a while."

He pushed back his rolling stool and picked up a bottle. "If you experience any pain, take a few drops of this and it should be all right, but don't take more than a few drops. Understand?"

The bank teller nodded and took the bottle. "I do, and I won't take it unless I really need it." He stood and grasped the edge of the bed for support.

Kate Monroe picked up the tray with the suturing supplies and equipment. "Aunt Mae will make certain you're comfortable, Mr. Fuller. She'll take good care of you."

The man's face, including his bald head fringed in gray, turned a bright red. "I'm sure she will, but I don't want her to go to any trouble."

Kate laughed. "It won't be any trouble. You know that."

Elliot turned to put the bandages back in the cabinet to hide his smile. Everyone in town knew Cyrus Fuller was sweet on Aunt Mae, and she didn't spurn his attention either. This was one patient he wouldn't have to worry about.

He walked with Mr. Fuller to the front door of the infirmary just to make sure the man was steady on his feet. At the door Cyrus shook Elliot's hand. "Can't thank you enough, Doctor Jensen. You did a fine job, and it hardly hurts at all. Tell your uncle I said hello." He lifted his hat to set it on his head, felt the stitches, and promptly put his hand down, still holding the hat.

Mr. Fuller took off in the direction of the boardinghouse, a few blocks down the street. Elliot continued to observe the man as he made his way home. Satisfied that he was all right, Elliot turned to walk back inside when he spotted Daniel in a buggy with a young woman beside him. Her golden brown hair peeked from beneath a black hat trimmed with yellow flowers, which matched the yellow dress she wore. She shifted her gaze toward him and locked with his. Something inside Elliot clicked, and a feeling he hadn't experienced in a long time came over him.

Elliot looked away and forced the emotion back into the deep recesses of his soul. He'd never let those feelings back into his life. They hurt too much.

A voice beside him caused him to blink his eyes and turn. "What did you say?"

Kate stood beside him. "I said that's Abigail, Daniel's sister. She was at his wedding, and she's come to live here in Porterfield. Remember I told you about her coming to set up a library for the town?"

"I remember." But he never expected her to be so pretty. He cleared his throat and hurried back into the infirmary. He needed to clean up the room where they'd just worked on Mr. Fuller, and it would help him forget the girl in yellow.

Kate's voice followed him. "If you don't have anything else for me, I'm going to run down to Aunt Mae's and meet up with Daniel and Abigail. I'll be there if you need me."

He waved her out. Kate was a good assistant. He and his uncle had come to depend on her for so many things at the infirmary. Doc should be back shortly, that is if everything went well at the Blalocks' place. Mrs. Blalock didn't usually have trouble with her deliveries, and as this was the fifth one, no problems were anticipated today.

Cleaning up didn't take long, and when he'd finished, Elliot went to the desk to fill out a report for Cyrus Fuller's medical file. The image of Abigail Monroe swam before his eyes. Porterfield sadly lacked young women of marrying age, so Elliot had no trouble staying away from what social life existed in town. He'd left Ohio with the vow that he'd never become involved with a young woman again. Everything had been fine until today when that little spark had jumped in his chest.

"I hear Cyrus Fuller had an accident. Get him all taken care of?"

Elliot jumped and dropped his pen. He greeted his uncle. "When did you come in? Yes, he's fine. How did things go at the Blalocks?"

His uncle grinned and set his bag on the desk. "Just like it should. This little boy decided to take longer than necessary, but he's good and healthy." He removed his hat and hung it on a hook then removed his coat. "I saw Daniel Monroe with a pretty young woman down at Mae's. Must be his sister from back east."

"It is. Kate was here to help with Cyrus, and then she left to go meet them."

"She's a pretty little thing from what I remember of last spring. It'll be nice to have a young woman like her around her for a change. You, Cory, and Philip Dawes are about the most eligible young men in town, and one of you ought to set your sights on her."

"There's a lot of men over at the sawmill, and many more on the ranches. That's why Frank Cahoon and Allen Dawes sent off for those brides. Remember?" So many other men in town would take an interest in Abigail and keep her busy. He'd managed to stay clear of any kind of relationship so far, and that was just the way he wanted it. Never again did he want to feel the pain he'd experienced in Cleveland.

CHAPTER
TWO

*D*ANIEL DROVE THE buggy down Main Street and pointed out the new businesses that had sprung up in town since it was named the county seat. That growth was what had sparked Abigail's idea for the library. A growing town like Porterfield needed one. Already the school had been divided into upper and lower grades, and that meant more children to check out books for reading and research.

They had already passed the building he'd picked for the library, the old land office building across from the infirmary. Daniel had pointed out the young doctor, Elliot Jensen, a most handsome young man. For a strange moment his gaze had locked with hers, and heat rushed through her body. Almost as tall as her brother, but not as broad, his face became embedded in her memory. How nice it would be to encounter him again. Getting sick or injured may not be such an unpleasant experience with him to treat her.

Then she turned her attention back to Daniel. She had not come to Porterfield to find a husband. No need to even let her thoughts wander off in that direction. Despite the handsome doctor and deputy, all her concentration would be on serving the town with the library.

They rolled down the street, and the boardinghouse came into view. Kate ran toward the buggy waving and calling Abigail's name. Kate's beautiful red hair gleamed in the sun with the bright rays creating a halo about her head. Envy crept into Abigail's soul. If only her mousy brown hair glowed with such beauty. The halo effect certainly suited Kate too. Everyone at the wedding had called her an angel because of her way with patients at the infirmary.

Abigail waved back at Daniel's wife and hopped down from the buggy as soon as it stopped. Kate wrapped her arms around Abigail, and Mrs. Sullivan ran out onto the porch to greet her. Such a warm welcome sent goose bumps to Abigail's arms. She already loved this town even after this short time.

Nathan and Rachel Reed pulled up in their buggy with Aunt Mabel seated in the back. Nathan helped Aunt Mabel down from her perch, and she headed straight for her daughter, Sarah, who had come out onto the porch with her husband, Donavan, holding their toddler son, Jeremy.

Kate hooked her arm into Abigail's and walked her up the sidewalk to the porch. "I'm so glad you're finally here. Daniel's been telling people about your library. Everyone's excited, especially Miss Perth and Miss Miller. Now they can have their students reading more. They're anxious to discuss a reading list with you."

The words rang like music to Abigail's ears. That's just the type of reception she'd hoped from the teachers. "The first load of books should be arriving next week, which should give us plenty of time to fix up the building Daniel found. I can't wait to see it."

Kate shaded her eyes from the sun and peered out to the buggy where Daniel unloaded the bags. "Daniel, when you get through with Abigail's belongings, take her down and show her the inside of the building you have in mind. I know she'd like to see it."

Abigail rocked on her tiptoes then back to her heels. "Oh, could you, Daniel? Please? I just saw the outside when we came through town, and I do want to see it better."

Nathan laughed and pounded Daniel on the back. "Got your work cut out for you. Guess we won't make it back to our offices this afternoon." He headed back to his buggy and called to Aunt Mabel, "I'll load these things onto Donavan's wagon so you can visit with them and play with your grandson before you head to their place. Daniel and I will bring the others out to the ranch and be there in time for supper."

Abigail drank in all the talk among the family members. The connections among them both amazed and delighted her. Three families, two from Connecticut and one from Texas, had blended together to form this noisy, happy group, and there were still more to come for supper. She needed to sit down later and sort through it all to get the relationships straight before then.

Daniel finished taking Abigail's belongings to Kate's old room in the boardinghouse. Then he helped her into the buggy and headed back to town and the old land office building.

At the building he stopped and jumped down to help her. "Well, here we are. I have the key, so we can go in. If you like it, the papers are drawn up and ready to sign. Mayor Tate will be glad to get that building out of the town's responsibility and into yours."

Abigail merely grinned. She already liked what she had seen on the outside. Two plate glass windows flanked the double doors. They'd be perfect for displays of new books.

Daniel unlocked the door and stepped aside for her to enter. She gasped at the size. It was much larger than she anticipated, but already she envisioned the walls lined with shelves filled with books. She clapped her hands then whirled around in a circle, spreading her arms out wide.

"Oh, I love it. It's absolutely perfect." She ran her hands over the counter toward the front. "This can be the checkout area for the library, and the tables and chairs for studying can be over there. " She pointed toward a corner. "And back over here is a perfect place for a reading corner."

If Andrew Carnegie set up libraries all over the United States, she could certainly contribute to having one here. The very idea of having her own library tingled her toes, and she pirouetted once again with her arms stretched out and her eyes closed.

Daniel laughed and caught her hand. "I'm glad to see you so happy about a bunch of books. I have my fill of them with all the new laws being made and the old ones to study."

"This is different. School children will be able to do research, and they'll be able to read for fun too."

"All right then. We'll get the papers signed tomorrow, and you'll have the keys to your own building." He dangled a ring of his own keys before her.

How good that sounded. She'd finally be doing something productive with her life. As the daughter of a wealthy investor, she'd had little to do except serve on committees in town and at church as well as help her mother with the endless number of luncheons and dinners she held. Once the library was opened and established, she could really contribute something of her own making to the town.

She followed Daniel from the building, still making plans in her head when she spotted movement across the street. The infirmary doors closed behind the same young man she had seen earlier, but this time an older man accompanied him.

Daniel hailed the duo, and they ambled across the street. Abigail's heart skipped a beat, and she sucked in her breath. The young man was even more handsome close up. His eyes were a shade of blue she couldn't quite describe, but they were darker than any blue sapphires she'd ever seen.

Elliot's knees shook as he followed his uncle across the street. He'd rather turn and head on down to their destination, but good manners meant they must stop and greet Daniel and his sister. He searched his brain for the name Kate had mentioned earlier. Oh, yes, Abigail.

They stopped at the edge of the boardwalk, and Elliot removed his hat, as did his uncle. He remained silent and let his uncle take the lead for conversation.

"I'm Doc Jensen, and you must be the sister Daniel has talked about so much in the past few months. I remember seeing you at the wedding, but didn't meet you then." He turned to Elliot. "This is my nephew, Elliot, and he's in practice with me."

Elliot's throat moved up and down as he swallowed hard. "Yes, I believe I saw you this afternoon when you first arrived in town. It's a pleasure to meet you." He'd been out of town when Kate and Daniel married. He would never have forgotten seeing a girl as pretty as this.

Her smile lit up her face. "It's a pleasure to meet both of you too. I hope I don't need your services anytime soon."

His uncle laughed at that and shook his head. "Just as long as you don't get into trouble like your brother here, you'll be fine."

"Only because he kidnapped a young girl to save her from the saloon owner. That's my brother, always willing to risk himself for others." She hugged his arm. "And I wouldn't have it any other way."

Elliot blinked and looked away from Abigail and toward the Graysons' store. He would not let himself be distracted by a pretty girl. He'd managed to escape both Kate and Erin Muldoon's charms, and now both of those ladies were safely married to fine young men. The other single women in town were much older, and that suited him just fine.

His uncle nudged him. "Isn't that right, Elliot?"

"I'm sorry, Doc, I didn't catch what you said."

His uncle chuckled. "I said I was glad we're going to have a library in town so I can read something other than medical journals."

"Oh, yes, that might broaden your horizons," Elliot teased.

Abigail smiled at him, and it flew straight into his heart. "Good, then I expect to see the two of you among my first patrons, especially since I'm right across the street."

Elliot stepped back. "Doc, it's best we get on down to Graysons' and pick up that shipment of medicine he ordered for us." He nodded to Abigail. "It was nice meeting you, Miss Monroe. I'm sure we'll see you quite often."

Doc placed his hat back on his head. "Yes, we must be going, and it's a pleasure to finally have you in Porterfield. You're just what this town needs." An impish grin crossed his face. "And I don't mean just the library."

Elliot shook his head. His uncle would be at it again. He and Aunt Maggie were of the same mind that it was time he found a girl and married. Every time a single girl came around, they got their hopes up. They'd never understood his reluctance to have a relationship.

Doc nudged him. "I say, you have a faraway look in your eyes. Does it have anything to do with that young lady we just met?"

Elliot shook his head. "No, it didn't." Well, in a way it did, but not in the way his uncle thought.

His uncle stopped and grasped Elliot's arm. "You're not thinking about Cleveland again, are you?" His blue eyes grew serious, as did his words. "Son, you have to put that behind you."

"That's what you say, but you didn't go through what I went through."

"I know, my boy. But did you ever read the psalm I told you about?"

"No, I haven't." To be honest, Elliot would have to admit he hadn't opened his Bible in many months. The Bible couldn't take away the hurt, so the words in it seemed pointless.

Doc shook his head and blew out his breath in a huff. "It would teach you something about life." He jerked his head toward the store. "C'mon, let's pick up our order."

Elliot didn't need the Scriptures to tell him about life. He was a doctor, after all, and had seen both life and death. Medicine was a science with truths he could rely on. Everything else was chaos and uncertainty.

CHAPTER THREE

ABIGAIL HUNG HER dresses in the wardrobe left behind by Kate. Such a nice room, and it was large and airy, a real necessity in the August heat. At least Daniel had warned her that the weather in Texas could be blazingly hot. She sat down at the desk by the window and drew a sheet of paper from her files listing the names of all the Muldoon and Winston families. Before going out to the Muldoon ranch for supper, she wanted to go over their relationships one more time.

Her brother had certainly married into a large family. She'd already met Cory again this afternoon, but Kate had three more brothers—Donavan, Brody, and Ian—along with their wives and children. Abigail barely remembered anyone from the wedding except for Donavan and Sarah. She knew them through their visits to Connecticut last year.

She studied the list. Since Kate married Daniel, that made her Abigail's sister by marriage, and thus, as Kate told her, a member of the Muldoon family. Her friend Rachel Reed's brother, Reverend Seth Winston, also married a Muldoon, the youngest daughter, Erin. So that made her best friend a part of the Muldoons also by marriage. Sarah was Rachel's and Seth's cousin, so they were related in two ways. Aunt Mae was Kate's aunt and insisted Abigail call her that too.

Abigail shook her head. The names and kinship were simply too confusing to try to straighten it all out. As many times as she'd tried, she still mixed them up. Forget the list. She'd enjoy the evening and learn names as she went.

She shoved the paper back into her satchel and changed into a simple skirt and shirtwaist for the ride out to the ranch for supper. All but a few of the dresses she usually wore still hung in her wardrobe back in Connecticut. The dressmaker in Briar Ridge had made up more suitable garments for the climate as well as the lifestyle. She much preferred the new, more comfortable clothing over the old.

After brushing out her hair, she pulled it back and fastened it at the crown with a tortoise shell comb. Kate had said not to worry with a fancy hat and had given her a plain straw one to wear. The wide brim would protect her face from the sun without the extra burden of a parasol. Satisfied with her appearance, Abigail followed the sound of voices coming from the parlor.

"There you are." Kate greeted her with a hug. "Daniel has the buggy all ready for us. Aunt Mae made arrangements with Annie's Kitchen to have supper for her other boarders tonight since this is a special occasion and she doesn't want to miss it."

"I wondered what they were going to do if she went with us. It's nice she has someone she can depend on to provide when she's not here."

Kate hooked her arm with Abigail's. "Yes, it is. Annie's

hasn't been open long, and the cooking isn't quite as good as Aunt Mae's, but none of them complained because this is such a special occasion for her."

They strolled outside to where Aunt Mae already sat waiting for them. She wore a navy blue hat with a blue bird attached among a few flowers. When Aunt Mae shook her head at them, the bird almost appeared to take flight. "It's about time. Ada will be pacing the floor wondering where we are. Sarah and her mother have already gone ahead with Donavan, and so have Rachel and Nathan."

"I'm sorry, Aunt Mae, I didn't realize I was taking so much time." Abigail climbed up into the seat beside the older woman. "I was trying to get all the names straight."

Aunt Mae's laugh floated in the breeze as Daniel clicked the reins and moved the surrey forward. "Honey, it'll take a lot more time than you ever thought to get all these people straightened out. The main thing to remember is that we're all family now, and you'll get to know everyone soon enough."

Aunt Mae chattered away about her nieces and nephews and their offspring all through the three miles to the ranch. Although already six in the evening, the sun still bore a great amount of heat as it pressed on overhead. The slight breeze from earlier no longer tickled the leaves and made them dance. At least the stillness kept the dust kicked up by the horses' hooves near the ground and not in their faces.

Such wide open spaces here in Texas! As she gazed at her new surroundings, pleasure spread through Abigail from head to toe. Cattle dotted the fields on one side of the road, and farmland graced the other side, giving life to the landscape.

Porterfield was now her home, and she would love every minute of it.

Nathan and Rachel Reed's buggy appeared not far ahead, so they'd be arriving about the same time. Abigail braced herself for all the hugs and greetings that would be forthcoming.

The Muldoon ranch came into view, and Abigail remembered it from her previous trip. The wraparound porch with its rocking chairs and swing offered a peaceful place for visiting and catching up on news. Children played in the yard with several adults sitting or standing on the porch. They all waved as the surrey rolled to a stop.

The ladies came out to greet them, and the men handled the horses. Sarah hugged Abigail first. "Welcome to the ranch. I'll stick close by and help you with all the names. It can be quite overwhelming at first, but you'll love them all."

"I can believe that since I already love everyone I've met." She stepped back from Sarah and into the embrace of Ada Muldoon, matriarch of the clan.

"Welcome to the Circle M, Abigail. I'm so glad you decided to come out here to live and give us that new library. It's something the town has sorely needed."

"Thank you, Mrs. Muldoon. I hope it's welcomed by everyone else as it has been by your family."

She waved her hands. "Oh, pshaw, it will be. Don't worry about that none. And please call me Ma. You're Kate's sister now, and that makes you like one of my own, or if that doesn't feel right, call me Ada, but none of that Mrs. Muldoon business, you hear?"

Abigail laughed. "Ada it will be, and thank you for having us to dinner tonight."

"Well, I figured the sooner you got to know everyone, the more comfortable you'd be around us all. We can get a might noisy sometimes."

That Abigail could tell from the din surrounding them now. The squeals from the children mingled with the deeper voices of the adults to create music that only loving families produced, and she thanked the Lord that she could now be a part of it.

Ada left with two of the other women and Aunt Mae to go in and get supper on the table. The rest mingled on the front porch and in the yard. Erin, Kate's younger sister and Seth's wife, sauntered over. Abigail's eyes opened wide at the sight of the obvious bump on her belly. Erin must be the other one Rachel mentioned earlier. Two more babies to add to the Muldoon family.

Erin now smiled at Abigail. "Welcome! Seth, Rachel, and Daniel have told us so much about you. It's wonderful to think that the four of you grew up together and now you're here in Texas, so far from your home."

"Rachel didn't say a word about you expecting a wee one. When is it due?"

"Right around Christmas time, and Ma's really excited about this little one. We asked Rachel not to say anything because we wanted to surprise you. We have another one that will be announced at supper tonight. No one else knows but Rachel and me. She was waiting for a special occasion to say anything, and this is it."

So, Erin wasn't the one Rachel meant. Abigail gazed at the other women. Which of them would it be? Maybe Kate? But she didn't have "that look" as Aunt Mabel called it. Before she could speculate further, Ada called out for everyone to gather around the table inside.

Where in the world would they put all these people? The number of adults now added up to at least nineteen if her math was correct. That's as many as some of her mother's dinner parties, and this was all family. When she stepped through the door to the house, she spotted a long table set with nine chairs and two high chairs. Another table sat a few feet away ready for the younger ones.

When they all gathered around, Cory joined his nieces and nephews. At Abigail's raised eyebrow, he shrugged. "I volunteer to corral them. They think it's fun to eat with a deputy, and it helps me keep them in line." He winked and sat down. Immediately the younger ones quit jostling and grinned at their uncle.

Abigail's spirits sank a bit. She had secretly hoped to sit by Cory during dinner. She glanced at the children and noted their adoring looks at their uncle. She actually envied them and wished she could join their table.

Callum Muldoon welcomed Abigail to the family table and stood to offer the prayer, but Sarah raised her hand and stood. "Before we say grace, I have an announcement." She beamed with delight as she reached for her husband's hand. "Donnie and I will be parents again come early next spring."

Of course, Abigail should have seen it, but she'd been so busy at the boardinghouse she hadn't noticed. Aunt Mabel jumped up and ran to hug her daughter, and the others all offered congratulations. Abigail glanced at Rachel, who winked. Sarah had even fooled her mother. What a wonderful family, and Abigail was delighted to now be a part of it.

Callum's grin grew as big as his range land, and he sent up a prayer of thanksgiving for not only the food but also the new lives coming into the Muldoon clan. When the blessing ended, conversation flowed, and food passed from one family member to the next. Never had Abigail seen so much food on a table at one time. At Mother's dinner parties, servants brought in and served each course one at a time, with only the individual plates of food set in front of each person.

She filled her plate with beef, potatoes, and vegetables along with freshly baked bread. The first bite rested on her tongue, and the savory flavor of the tender beef gave proof that all of the food would taste as good as it looked and smelled.

She sat back to enjoy both the delicious meal and the animated company that filled the room with laughter, love, and fellowship.

Cory bantered with his young charges, but his gaze wandered to the main table and Abigail. Now there was one pretty little lady. But when he became a lawman, he'd vowed never to put a woman through the worries and dangers of his profession. Miss Monroe would make someone a good wife someday, but she just couldn't be his.

Then she happened to glance his way, and their gazes locked for a moment that sucked the breath clean out of Cory. He swallowed hard and finally looked away. Something had happened in that moment, and if he wasn't careful, all he'd vowed would disappear in a blink of the eye.

He turned his attention back to the children at the table.

His oldest nephew regarded him with one eye squinted closed and an eyebrow raised.

"What's the matter, Patrick. Something in your eye?"

An impish grin filled his face. "I saw you looking at Miss Abigail. You sweet on her or somethin'?"

Heat filled Cory's face. Trust the twelve-year-old to notice. "No, I'm not. We just happened to look at each other at the same time."

His ten-year-old niece giggled and held her fingers over her mouth. Cory put on his sternest sheriff look and stared at each of them. Neither said another word, but nothing could suppress the grins on their faces.

Cory's insides churned with the knowledge that Patrick had come close to the truth that had begun to dawn on Cory. The problem was what he was going to do with it.

The aroma of Aunt Maggie's fried chicken drifted in from the kitchen. Elliot stretched his arms above his head and breathed deeply. He imagined what she'd prepared to go with the meat and could already taste fresh green beans, mashed potatoes, creamy gravy, and melt-in-his-mouth biscuits.

One of the perks about being a doctor in a farm and ranch community was the good food patients liked to give them. Most of the time it was in payment for services, but sometimes it was just a thank-you even though the bill had been paid. And Aunt Maggie made good use of the produce and meat they were given. Not only a good cook but also an excellent baker, Aunt Maggie kept the cookie jar and bread box full, and the treats beckoned when hunger pangs attacked.

He closed the book he studied. It contained some of the latest innovations in medicine, and he planned to do everything he could to keep up with them. His uncle did the same. Doc even had the latest in sterilization equipment and kept the clinic as clean as possible with disinfectants and constant hand washing. One thing Doc insisted on, they all had to wash their hands with disinfectant between patients. He was a firm believer in the recommendations from Joseph Lister. They even had to remove aprons or shirts if a patient was highly contagious. Kate kept several aprons available for just that reason.

Elliot gazed around his room. The striped wallpaper had begun to peel a bit at the corners, and the carpet had grown thin, but in another month or so they'd all move into the new house down the street, and renovations to turn this building into a six-room hospital would begin. He'd been living with his aunt and uncle above the infirmary for the time he'd been in Porterfield and had grown to love the place, but moving would be good for Aunt Maggie.

She called to him now. "Elliot, supper's ready."

He pushed back from his chair and went to the washstand to clean up. A few minutes later he joined his aunt and uncle for the meal. Aunt Maggie set the food on the table, and he sniffed with a deep breath. "Hmm, I've smelled that apple pie baking all afternoon. It's enough to make a man forget what he's doing."

Doc laughed and patted his stomach. "Yes, sir, the old stomach's been rumbling since after lunch."

Aunt Maggie waved her hand at both of them. "There's plenty, and you can have as much as you want…both of you, but I'd go easy on the fried food, Nehemiah." She pointed a finger at him.

"We'll see about that. Now c'mon and sit. Food's getting cold."

She sat and Doc said grace. No one spoke for a few minutes as plates were filled and bowls passed around. This was Elliot's favorite time of day with his aunt and uncle. With their children all grown and moved away from Porterfield, they had taken him in like a son, for which he had been most thankful.

Although Elliot had the skill to be an excellent doctor, he'd nearly quit after the tragedy in Cleveland. If not for his uncle, he'd be holed up somewhere lost and alone. God had abandoned him at the time Elliot needed Him most, but Uncle Nehemiah had saved his life.

"I talked with Mae Sullivan today, and she certainly had great words of praise for Daniel Monroe's sister. She arrived this afternoon."

Aunt Maggie's voice snapped him back to attention. He didn't comment for fear of allowing his emotions to color his voice.

His uncle sipped his coffee and peered over the rim at Elliot. "Yes, Elliot and I met them over at the vacant land office. Seems Daniel and Nathan have made arrangements to purchase the space for a library. She's quite pretty and about as petite as Daniel is big."

Elliot cringed at the apt description of the young woman he'd met. He recalled her eyes as dark brown as the plain coffee his uncle now drank, and her golden brown hair enhanced her creamy complexion. He almost choked on a biscuit. He hadn't thought of a girl in those terms since Cleveland. Best to keep his mind on the food before him.

"It's nice to have another single young woman in town, don't you think, Elliot, since there hasn't been one since Kate married Daniel."

Elliot kept his head bowed over his food as he answered his aunt. "I imagine there will be a lot more of the boys from over at the sawmill visiting once they learn she's here." He glanced up and managed a grin. "I would also imagine her library will be quite busy on Saturdays." If he thought of her only in terms of being a librarian, maybe his mind wouldn't dwell on the fact that she was also very pretty.

Aunt Maggie shook her head. "Seems to me that you'd take notice yourself. It's time for you to find a wife. You're too fine a young man to be spending your life living with an old aunt and uncle."

Doc snorted. "Speak for yourself, Maggie dear. I'm certainly not old."

She swatted at his arm. "Oh, you know exactly what I mean, you old coot."

His uncle's eyes sparkled as he caught her hand. "Yes, I do, but for the record, you're a long way from being old." He wiggled his eyebrows and grinned.

Elliot swallowed hard. So much love flowed between these two. It reminded him of what he could have had if things had been different. He gulped down a swig of tea. Right now he was satisfied with the way things were. Miss Monroe may be attractive, but he preferred to keep his heart under lock and key—where it would be safe.

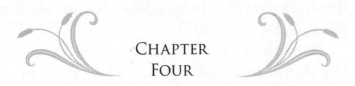

CHAPTER
FOUR

*M*ONDAY MORNING ABIGAIL walked out of Daniel's office with the keys to the new library. She had so much to do in order to be ready to open on time. She'd spent Friday getting settled into her room at the boardinghouse, and Saturday she looked at lettering options for the new sign on the door. She couldn't wait until her books arrived. She skipped down the sidewalk with anticipation filling her heart.

Daniel trailed behind chuckling. "If I'd known you were going to be this excited, I'd have made sure you came out here earlier."

"Oh, no, this is perfect. With school opening soon, I'll have things up and running for the children to check out books in no time. Miss Perth, Miss Miller, and I will be meeting in the next day or two to go over a list for them. What I don't have I'll order." She pirouetted again with her arms spread out to her sides. A few grins and smiles greeted her as she twirled.

He caught up with her and hugged her. "You know, just

being around you makes my heart glad. You were always fun to be around, and now I realize how much I missed you."

Abigail cast a glance at him with one eyebrow raised. "Hah. How could I have been much fun when you were always making my life miserable?"

He reached up and tweaked a strand of hair. "Because you were always a good sport. You and Rachel laughed a lot and always saw the good in life, especially people."

"You're right about Rachel. Look at how she believed in Nathan, even when he was gone for so long." Her best friend had seen something in Nathan that prevailed in spite of his challenging past. "Now look at them. Married and looking forward to their first little one."

Daniel chuckled as she unlocked the door to her library. "You must hand it to the Muldoon family. They're doing their part to populate Porterfield."

Abigail grinned and nodded, wanting to ask when he and Kate would be added to that list, but that was a private matter, and she wouldn't be nosy even though he was her brother. Then she stepped over the threshold and forgot everything but what she wanted to do with the space. Consisting of three rooms, two small rooms in the back, and one large one in front, she had space for an office, storage, and the library.

A railing divided the front space into two parts. She ran her hand across the wood. "If we move the railing over here, it will make a perfect checkout area for the library. But I want to be sure to save what we remove. I have an idea about how I might want to use it later." She strode across to the windows.

"Mr. Hinkle said at church yesterday he'd come over and start on the lettering for the windows soon as I give him the word. If he can start after dinner today, that would be wonderful. My crates and some furniture should be arriving on the afternoon train. Can I get you and Nathan to help with that?"

"I think so. I won't be very busy today, but I'll have to check with Nathan." He glanced around the space. "You know, Erin helped me with my office, and I'm sure she'd be glad to offer some suggestions to you."

"Hmm, I'd like that. I'll run over to the parsonage later and talk with her. She's really a sweet girl and seems to be perfect for a minister's wife." She laid her finger against her cheek. "Even though they're both young, they do have a maturity about them that is rare. Seth's sermon yesterday touched my heart. He's so like his father, and I loved his message." The senior Reverend Winston, Seth's father, had been her pastor for almost her whole life in Briar Ridge.

She hooked her arm through Daniel's. "I really worried about missing Briar Ridge, but everyone was so nice and friendly yesterday. They all made me feel welcome and were really interested in the library. I'm not going to miss Briar Ridge near as much as I feared I might."

"I hope you'll be happy here because I am delighted you decided to come. It's a wonderful thing you're doing with your inheritance from Grandfather." He pulled a pocket watch from his vest. "Enough chatting, Aunt Mae will be serving the noon meal soon, and we'd best get you back there so you won't be late."

"Then let's lock up and head that way. Oh, but first I need to see Mr. Hinkle." Abigail strode out the door and onto the boardwalk. Such a beautiful day, even if it was warmer than she'd anticipated. Perspiration dotted her brow, and her dimity blouse clung to her shoulders. Even her small hat weighed a ton atop her upswept hair.

They crossed the street, if she could call it that. Even though constant traffic had smoothed the ruts, her shoes and dress hem still kicked up dust as she walked. She gave the infirmary only a cursory glance and headed for Mr. Hinkle's little shop a few doors away.

When she entered, the bell tinkled overhead to announce her arrival. Mr. Hinkle looked up from the drawing board where he sat hunched over his latest endeavor. He grinned widely and hopped up to greet her. He wore a visor to protect his eyes from the bright glow of a lamp on his desk. "Hello, Miss Monroe. I take it you're ready for your window signs."

"Yes, I am. I still want the green and gold lettering I admired Saturday. Will that be a problem?"

"No, ma'am, it sure won't." He reached beneath the counter. "Got the perfect color right here, and some lettering samples for you to see." He set a bottle of green ink before her and pulled out a piece of heavy paper with sample letters on it.

He was right. It was exactly the shade she'd had in mind. An emerald green for the main part of the letters and then an outline of gold were just as she imagined. "Oh, it's wonderful, Mr. Hinkle. You do beautiful work. When can you start on it?"

"First thing in the morning. I'll be finished with this other project this evening, so you're next in line."

Not this afternoon, but it would do. "Thank you. I'll be over there working on the inside." She extended her hand. "Until tomorrow."

He shook her hand and grinned. "It'll be my pleasure, Miss Monroe."

With that errand accomplished, she joined Daniel on the boardwalk for their walk to the boardinghouse.

Elliot couldn't help but notice the activity across the street. He had dried his hands and stared out at Daniel and Abigail as they crossed the street. When her glance had cut in the direction of the infirmary, he had jumped back from the window and hoped the glare from the sun would shield him.

They had gone down a ways and into Mr. Hinkle's shop. She looked almost like a young girl beside her brother, who stood well over six feet in height. Daniel and Cory Muldoon were both tall and broad across the shoulders. They made Elliot, two inches under six feet and slender, look much smaller, but then Frank Cahoon outdid both of those boys.

He arranged instruments on a tray and tried to erase the image of Abigail Monroe from his mind, but she persisted in waltzing in without the least bit of warning. The white dress with green flowers she wore today had flounced about her feet as she walked beside her brother. Elliot imagined he could circle her waist with both hands and have his fingers touching each other. To stay that tiny, she must skip a few meals, and that wasn't healthy. But her rosy cheeks and bright eyes didn't have the appearance of someone starving herself in vanity.

He blew out his breath and shook his head. What was wrong with him? He'd steered clear of all the young women in Porterfield thus far without even thinking about it, but Abigail had pricked a hole in that wall around his heart. He had to be careful, or she'd start poking and scraping until it broke through completely.

"You about through straightening that tray of instruments? You've been standing there a good ten minutes just moving them around."

Elliot jumped and dropped one of the clamps. "Oh, sorry, Doc, I guess I was distracted."

His uncle's eyes twinkled behind his wire frame glasses. "Hmm, could it be that pretty little gal I saw across the street a little while ago?"

Heat filled Elliot's face. "No, I was just thinking about the patients we saw this morning." He'd say anything to keep his uncle from getting any ideas about Miss Monroe.

"Not much different from any other morning. A few cuts, scrapes, sore throat, and mashed thumb. Nothing I can see to worry about." He strolled over to the pegs beside the door, retrieved his hat, and set it on his head. "It's about lunchtime. How about we make a visit to the boardinghouse since Maggie is over in Carthage visiting her sister?"

Elliot hesitated. Going to the boardinghouse meant he would most likely see Miss Monroe again since she lived there. He debated the pros and cons until his uncle shook his head and left the building.

Elliot jumped into action and ran after Doc. "Wait up. I'm hungry, and Mrs. Sullivan's food is about as good as it gets when Aunt Maggie's not cooking."

"Good. I was beginning to think you might be sick or something yourself." But his smirk and the lilt to his voice evidenced his true thoughts.

If Miss Monroe so much as glanced his way, he'd have to…to what? Be polite and speak to her was his only choice if he didn't want to appear rude.

When they entered the dining area, she was already seated beside Cory at the boarder's table. Doc waved at Mrs. Sullivan and took a seat at one of the extra tables set out for those who made reservations early for the noon and evening meals. When Aunt Maggie went over to visit her sister and mother once a month, Doc always made sure he had a place at the boardinghouse.

Once seated, Elliot glanced up and realized Abigail sat directly in his line of vision. After Cory said grace, everyone filled their plates from the family-style platters on each table. Abigail's musical laughter rang out. Apparently Cory must have made a humorous remark as the deputy's face flushed bright red.

He stabbed a piece of meat. Why should her laughing and talking to Cory be of any concern to him? He stuffed the meat into his mouth and chewed. He had to get his mind off Miss Monroe. "This pot roast is just like Aunt Maggie's. Wonder if they use the same recipe."

Doc lifted the napkin tucked into his collar and swiped at a dab of gravy on his chin. "It wouldn't surprise me any. Those two women are always exchanging recipes. That is, all except a few. Maggie won't tell anyone her secret ingredient in her chocolate cake, and Mae won't tell anyone her secret for that wonderful pound cake she makes." He leaned over in a conspiratorial manner. "If you ask me, I think she uses buttermilk instead of sweet milk, but you never heard it from me."

Elliot shrugged and gulped down a swig of sweet tea. His knowledge of cooking was limited to making decent coffee. He certainly didn't know what difference the kind of milk used would make. He ate food to enjoy it, not analyze what was in it.

As hard as he tried, he couldn't keep his gaze away from Abigail Monroe. Her voice carried to his table as she described some of what she wanted to do with her new building.

"Like I said, she's a pretty little girl."

Elliot's fork clattered to his plate. "Who is?"

"Miss Monroe. As if you weren't sitting here staring at her."

Heat flooded his face. Had he been that obvious? He'd have to be much more careful in the future. She was simply another young woman like any other. If she wanted a husband, the town held plenty of men who would be interested, and it looked like Cory was already one of them.

A commotion at the door grabbed his attention. Miss Miller, one of the teachers at the school, raced into the room. "Doc, you have to come quick. It's Sally Davis. The boys were playing ball, and she got hit in the face. I think her nose is broken, and she's bleeding something awful. Miss Perth is with her now."

Doc jumped up from the table with Elliot close behind. They followed her outside and up three blocks to the schoolhouse. Sally sat on the steps with Miss Perth beside her holding a bloodied rag to Sally's face. Three boys, including Sally's brother Pete, stood to the side with guilt and fear written on their faces.

Doc examined her then pulled out his clean handkerchief. He replaced the blood-soaked one with it and turned to Elliot. "I want to take her down to the infirmary and check her out good. Can you carry her that far?"

Elliot picked her up. Despite his wiry frame, he was strong and held her with ease.

Miss Miller grabbed his arm. "Bring her over here. I have the wagon hitched up. It'll be faster."

Doc thanked her and helped Elliot place Sally in the wagon. Miss Miller had even found a blanket and folded it to make a cleaner place for Sally to sit. Elliot climbed in back with her and helped hold her head and the cloth to stop the bleeding, and his uncle drove the wagon.

Tears streaked her bloodied face. "It hurts, Doc Elliot."

He wiped away the tears with his own handkerchief. "I know it does, but Doc Jensen will get you fixed up in no time." He remembered the girl from last fall when her family's home had burned and injured her parents and younger brother and sister. She had been so brave then and had helped Kate Muldoon care for little Carrie and Lenny until her parents recovered.

By the time they reached the infirmary, Sally's parents were there to see what had happened. Doc took over and had the situation well in hand, so Elliot washed up and went back to the boardinghouse to retrieve the remains of the meal that had been interrupted. Mrs. Sullivan always took care of the doctors, as this wasn't the first time a meal had been interrupted by an emergency.

The dining room had emptied of all its patrons, and Mrs. Sullivan cleared the tables. She grinned when she spotted him. "Have your food all ready in a basket for you. I kept it warm on the back of my stove."

She disappeared into the kitchen, and Elliot gazed around the room. At least he didn't have to encounter Abigail Monroe again. He could get on back and help Doc clean up then finish eating.

"Oh, Doctor Jensen, how is the girl?"

He turned to see Abigail standing near the stair landing. So much for not having to encounter her again. "She's fine." He moistened his lips. "People around here call me Doc Elliot and my uncle Doc Jensen so as not to get us confused."

"Well then, Doc Elliot, I'm glad she's going to be all right." She brushed past him, leaving a scent of rosewater as she did so. "I'm going to help Aunt Mae with cleaning up. She saved your meal for you."

All he could do was nod. If Mrs. Sullivan didn't hurry up with the basket, he might have to leave without it. He'd miss the rest of his meal if he had to just so he could get as far away from Abigail Monroe as possible.

CHAPTER
FIVE

ON THURSDAY, ABIGAIL sat in the middle of the room in the only chair she had surrounded by boxes and crates delivered on the Wednesday afternoon train. Since Monday, she'd swept and cleaned until the wood floors shone almost like new. Frank Cahoon and his bride, Suzanne, had stopped in to help. On Wednesday Frank had moved the railing to the positions she wanted, and Suzanne had helped clean the plate glass windows and doors on the inside.

The willingness of everyone to help thrilled Abigail. It added to her excitement as she tore into boxes filled with books mostly for the library. She picked up each volume and caressed the cover before setting it in a stack to be catalogued and shelved. Later this evening she'd finish writing down the information for her card catalog and for the bindings of the books.

"Hi. You need any help?"

Abigail glanced up and grinned. "Kate! Come on in. I'm

glad to see you. All these boxes and crates need to be unpacked. I've started with the books that came today."

Kate strolled across the room, her gaze darting about the space. "You've done a great job here. It's as clean as Doc keeps the infirmary. How'd you like the surprise Nathan and Rachel had for you?"

Abigail eyed the floor-to-ceiling bookshelves lining one wall. Three of them had been installed this morning, and three more were to be delivered the day after tomorrow. "I love it. She didn't say a word about it in all the letters we exchanged in the past few months. They fit perfectly."

Kate laughed and ran her hand across a shelf. "Lester Williams did a fine job building them. You might want to check out his store for some other items."

"I meant to go down to his shop today, but I haven't had a lick of time to do anything but fix things up here. I'll have to work extra hard to have everything ready for my grand opening on Saturday." Nathan and Daniel had both promised to help, as had Frank and Cory. She prayed they wouldn't forget.

Kate waved a hand toward the windows. "I see Mr. Hinkle got the signs done. They really spruce up your windows and make this look like a real library."

Indeed, the lettering he'd done was just about perfect. He concentrated so hard on his work that he hadn't even heard her when she'd offered him a cool drink of lemonade. "I love what's he done, and he's so meticulous."

Kate opened a box of books. "How are you sorting these? By alphabetical order?"

"No, the ones I sent from home are packed by subject

matter so it'll be easier to catalog them tonight. The other ones we ordered have to be put in the correct stacks. Here, I'll show you."

Abigail lifted a few of the books and showed Kate the stacks for subjects like science, biographies, arts, and history. The fiction books were set aside for later as they were the easiest to sort and label.

They worked in silence for a few minutes, but it was a companionable silence that filled Abigail with joy at sharing her work with her sister by marriage.

Kate stood and arched her back. "I'm not use to sitting on the floor. Think I'll go borrow a chair from the infirmary."

"Oh, my, I didn't even think about that." Abigail jumped up. "Here, you use this one for a while. I want to check out how the books look on the shelves anyway. I guess I also need to find the crates with the chairs I ordered and get Daniel to open them for me so I'll have them available for seating."

"OK." She sat on the chair and opened another box. "By the way, what do you think of the men you've met so far?"

Abigail tilted her head and peered at Kate. "I'm not sure. I haven't really been around them enough to form an opinion one way or the other, and I'm really not interested now because I want to get the library established first."

"I think Cory and Elliot Jensen are about the two most eligible in town, especially since I think one of the hands at the ranch is interested in Jessica Miller. Of course there's lots of others on the ranches and over at the sawmill. You'll get to meet a bunch of them on Friday night for this month's town social, and you'll have ample opportunity at church gatherings as well."

Kate then laughed. "Listen to me. I hated it when Erin and Sarah fussed about marrying me off, and here I am trying to do the same to you."

"I don't mind. I look forward to the socials. Cory and Dr. Jensen are both very nice, and your brother is quite handsome. He seemed to enjoy his nieces and nephews too."

Kate laughed. "Cory certainly has a way with them." She sent a sidelong glance to Abigail. "He's ambitious too. He wants to become a full sheriff or even a marshal one of these days."

"Why doesn't he join the Texas Rangers that I've heard so much about?" She pictured him as a Ranger fighting battles with outlaws, and it sent a little smile to her heart.

"He likes it here in Porterfield. Sheriff Rutherford will be ready to retire in a few years, and Cory would most likely be voted in to take his place. No one's opposed Rutherford so far, and it doesn't seem likely anyone would run against Cory."

Ambition, good looks, and well liked. What more could she ask for in a man? Even if she didn't plan on marrying anytime soon, Cory would be fun to have as an escort. "I must say he's nothing like any other men I've met, either here or in Connecticut."

Kate made no comment, but she grinned in that knowing way Abigail had come to recognize in the few days she'd been in town. Most likely Daniel would hear about this conversation and have a few words to share on the subject as well. Big brothers could be a tease.

A few minutes later Kate stood and stretched. "I have to go back to the infirmary to check on a patient there and then I'll head home. It's getting on to suppertime."

Abigail glanced at the watch pinned to her shirtwaist. "Why, so it is. Where has the time gone? I'm not nearly through the list of things I need to do." She sighed and walked back to the stack of boxes. "Looks like I'll need to come back this evening and work some more."

"Daniel and I can come to help if you need us." Kate headed for the door.

"Thank you. I'll let you know."

Kate hurried across the street, and Abigail surveyed the chore ahead of her. It'd take at least another day to get them all unpacked and sorted and then several more days getting labels made with the decimal system.

Right now, however, hunger for one of Aunt Mae's good suppers beckoned. She picked up her handbag, retrieved the key, and stepped through the door. After locking it securely she turned to walk away. Suddenly she found herself falling face forward. A sharp pain pierced her ankle and shot up her leg.

She winced and pulled her skirt aside to observe her foot. The toe of her shoe had caught against a piece of loose board and caused her to trip. She bit her lip against the pain in her ankle and tried to stand, but that caused even more agony. She clung to a post in front of the building. Footsteps pounded across the street.

"Abigail! Are you hurt?" Cory jumped up onto the boardwalk and grabbed Abigail around the waist.

"I'm not sure. I tripped over a loose board and fell. Now my ankle hurts something terrible."

"Sit here on the step and let me have a look."

Abigail eased down and lifted her skirt. Heat infused her face as Cody unlaced her shoe. "It's beginning to swell. I'm getting you over to the infirmary so the doctor can examine it." He lifted her up to one foot and put his arm around her waist.

With her shoe in one hand and pink in her cheeks, Abigail placed the other hand on Cory's back and limped across the street on one foot, berating herself for her clumsiness.

Elliot glanced out the window and spotted Cory helping Miss Monroe across the street. The young woman appeared to be injured. Concern as well as a snip of jealousy shot through him, and he raced through the door to help.

He grabbed Abigail's free arm and draped it across his shoulder. His arm slid around her waist above Cory's. A little shock of surprise bolted through him when he realized he didn't feel thick stays beneath her garment. His hand burned with the contact, but she needed to get off that ankle.

"What happened to you, Miss Monroe?"

Her cheeks flushed red, and she bit her lip. "I tripped on a loose board and fell flat on my face. I feel so silly."

"Nothing silly about that." He helped her up the steps and into the infirmary. "Let's get you on the table over there, and I'll take a look at that ankle. Thank you, Cory; I'll take over from here."

Cory released Abigail and stood back as Doc Elliot helped her up onto the examination table. "I don't think it's broken, but it had already begun to swell, so that's why I took off her shoe." He glanced around the room. "Where's your uncle?"

"Very good thinking." Cory's action with the foot probably saved having to cut the shoe from Abigail's foot. "Doc's over at the Davis place. Carrie and Pete came home from school not feeling well, so he went to check on them. Now let me see what we have here, Miss Monroe."

Kate entered the examining room and rushed to Abigail's side. "What in the world happened to you?"

Abigail lifted her skirt again and explained to Kate while Doc Elliot examined a very red and swollen ankle. She had certainly twisted it without a doubt, but as Cory surmised, it didn't appear broken. He nodded to Kate. "I need a cloth saturated with cold water. I'll wrap her ankle with it, and that should help the swelling go down." He turned back to Miss Monroe. "I'm afraid you won't be able to use your foot for several weeks."

He noticed Cory turn and leave without saying good-bye to either his sister or Miss Monroe. That was strange, but Elliot had no time to think about it.

Abigail's face scrunched into frown followed by a moan. "Oh no, that isn't possible. I have to get the library ready to open."

Kate returned with the cold water, chipped ice, and cloths. "The town has gone this long without a library, so another week or so isn't going to make that much difference."

A tear slipped down Abigail's cheek. "It will to me." She flinched when he placed the icy compress around her ankle.

"I'm sorry. I know it's cold, but it'll help the swelling."

"Actually, with this hot weather, it doesn't feel so bad now, and it does numb the pain." She reached down to touch the wrapping around her ankle.

He gazed up into her eyes that had become liquid pools. Her simple beauty struck a chord in his soul that he didn't want to hear. Breathing became difficult with her rosewater scent so close. He had to get away from her. "Excuse me, I'll go into the next room and find crutches for you to use."

Her voice moaning over the fact she couldn't work in her library followed him to the next room where his uncle stored medical equipment. She'd need some practice to use the crutches correctly. Kate could do it. He'd assign her to help Abigail learn how to maneuver with them.

When he returned, Kate was reassuring Abigail that everyone would pitch in and help get everything ready for her to open next week. "It may not be this Saturday like you first planned, but it will be as soon as we can get it put together. What can you do to supervise and stay off your feet?"

Abigail bit her lip. "I suppose I could go ahead and do the labels for the library books. I have the invoice list and can go from that and the Dewey system information book. Then I guess you could put them on the shelves."

"OK, I'll get Daniel to help me round up a few helpers and organize them."

Elliot shook his head. What would this town do without Kate Monroe? He hoped he'd never be around to find out. "Excuse me, Kate, but I have the crutches here, and if you'd be so kind as to instruct her how to use them, I'd appreciate it." It would also keep him from having to be so close to her.

Kate helped Abigail down from the table and positioned the crutches beneath Abigail's armpits. "I'm sorry these don't have padding, but if you don't put all your weight here at the top on the cradle and put all the weight on your hands, your arms won't be as sore."

Elliot busied himself with cleaning up the area as Kate led

Abigail outside. The few blocks to the boardinghouse were not going to be fun for Abigail, but at least she had help. He pulled in several deep breaths and exhaled to ease his thumping heart. It had been two years since he'd been so affected by a young woman. And he didn't welcome the feeling.

Chapter
Six

*A*FTER BREAKFAST FRIDAY morning, Abigail sat on the edge of her bed staring at her ankle. At least her room was on the first floor and she didn't have to climb the stairs. How could she have been so clumsy? This was the worst possible time for such an accident. Even though it had been wrapped securely, the ankle throbbed with pain. Tears misted her eyes. How would she ever get anything done like this? The library had to be open by next week, or she would be a failure at her first endeavor on her own.

Aunt Mae appeared in the doorway with two pillows in her arms. "Child, you're supposed to have that foot elevated." She marched over to the bed and stacked the two pillows at the bottom then swung Abigail's injured leg up onto them. "There, that will keep it up while you rest."

"Thank you, that does help, but what am I going to do about getting around and taking care of the library?"

"I've already spoken to Daniel and Nathan about that, and they're rounding up members of the Muldoon family to help you get everything ready. You can sit in the middle or wherever and give instructions to everyone."

"They'd do that for me?"

"Of course, dear, and if you need anything, just ring this to let me know." Aunt Mae pulled a small hand bell from her pocket. "I'm right next door, and I'll come help."

Abigail blinked back tears. So many good people in Porterfield had welcomed her and now were ready to help fulfill her dream. "How can I ever repay everyone for their kindness and generosity in helping me?"

Aunt Mae planted her hands on her hips. "Why, by having the best library you'll ever see. This is what our town needs, and you're just the one to do it. We're all so glad you're here, and we'll do anything we can to get things started."

"As soon as the books ordered match the bill of those received, I can get them catalogued, start writing the labels for them, and get them glued on. I have the labels all ready with the categories, so all I need to add is the title, author, and number."

"If you say so, dear; I don't know anything about that. Now don't forget; Cory and Henry will help you get over to your building, and as soon as everyone arrives, you can start supervising. Let me know when you're ready to go, and I'll send the boys to get you." With a little wave she stepped back in the hall and closed the door.

Abigail intended to do no such thing. She had the crutches, and she could make her way to the library on her own. She hopped over to the vanity table and inspected her appearance in the mirror. After smoothing back her hair, then biting her lips and pinching her cheeks to give them a bit of color, she reached for her crutches leaning against the wall.

She positioned them under her arms and swung toward the door. Using them was more difficult than it looked. She wrestled with the door a minute or so before she managed to get it open and then herself through it.

The thumping of her crutches must have been loud enough for Cory and Henry to hear because they both jumped from their chairs and rushed to meet her.

Cory stopped her with his hands on her shoulders. "Where do you think you're going?"

Abigail straightened her shoulders and lifted her chin. "Where else but to my library?" She twisted her body to get loose from his grasp, but he held tight.

"Not without our help you aren't. I'll carry you if I have to. No sense in wearing yourself out before you get there. It's going to be a long day." He nodded to Henry. "C'mon, Wilder, get on the other side so we can help her down the street."

She started to protest, but the determined expression on Cory's face halted that idea. Besides, his curly red hair and green eyes made walking with him a bit more interesting than going alone. Cory Muldoon was indeed a handsome man. She couldn't forget how he'd helped her yesterday. For a big man, he had a gentle touch.

Then she remembered the town social tonight and how much she had begun to look forward to meeting more towns-people. With her ankle in the shape it was, she'd have to sit on the sidelines and watch others have fun. Better that than to sit in her room and feel sorry for herself.

Daniel's sister was about as stubborn as her brother had been. Cory glanced down at her as he wrapped one arm across her back. She had to be a good foot plus an inch or so shorter than he was, and she weighed hardly anything. She had a spirit of determination about her that he had grown to admire too.

He grinned down at her as they descended the steps from the porch. "Henry here said he wanted to interview you for an article for the newspaper."

Abigail turned on her brightest smile for the reporter. "Why, Mr. Wilder, how nice of you. I'd love to give you an interview. When did you want to ask me some questions?"

Henry's round face and balding head heated a nice shade of pink. "Um, this morning, ma'am, if you don't mind."

"I don't mind at all, and please call me Abigail. Ma'am sounds like I'm an old woman." Her smile continued and now turned to Cory.

"I only have one chair in my building at present. Could you possibly bring in another one? I haven't yet unpacked the crates with the ones I ordered for the library."

"Of course I will. It'll make things easier for you and those who are stopping by today to help." He'd do just about anything she wanted him to do. Besides, she didn't need to be opening any heavy crates today, especially with that injured ankle. Maybe he should use his position as deputy to convince her to let him help her with some of the heavier work.

When they reached the building, she handed Henry the key, and he unlocked it for her. Once inside, she sat on the lone chair. To make sure she stayed put, Cory propped the crutches against the railing up front. Knowing her, she'd grab them and move around too much.

When she frowned at him, he laughed. "Now that's to make sure you don't get up every few minutes and try to do things. If you need help, ask for it. Someone will be here all the time. Kate said Doc Elliot gave you strict orders to stay off that ankle for several days and to keep it propped up, and I aim to make sure you do."

Her eyes flashed in anger. "And just how am I supposed to do that? I don't see anything to prop it up on."

Cory laughed again. She was a feisty one, almost like Kate. "I'm going to take care of that now." He turned to leave. "You answer Henry's questions, and I'll be back in a few minutes."

Once out on the street, he strode across to the infirmary where Doc Elliot had said he'd have a pillow and stool for Abigail to use. Now all he had to do was to make sure she kept that foot up. Sarah and Rachel both planned to be there this morning, and Kate would most likely be over there herself half a dozen times or more. Independent Miss Monroe may not like it, but she would be surrounded by watch dogs today.

He entered the infirmary. "Hey, Elliot, I've come to fetch the stool and pillow you wanted for Miss Monroe."

"Um, sure thing, Cory. I have it right here." He ducked his head and darted into another room.

The doctor's face glowed pink. Cory frowned and shook his head. What had Elliot been doing to cause such embarrassment that he turned red and wouldn't look at Cory? He shrugged and turned to gaze out the window. He spotted Rachel and Sarah entering the library building. Good. They'd take care of Abigail, and he could get on about his business soon as he delivered the stool and pillow.

Elliot returned with the items. "Be sure to remind Abigail to sit down as much as possible and to use those crutches when she really needs to walk somewhere. I don't want her putting weight on that ankle."

Cory shook his head and chuckled. "That gal is as stubborn as Daniel, and I'm not sure she'll take orders or advice from anyone but you." An idea struck him. If he went to the office right now, he could finish his work and get back to the library to help Abigail. "Since you're just across the street, why not go over and check on her yourself? You can take this stool and pillow over to her."

Doc Jensen strolled into the room. "Good morning, Cory. Elliot's patient isn't behaving herself?"

"She's got a mind of her own, and if Henry and I hadn't been there when we were, she'd have tried to walk all the way from the boardinghouse to the library. I know it's only a few blocks, but she hasn't really got the hang of those crutches yet, and I could see her falling in the street." Of course any number of men would have run to help her, but she didn't need that kind of attention right now.

Doc Jensen stroked his chin. "Hmm, she's a little thing, but it sounds like she's a ball of fire. I bet she can't wait to open that library."

"That's about it. Elliot can check on her when things aren't busy here. Aunt Mae would be a lot happier if we kept a close eye on her newest boarder." If somebody didn't keep tabs on Miss Abigail Monroe, he'd do it himself to satisfy Aunt Mae—and to get to know the librarian a little better.

Elliot turned his back and began straightening a tray of instruments. Cory shook his head. Looked like the young doctor didn't want to be bothered by Abigail. That was strange, since he'd always shown concern for his patients before. He headed for the door. "I've got to get down to the jail and relieve the night deputy until Rutherford gets back. We had a couple of drunks locked up last night for causing a disturbance at the saloon. Since both of you are here now, I'll just leave the things for Miss Monroe for you to deliver, Elliot."

Doc Jensen walked with him to the door. "That's fine. We'll take care of it. Kate will be in soon, and one of us will keep an eye on Miss Monroe. From the traffic going into her building, she should have plenty of help today."

"Thanks, Doc. Rachel and Sarah are there now, and Frank, Daniel, and Nathan are to come and help put up more shelves. I'll be back to help this afternoon." Cory strode through the door and down the sidewalk toward the courthouse and the sheriff's office. He could rest easy. Abigail had plenty of others to watch over her for now.

Elliot stood by the infirmary door and watched Cory make his way to the courthouse at the end of Main Street. First yesterday and then today Cory had been with Miss Monroe. The last thing he wanted today was to be near Abigail Monroe, but unless he could think of a good reason not to take this stool over there, he'd have to. He didn't care for the closeness that had developed between the deputy and the librarian.

His fists clenched at his side. He didn't have time for this.

Let Cory do whatever he wanted. Still he envied the ease with which the two seemed to get along with each other.

"Yoo-hoo, Doc Elliot."

He glanced over to see Rachel Reed standing on the boardwalk in front of the library building with her hands on her hips. "What is it, Rachel?" As if he didn't know she wanted the stool. No excuses now.

"I thought someone was to bring a stool and pillow to prop up Abigail's ankle. We need them now. I don't want her ankle swelling up again."

"I'll be right there." When she turned and reentered the building, Elliot sighed and picked up the objects like they were hot coals.

"You might want to give that ankle another look see while you're there, son." His uncle hooked his glasses over his ears and picked up a patient's folder. "You gonna stand there all day, or are you going to take that stuff over to Miss Monroe? Seems like I heard a bit of impatience in Mrs. Reed's voice."

Elliot jerked his head up. "I'm doing it now." He grabbed the stool and pillow and hurried across the street. At the door to the library Elliot took a deep breath then exhaled. He had to brace himself against the charms of Abigail. It'd take some doing, but he had to keep this meeting strictly a doctor-to-patient one.

Henry Wilder pushed through the door and almost ran into Elliot. "Sorry, Doc, I didn't see you. I finished my interview with Miss Monroe, and I must say she's much more cooperative than you've been with me."

"Sorry about that, Mr. Wilder, but I don't see what possible interest anyone could have in my life." For nearly a year now Elliot had been able to avoid Wilder's numerous attempts to write a story about the new doctor in town. "After all, I've been here awhile, and most people know me well enough."

"You're probably right, but I'm not giving up." He tipped his hat and strode off in the direction of the newspaper office.

Knowing Wilder, he wouldn't give up. Elliot clenched his teeth and walked into the room to find Frank and Daniel positioning a new set of shelves against the wall, and Rachel and Sarah seated on two chairs unpacking books with Abigail. He'd have to think about Wilder later.

Rachel hopped up and glared at him. "It's about time you got here. Cory was supposed to have brought them over. I don't know where he disappeared to or why he didn't return." She grabbed the pillow and stool then knelt and propped Abigail's foot on the stool. "How's that, dear?"

"Just fine, and it feels much better now. If we're going to open on Saturday, we still have lots of work to do."

"Well, it won't be this one, but a one-week delay won't make that big a difference." She knit her brows together and tapped her chin. "I still think the doc should take a look at your ankle."

Elliot nodded. "Of course, I intend to do just that." He knelt beside Abigail to examine the injured ankle and fought the emotion rising in his chest. The scent of rosewater wafted to his nose and reminded him of his mother's bushes in the garden back home. He pushed back memories of Cleveland. That's the last place he wanted to remember today.

"Looks good, but you do need to refrain from putting any weight on it for a few more days. Are you doing all right with the crutches?"

He gazed into her brown eyes, and a smile sweet as sugar graced her lips. "They're a little cumbersome, but I'll get better if I practice. I'm not an invalid, you know."

Why did she have to be so attractive and nice? "Yes, I know, but you are injured, and we do want it to heal properly and quickly." He stood and stepped back. "Ladies, make sure she doesn't do too much, and I'll check on you again tomorrow."

Abigail peered up at him. "Will I be able to go to the town social tonight if I promise to stay seated and not dance?"

"If you can keep that promise, I see no reason for you not to attend."

"Will you be there to check on me and make sure I don't?"

Elliot's hands clenched at his sides. "You don't need me to do that. Plenty of others will be there like Kate and your brother and Cory."

He turned and strode through the door. If he didn't get away now, the wall around his heart might crack. He couldn't let that happen. Still, a tiny prick of jealousy for the attention she'd get from Cory Muldoon poked Elliot's heart. Maybe he'd be at the social after all.

CHAPTER
SEVEN

ALONE IN HER room, Abigail smoothed the sides of her bright blue skirt over her hips. The three petticoats she wore beneath it gave it the fullness she desired. Of course she wouldn't be whirling about the dance floor in it, but it would drape in an attractive way while she sat and observed. Maybe it was silly to go when she couldn't really participate, but if she truly wanted the library to be a success, she had to let people know she planned to be a part of the community.

Cory and Mr. Wilder waited in the parlor to accompany her to the town hall. She positioned the crutches under her arms and clumped out to meet them, greeting them with a smile. "I appreciate your taking me, but are you sure you want to be burdened?"

Mr. Wilder grinned and bowed. "We're at your service, dear Abigail, and your carriage awaits."

"Carriage? I thought we were going to walk. It's only four blocks down Main Street."

Cory shook his head. "Oh no, young lady, that's too far for

those crutches. I have Aunt Mae's buggy outside. You'll arrive in style." He opened the door for her to walk onto the porch.

True to his word, Danny Boy stood hitched to the one-seated vehicle. "Who's going to drive it?"

Henry doffed his hat and bowed again. "I am. Now let me help you aboard." He lifted her up so her good foot hit the flooring under the seat.

She settled in the seat and turned her gaze to Cory, who stowed the crutches in the space behind her. "How are you getting there?"

"I'll be on my horse right beside you." He strode over to where his horse was waiting and swung himself up and over the saddle.

Henry clicked the reins, and they moved ahead to join a few other wagons and buggies coming into town for the social. "They have these socials every few months here in town. Not many women around, so the ones who are get plenty of dancing. The married ladies dance with the single men to make it more fun. Even Miss Perth and Mrs. Bennett join in at these events."

So that's what had the two women all atwitter at supper as they discussed the social. Mr. Fuller had invited Aunt Mae, and they had left only a few minutes before she had.

At the town hall Cory dismounted and lifted Abigail down from her perch then handed her the crutches. "Now you be sure to stay in one spot and get up only if you have to, and I'd better see these crutches under your arms if—no, when—you do. I can't see you sitting still all evening."

"I promise to be careful." His attention sent butterflies to her stomach. If only she could dance with him tonight. She sighed and glanced around at the crowd entering the building. So many unfamiliar faces in this town she now called home, but she determined to get to know a few more of them tonight.

Henry hitched Danny Boy to the railing and followed Cory and Abigail indoors. Cory led her to a chair among a line of them set against the wall, and Henry headed for the refreshment table.

"Thank you, Cory. I'll be fine here." Although she didn't want him to leave, she couldn't monopolize his time. She reached out to position the crutches against the wall.

When she looked back up, Elliot stood in the doorway. He'd said he wouldn't be here. His gaze locked with hers for one instant then jerked away. He strode to the far side of the room. Abigail shook her head. And men said women were hard to understand.

Cory leaned over. "I see the good doc is here. He'll make sure you behave, so I don't have to worry about you the rest of the evening."

His lopsided grin produced a giggle and set her heart to fluttering. "I'm flattered to think you were going to worry about me."

He placed his hand on her shoulder. "You're Daniel's sister, so that makes you family, and the Muldoon men take care of their women." He winked then walked away.

Abigail sighed. He'd never see her as anything but someone to watch after. If she didn't have these crutches, she'd show him a thing or two on the dance floor.

She'd only been in town a little over a week, but she still recognized a few of the townspeople. The Graysons' daughter had just turned eighteen, and her parents hovered about her as several of the young men showed an interest. A little on the plump side, Marabelle was still pretty enough with her blonde hair and blue eyes that she'd have no trouble attracting a husband. Maybe if her hair was that color and her eyes a prettier shade, she would be attracting some of the attention.

The musicians began playing, and a few couples swung out onto the floor to the tune of "Turkey in the Straw." Abigail blinked then shook her head. This dancing certainly wasn't anything like she'd seen or heard back home. Here they called the violin a fiddle, and the music coming from it sounded quite a bit different from the music she had danced to at home. Relief that she didn't have to try to keep up with the dancing filled her, and for once she offered thanks for her sprained ankle.

Her gaze swept across the room. In addition to not having to worry about keeping up with the new dance steps, sitting gave her an opportunity to observe people and learn more about them. Elliot entered her line of vision, and she stopped to study him. He stood at the refreshment table with his back toward her.

Now there was a young man hard to figure out. Usually she could tell so much from a person by his conversation and demeanor, but Elliot gave no clues at all to his true personality. He was a doctor, a professional through and through. And she'd seen none of that bedside manner Kate had gone on about earlier in the week. He was a mystery for sure, but she didn't have time to solve mysteries.

She shrugged and turned her attention back to the couples swirling in time to the music.

He shouldn't have come. Despite knowing Abigail would be there, he'd thrown caution to the wind and attended the event for the first time in more months than he could remember. Elliot's throat closed, and all desire for the cool punch he'd just picked up vanished. He set it to the side on a tray provided for empties then swiped his hand down his trouser leg. Cory had left her alone, and that was his cue to speak to her if he could get up his nerve.

The music stopped, and people all around applauded. In a minute or two they'd strike up a new tune. Maybe if he danced first he could get up the courage to approach Abigail. Elliot spotted Miss Perth a few feet away. He strode toward her and stopped by her side. "Miss Perth, may I have the honor of the second dance?"

Her gray-blue eyes sparkled. "That would be lovely, Doc Elliot, but wouldn't you rather have a spin with one of the younger ladies?"

"Now if that's what I wanted, I would have asked one of them." The music began, and he reached for her hand.

Pink tinged the older schoolmarm's cheeks as she followed his steps across the floor. He smiled at her. "I must say that you are very good. I can tell you have experience."

"Oh, yes. I was quite the dancer in my younger years, but I've never lost my love for music and toe tapping." She glanced over his shoulder. "Too bad Abigail has that sprained ankle. She'd be swamped with requests to dance. Look at her; the young men are buzzing about like bees around spring flowers."

They turned in one of the steps, and he spotted Abigail.

Indeed, three young men vied for her attention, and a swift stab of jealousy pierced his heart. The ugly beast reared its head for the second time this week. He had nothing to be jealous about. After all, he didn't really care whom Abigail Monroe attracted tonight.

He swept Miss Perth in the other direction and turned his back to Miss Monroe. When the music ended, he led the teacher back to her seat. "Thank you, Miss Perth. You were a most delightful partner."

Before he could control his feet, they led him straight to where Abigail sat. He stood before her and nodded. "I see that you're keeping your promise to sit on the sidelines tonight. You will be thankful for that later."

"I must admit the thought of being on it for even a few steps gives me pain. To tell the truth, I'm enjoying sitting here and getting to know the good people of Porterfield."

He swallowed the lump rising in his throat. "May I get you a cup of punch and a cookie or two?"

Her smile brightened. "Oh, would you? I've been eyeing it and wishing for a bit to drink."

Why did she have to be so pretty and so friendly? "I'll be back in a moment." He turned and hurried to the table laden with two punch bowls and platters of homemade cookies. Now he'd have to spend a few more minutes with her to be polite after bringing her the food and drink. That had not been his intention at all.

Aunt Maggie stepped to his side and picked up a plate. "I saw you speaking to Abigail. Is that plate and cup for her?"

Heat filled his face. "Yes, it is. She's sitting out the dances like I ordered her to do because of her ankle. The least I can do is provide something for her to eat and drink."

"Of course, how considerate. She certainly looks pretty in that bright blue. If she wasn't incapacitated, she'd have her pick of young men for partners."

He glanced back across the room. Cory stood at her side. She gestured toward Elliot and the refreshment table. Cory glanced his way and frowned. Elliot grinned and held up the cup and plate.

Aunt Maggie laughed. "Well, looks like you better get back over there before the competition takes over. I'm glad to see you having a good time."

Elliot groaned and grit his teeth. Aunt Maggie would not let this gesture of kindness pass without making something else of it. He headed back, dodging dancers across the way. Was it only an act of kindness, or was it something else? His fingers gripped the plate, and he refused to even visit the notion that this was more than a doctor watching out for his patient.

Cory still stood by her side. She smiled again and grasped the plate with the cookies and punch. With one hand she spread a napkin across her lap and held the plate in the other. Then she rested the plate on the napkin, still holding the edge. "These cookies are the ones Aunt Mae made this morning." She glanced up at Cory. "I saw you try to snitch a few and Aunt Mae rap your knuckles. Nobody can get away with that, not even you, Deputy Muldoon."

Elliot cut in. "That reminds me of a time when Aunt Maggie swatted me with a wooden spoon when I swiped my finger through the frosting she was putting on a cake. Best to stay away from cooks until they offer their goods."

Abigail giggled at that. "I guess we're never too old for a little punishment. Right, Cory?" She bit into a cookie then offered one to Elliot.

"No, thank you. I'm still full from Aunt Maggie's dinner." He stood in silence for a few minutes. No stream of conversation came to his mind.

Cory leaned over and said, "Whenever you get tired of sitting, I'll be here to help you with the crutches. And let me know when you're ready to go home. I'll be ready whenever you are."

As Elliot watched Miss Monroe smile up at Cory, he winced. Coming here was a stupid idea. He should have known Cory would take up her attention.

When Miss Monroe turned again to him, he nodded shortly. "I see that you're in good hands, so if you'll excuse me, I'll be on my way."

He turned and strode across the room and to the door. He wouldn't make this mistake again. Abigail Monroe was not worth a broken heart. He was sure of it.

CHAPTER EIGHT

ABIGAIL LEANED ON her crutches to observe the hustle and bustle of people looking at books. After a week of supervising others in getting books shelved, today, the first Saturday of September, the library had officially opened, and patrons came in a steady stream to browse and sign up for library permits. Aunt Mabel had come into town with Sarah to help with the opening, and she now answered questions with great delight. Abigail couldn't help but smile at the plump gray-haired woman who once held court in Boston society and now conversed at ease with the citizens of Porterfield.

All the shelved books bore the proper labels and were ready for checking out. Abigail hobbled over to the library desk, where Sarah issued library permits.

"Thank you for sitting in for me while I went to have my ankle checked. The doctor said by tomorrow I should be able to put my weight on it, and for that I am very grateful." She pulled up a chair and sat down.

"I'm glad to hear it," Sarah glanced up from her work. "Did you see Elliot or Doc Jensen?"

"Both were there, but Elliot did the exam. He sure is a quiet young man. He's hardly talked to me at all except to give me directions on taking care of my ankle, and even though he brought me refreshments at the social, he barely spoke to me." His lack of interest in anything but her injury bruised her ego since she'd never had trouble attracting young men before. At Brighton Academy and again in Boston they'd paid notice to her, and Charles Wentworth had even courted her. But apparently she didn't much interest this young doctor.

Sarah handed a form to a man and his wife. "He doesn't talk much when I go in to see his uncle for my monthly checkups for the baby either. Ma Muldoon says my going seems a waste of time to her. She never had the doctor for any of hers until time for their birthing. However, I rather like the idea of having a doctor keep a close eye on how this little one develops." She walked around the counter to the railing. "I see Donavan out there waiting for me, so I suppose he wants to get back to the ranch."

"I really appreciate your coming in and giving me a hand today. It's been a big load off my mind." Without the help of her friends, today could have been a disaster with her not being able to get around very well. As it was, the opening ran smoothly without anyone complaining about waiting for anything.

Sarah walked toward the door and waved at a young man who approached the desk where Abigail sat. He leaned on the counter and rolled the brim of his hat in his hands. He looked familiar, and dimples winked when he smiled. "Miss Monroe, you do make a pretty picture as a librarian."

Heat rose in Abigail's cheeks. "Thank you. May I help you with something?" He was the first young man to approach her in such a way, but something about his eyes reminded her of someone. Had she seen him in town before today?

He shoved his hat back on his head then quickly removed it again. "Sorry, Ma always said not to wear my hat indoors." He gulped, and his Adam's apple moved up and down. "I'm thinking about gettin' one of them library permits and check me out some books."

"Very well; here's the application and a pen. Just fill it out and return it to me. Are you from in town?" Maybe he'd give her a clue as to why he seemed familiar. She handed him the paper and hoped he'd be able to read it.

"No, ma'am. I'm out at the Muldoon ranch. I heard about this here place and decided to look at some books. I used to love reading, but I haven't had much time for it lately." He moved to the side to fill out the form.

That explained it. He must have been at the ranch when she went there for dinner that first night. He fit in with the ranchers and cowboys she'd met so far. Not much in the way of society here. Everyone seemed to be cut from the same cloth. The only ones she'd seen that anywhere resembled those back home were Mr. Fuller, the bank president, the two doctors, and Mayor Tate. Also, Daniel and Nathan wore suits most of the time, but all the other men appeared in denim trousers and cotton shirts and wide-brimmed hats like the young man before her.

She glanced down at her ruffled shirtwaist and the green

and black plaid taffeta skirt she now wore. Perhaps these were
a bit dressed up for today when most of the women wore
simple solid-color sturdy skirts and either a top matching the
skirt or a white shirtwaist, but this was a special occasion, and
she wanted to look her best.

The young cowboy returned with his application. She
raised her eyebrows at the very neat handwriting for each
space. "This looks very good. If you want to check out a book,
browse around until you find what you want, and I'll write it on
your checkout sheet here." Where had he learned to write so
clearly? Most young men she knew had atrocious handwriting.

He smiled and headed over to the history section. She
shook her head. That's the last place she would have picked for
his interests. She straightened up the stack of sheets already
filled out and placed the new one in its proper place in the
alphabet. James A. Lowell; such an unusual name for a cowboy.
It sounded more like a poet or writer. Surely the others didn't
call him James, maybe Jimmy, but it was probably more like
Slim, Buck, or even Dusty. Well, it was none of her concern.

Abigail sighed and reached down to rub her ankle. Though
not as sore, it still gave a twinge of pain every now and then.

James Lowell returned to check out a book about the
Revolutionary War. "It's nice to see young people interested
in history." She wrote the name of the book and author on his
permit sheet.

His cheeks burned red. "Yes, ma'am. I enjoy reading about
how those men got together and set up a government that
gives everyone their rights." He clasped the book to his chest
and scurried out of the building.

Aunt Mabel ushered a young couple out the door. Abigail

recognized Allen and Penelope Dawes from church. Kate told her Penelope was one of those mail-order brides like Suzanne Cahoon. The two ladies arrived in town at the same time and married the men who sent for them. It was a strange way for a man and woman to get acquainted and marry. She'd have to know a man through more than letters before she'd even consider courting, much less marriage.

Aunt Mabel dusted her hands together. "Well, I think we'll probably have a quiet spell here for a while. Anything you need me to do?"

"No, but how are you going to get back out to Sarah's place? Donavan's already picked her up."

"Cory said he had some business with his brother and would take me out there when he goes." She ambled over to pull up a chair and sit beside Abigail. "You know, he's a right handsome young man with that curly red hair and greenish eyes like Kate's."

"Yes, he is, and I enjoyed being with him at the social last week."

"He's not exactly from our social standing and probably not what your parents have in mind for your future, but he does have a way about him."

She agreed on all counts, but what could one expect in cowboy and farmer country? "You've seen how he is with his nephews. They dote on him and look at him like he was their hero. I'm not sure he sees me as anything more than one of the family."

"Well, it seems to me that the young doctor is more to your standing. He's from a city and knows more of the ways of society."

"That may be, Aunt Mabel, but neither he nor Cory are interested in me like that."

"Then they're both blind as bats if they don't take notice of a pretty thing like you. Don't worry about either of them, though. If the right man is here, you'll know it soon enough."

"Thank you. I just hope I do recognize it when it happens."

She glanced at her watch. Miss Miller planned to stop by with her list of books for Abigail to order for her older students. Yesterday Eloise Perth had given her a list of books for the younger children and set up a time for them to visit when the books arrived. Soon the shelves would be full of books children of all ages could enjoy.

Aunt Mabel stood and stretched her arms above her chubby body. "Gotta kink in my back and need to stretch." She moved her shoulders around and rotated her neck a few times. "Aah, that feels better." She sat back down. "Now, as I was saying—"

"Pardon us, Miss Monroe, but we'd like to apply for a library permit."

Abigail breathed a sigh of relief, thankful she didn't have to listen to a lecture on love from Aunt Mabel. Much as she loved the woman, she had heard the love story of Aunt Mabel and her Franklin numerous times already.

She smiled and handed the newcomers a form. "Just fill this out and you can check out books today if you'd like."

They thanked her and stepped aside to fill it out. An older couple Abigail didn't recognize came into the library, and Aunt Mabel hurried to greet them.

Aunt Mabel's heart may be in the right place, but running the library would leave little time for courtship. And she had no idea what kind of man would be right for her anyway. God would have to knock her on the head to let her know when the right man came along, if he ever did.

Elliot wandered up to the front windows during a space between patients. More and more people came in for checkups or for minor ailments on Saturdays now when they came to town. He usually took care of them to free Doc up to make house calls out in the country.

A steady stream of men and women entered and left the library across the street. When he saw Miss Monroe earlier, she'd been a pretty picture in her plaid skirt and white blouse. She was getting more adept at using those crutches too.

He imagined her now holding people spellbound with her charm and knowledge of books. That was not the direction he wanted to go. He turned from the window to bump into his uncle.

"Looks like our library will be a success." Doc smiled and inclined his head toward the building across the way.

"Yes, it does, and I'm happy for Miss Monroe. Her enthusiasm is catching."

"And she's the kind of girl you ought to consider for a wife. Doctoring can be mighty lonely if you don't have someone to welcome you home after a particularly hard day. Don't know what I'd do without Maggie."

Elliot clenched his hands into fists at his side. Why did everyone want to see him married off? He liked his life, and it kept his heart shielded from more hurt. He said nothing but continued to stare out the window.

Doc placed his hand on Elliot's shoulder. "Son, it's been long enough to grieve. What happened was tragic, and you did all you could."

A lump formed in his throat. "Yet it still wasn't enough. I should have done more."

"Elliot, you've been in medicine long enough to know that some of our patients can't be saved. Since God knows us from the moment of our conception and ordains our days, none of us will go before it's our time, and when God calls a person home, it's the end of their days. Have you read that psalm I gave to you? If not, then you must read it. Psalm 139 tells you everything you need to know about God's plan for your life. God doesn't blame you for not saving Angela, nor does anyone else."

Elliot pulled away. "Doc, you didn't see the look on her parents' faces at the funeral. They wouldn't even speak to me. They knew I had failed as a doctor. God should have been able to keep her from dying. He could have shown me what to do and guided my hands, but He didn't. I'm not ever going to put myself in that position again. I'm thinking it may have been a mistake to let you talk me into staying in medicine and coming here with you and Aunt Maggie."

"I don't want to hear that from you. You're a good doctor, and your colleagues in Cleveland thought so too. They all had high praise for you. Remember, I told you I wouldn't consider letting you share my practice if I didn't believe in you as a doctor. You've done a wonderful job here, and the people of Porterfield appreciate you very much."

Elliot did like the town and did enjoy helping the people who came through the infirmary. He had begun to regain some of the confidence lost back then, but in the back of his mind the question of what if it happened again plagued him.

Doc tightened his grip on Elliot's shoulder then released it. "I see Mrs. Pettigrew coming up the walk with that determined look on her face. Wonder what ailment she's come up with now." He stepped away. "I'll take care of her, and you think about what I said. Forgive yourself, and you'll be much better off."

His uncle greeted Mrs. Pettigrew, who immediately began to list her complaints. Doc's final words presented the problem for Elliot. He didn't want to forgive himself. Because if he did, he could make that mistake again. And that was something he had vowed never to do.

CHAPTER
NINE

O N SUNDAY AFTER church, Abigail rode out to the
Muldoon ranch with Kate and Daniel. "Everyone was so nice
this morning, and they told me how much they appreciated
having the library. I'm so glad we were able to open it in spite
of my accident."

Kate nodded and turned in her seat. "Me too. I don't think
I've ever seen the town this excited about a new enterprise since
the bakery opened several years ago."

Daniel nodded. "I'm really proud of my little sister. You've
accomplished more in two weeks than most people achieve in
a lifetime."

Abigail laughed. "I learned it all from our father. He said
if I was going to go out on this adventure, he wanted to be
sure I did it right. He didn't want me to waste the inheritance
Grandfather left me. He taught me how to keep accurate
records and how to be organized and on top of things." She
remembered the many hours he'd sat with her as they'd made
plans for the library's holdings.

"Looks to me like you learned well. Anytime you need Daniel or me for anything, just let us know."

"That I will for sure." She wrinkled her brow. "Kate, I noticed Doc Elliot was not in church this morning. He wasn't there last Sunday either. Was there some emergency at the clinic?" With Kate here, that probably wasn't the case, but what other reason could there be for his absence?

Kate shook her head. "Elliot hasn't been to church but once or twice in the time he's been here. He's a wonderful doctor, but he once told me he had no use for religion."

Now that was strange. How could a man be in the business of healing people and not see that a Greater Physician than he took care of people? Besides, he wasn't a drinking or carousing man like most of the men who weren't Christians, but then Elliot hadn't said he wasn't a Christian, only that he had no use for religion.

"That's too bad. We ought to do something about that."

Daniel's eyebrows arched, and he turned to peer at her. "Abigail Monroe, you need to think twice about prying into a man's private life."

"I'm not going to pry. I'm only going to show him what it means to have God in his life and how important it is."

"I'm just saying don't go asking a lot of questions."

Kate nodded. "He's right, Abigail. There's something in Elliot's past he doesn't want to discuss, and he closes up whenever it's mentioned. He wouldn't even give Henry Wilder an interview for the newspaper when he came to town."

"What was his answer for not doing it?" Henry had hinted at such when he'd interviewed her and asked questions about how the doctor had treated her. None of that had been in the article printed in the newspaper last Friday.

"He said that if people wanted to know more about him and his skills, they could come to the infirmary for treatment of any ailments they might have."

Abigail laughed. "Sounds like a good answer to me." Still, she intended to get to know more about the younger doctor. After all, it was her Christian duty to witness to unbelievers.

She glanced down at her ankle. Had it not been for her injury, she might not have had any contact with him thus far. The only reason he'd spoken to her was because he wanted to check on her ankle. The mystery intrigued her and whetted her curiosity. In spite of her brother's warning, she determined to find out more about the mysterious Dr. Elliot Jensen.

Elliot sat in his room and enjoyed the aroma of Aunt Maggie's cooking. Her pot roast was the best he'd ever tasted, and she said her recipe was foolproof. The most important step was to put it on a low burning flame and go to church, leaving it to cook itself done. Must work, because he relished the meat, potatoes, carrots, and onions swimming in rich gravy.

The sounds of dishes clattering and silverware clinking told him dinner would soon be ready. He closed his book, ambled over to the washstand, and cleaned up. The house had been quiet while Doc and Aunt Maggie had been at church, but now the sounds from downstairs beckoned him.

He entered the kitchen and went over to plant a kiss on

his aunt's cheek. "My stomach's been craving that roast all morning, and as always it looks as good as it smells."

The heat of the late summer day added to that of the kitchen gave a rosy glow to her cheeks. "Well, you can sit yourself right down there at the table, and I'll have it on the table quicker than you can unfold your napkin."

Elliot laughed and joined his uncle, who was already seated. True to her word, plates of hot meat and vegetables appeared on the table in minutes. He bowed his head as much from habit as from respect and waited for Doc to say grace.

After the dishes made their rounds, Aunt Maggie peered over at Elliot. "You missed a good message this morning. Reverend Winston is a fine young preacher. You ought to go hear him sometime."

She knew he wouldn't, but she said the same thing every Sunday anyway. Elliot gave the same reply in return. "Maybe I will someday."

Today she didn't stop with that as she usually did. "Abigail Monroe was there with her crutches and appeared to have only a slight limp. She must be following your instructions to have it do so well."

That stubborn girl was bound to have her way. "I told her to keep off that foot for several weeks, and it's only been a little over a week."

Aunt Maggie shrugged. "She looked fine to me, and she was mighty pretty in a yellow dress with a straw hat to match. I still say she'd make a fine wife. She's smart too."

Aunt Maggie was bound and determined to find him a mate, but so far he'd managed to escape her matchmaking efforts. This time would be no different. "I'm sure a lot of young men in town have noticed that as well. I saw plenty of them coming and going from the library yesterday when it opened."

Aunt Maggie reached over and grasped his hand in hers. "Son, it's time for you to let the past go and look to the future. Like the apostle Paul said to the people at Philippi, forget the things that are behind and press on to find what God has in store for you."

Elliot hid a smile. The verse didn't go exactly like that, but then Aunt Maggie always put her own spin on the Scriptures. "But I don't want to forget Angela and the wonderful times we had together."

"That's not what I meant, and you know it. You don't need to forget her, just what happened and how it happened."

"I can't." He couldn't even admit how panic had almost set in last year when the Davis home burned and the family had been injured. Fortunately, the injuries had not been life threatening, and he'd made it through the emergency.

Aunt Maggie sat back and shook her head. Doc laid down his fork. "I've told you over and over again that none of that was your fault. For one thing, doctors at the hospital didn't want you to resign. None of them blamed you, or you would have been reprimanded and put on notice. Did her family accuse of you of letting her die?"

Doc knew the answer to that, but he kept insisting on asking. Elliot's appetite disappeared, and he shoved back from the table. "I don't want to talk about this anymore."

His uncle reached out to stay his departure. "You still haven't read that scripture I recommended, have you?"

Elliot shook his head. He hadn't read it, and he didn't have any plans to read it. It wouldn't make any difference anyway.

Nothing could change what happened. "Excuse me. I have some more reading to do this afternoon."

They'd continue to discuss the situation after he left, but he didn't care about that as long as he didn't have to be around to hear what they had to say. His plans for the future did not include taking a wife. He had plenty to do to keep him busy helping his uncle take care of the good people of Porterfield, and that's all he needed.

Back in his room, he tried to concentrate on the latest medical journal, but one face kept intruding. If he had no room for a wife in his future, why did Abigail Monroe's image keep popping up on every page? Maybe it was time to get out of the house and take a walk to clear his head.

Henry Wilder stood on the front porch of the boardinghouse and scanned the street leading out from Mae's to downtown. He spotted a familiar figure on the boardwalk a block away. Why would the young doctor be outdoors on a hot afternoon like this? That man had eluded every attempt to interview him. The only information gleaned so far had come from Doc Jensen and Kate, and that hadn't been much at all.

He shoved his hands into his trouser pockets and rocked on his heels as he observed Elliot Jensen. Since he was so secretive, the doctor must have something to hide, but so far his sources hadn't provided him with anything worthwhile.

On impulse, Henry strode out to the street and in the direction of Elliot. Maybe a casual meeting like this would open up the young man and reveal something interesting. "Doc Elliot, wait up a minute."

Elliot turned at the sound of his name. He stopped, stared at Henry a moment, and took a few steps away. Then, as if he'd reconsidered, he stopped and waited for Henry to catch up. "What can I do for you today? Are you ill? Injured?"

"No, no, nothing like that. I just wanted to visit with you. Things are pretty quiet around here on Sunday afternoons." He swept his hand to the side. Every place of business was closed up for the day, and no one walked the streets save for the two of them.

"Yes, they are. I actually came out here to walk because of the quiet." He raised his eyebrows to get his point across.

"I see. Well, I won't bother you then." Henry turned around to head back to the boardinghouse.

"No, wait. As long as you don't probe into my background, we can walk along together."

Henry rejoined Elliot. Something was better than nothing, and who knew what a little casual conversation might reveal.

Elliot proceeded to stroll along the boardwalk. "I have never understood why you have been so interested in me in the first place. I'm just another doctor who came to town to practice medicine. What makes that newsworthy?"

"A reasonable question, but the good citizens of Porterfield like to know about the people who come here and set up business. Of course doctoring isn't a business as such, but you're still treating them and taking care of their ailments, so they like to know all about you." He and Elliot had arrived at the same time, but Henry had never been able to really make friends with the doctor.

"It's a little late for that since my uncle and I have treated just about everyone here in Porterfield, including you when you had that chest cold and were so sick last year."

"Maybe so, but it'd still be interesting for people to know about your life in Cleveland. You've never talked about it."

Immediately a veil fell over Elliot's eyes, and Henry wished he could take back the statement. He'd broken the first request made, but Elliot himself had opened the door.

Elliot stopped then turned and headed back toward the infirmary. "Suffice it to say that is one thing I don't want to discuss. I left all that behind to come here, and so far it's been a good thing. Leave well enough alone, Wilder."

Henry opened his mouth to comment further, but then snapped it shut. If he had any hopes of ever learning anything about Elliot Jensen, he must be more careful with his words and approach. This young man had hurt written all over him, and Henry would give anything to learn the reasons for it.

They walked in silence for a few minutes before Elliot spoke again. "That was a nice article you wrote about Miss Monroe and the library."

"Thank you. She is a most delightful person and is likely to be snared by some lucky young man in town. If I was a few years younger, I might consider courting her myself." Henry noted the mixed emotions now playing about Elliot's face. "Have you considered that for yourself?" he asked.

That question brought storm clouds to Elliot's eyes. "No, I haven't, and I don't intend to. I'm not in the market for a relationship." With that, he pounded his feet on the boardwalk and entered the infirmary.

That had touched a nerve in Elliot. Henry could only speculate, but he'd bet his last dollar that the sadness in the doctor came because of a woman. But how was he ever going to find out if Jensen wouldn't talk to him? He sighed and turned back to the boardinghouse.

CHAPTER
TEN

ANOTHER WEEK AND a half passed, and Abigail decided to discard her crutches. Her ankle had only a slight twinge of pain now, and she had grown to hate the crutches. Now she sat at her desk in the library checking the list Jessica Miller gave her against the box of books just delivered. The students showed great excitement about the library and were due in for a tour in the early afternoon. She looked forward to seeing them and telling them about the library. As she wrote labels to be pasted to each book, the stories raced through her mind. Bronte and Dickens were two of her favorites, although sometimes Dickens could be depressing.

She stood to test her ankle. Satisfied that only the twinge remained, she walked across to shelve some returned books. At least she'd been able to walk in church a few days ago. She needed to take those crutches back to the infirmary later today and get rid of them for good. A smile played about her lips. She could see Doc Jensen without being injured this time.

Now why did that give her pleasure? He had no interest in her, and she shouldn't have any in him.

During the week not many people came into the library as they had chores and business to attend to, but last Saturday had been so busy, she'd hardly had time to sit down. The cowboy named Lowell had returned his book and checked out another one. Jessica Miller had been there, and Abigail noticed a spark of interest between the two when the cowboy greeted the teacher.

They would make a nice pair. If Aunt Mae or Aunt Mabel saw the two of them, they'd be in their matchmaking mode faster than Abigail could count to ten. She'd even heard the two of them whispering after church last Sunday and glancing her way a time or two. It'd be interesting to find out with whom they were trying to pair her. Cory or Doc Elliot? Neither of the two men had shown any interest lately. She sighed and picked up another book. She hadn't come to Porterfield to get a husband, and she needed to remember that.

The bell over the door jangled, and Kate stepped through. "Good morning. I'm on my way to meet Daniel for dinner at the hotel. I thought you might want to join us."

"Oh, that sounds lovely." Abigail laughed and swept her hand to the side. "As you can see, I'm so busy I can't find time to think."

Kate joined in the laughter. "Not that many people come to town during the week, and most of the men are hard at work on the ranches or over at the lumberyard."

"That I've learned this week." She reached behind the counter and grabbed her handbag. "Eating with you two sounds much more interesting than sitting her and twiddling my thumbs until Jessica Miller brings over her charges."

"Let's go then." She reached over to open the door and raised an eyebrow. "I see a limp. Are you sure you're OK without the crutches?"

"Of course I am. Mother always said I healed faster than any child she ever knew. I'll be fine."

After locking the door, she joined Kate to walk the two blocks to the hotel, mindful of her ankle every step of the way. They passed the saloon, and Kate frowned when they heard the tinny sound of the piano and the laughter of men. "Guess a few men decided to spend their noon hour in the saloon wasting their money on whiskey and those girls. Cory and Daniel should have run them all out of town after that business last year."

She marched by with her head high and shoulders back. A good four to five inches taller than Abigail, Kate created a picture of a no-nonsense, don't-fool-with-me woman. Daniel had truly met his match when he married Kate Muldoon.

When they passed the mercantile, Mr. Grayson stopped his sweeping and nodded to them. "Good day, ladies." He leaned on the broom handle. "Miss Monroe, I finished that book I borrowed. I'll send the missus down later to turn it in."

Then he wrinkled his brow. "On second thought, I just might come myself so's I can check out another one."

"You do that, Mr. Grayson. I'm getting in more books every week. I'm sure you'll find some to your liking," Abigail replied.

Kate led the way into the hotel, where Daniel waited for them. He lifted his eyebrows in surprise when he saw her. "I

wasn't expecting you, but it's good to see you all the same."
He narrowed his eyes. "I thought you'd still be using your
crutches. Are you sure it's wise not to?"

Before Abigail could respond, Kate said, "Don't waste your
breath. I've already scolded her, and I can see she's cut from the
same cloth you are with her stubbornness."

Daniel said nothing to that but grinned and bowed slightly.
"After you, ladies."

Once they were seated and had ordered their meal, Abigail
spread her napkin in her lap. "Kate, I've been meaning to ask
you about James Lowell. He said he works on your pa's ranch."

"He does, but he's more than just a ranch hand. He's my
cousin from Dallas and is Pa's sister's son. He was hankering
to work on a ranch, so Pa invited him to come here and be a
cowboy. Jimmy loves it and won't let us treat him like one of
the family. He says he wants to be with the boys in the bunk-
house, so Pa and Ma leave him be except for special family
occasions, and then they make him come to the house and help
celebrate."

"So that's why he looked so familiar. He has a resemblance
to Donnie and Ian, and he writes so well and likes to read. Not
that other cowboys don't, but he just seemed different." Add
one more to the ever growing list of Muldoon family members.
"I think the schoolmarm, Jessica Miller, may be sweet on him."

Daniel chuckled. "You're as bad as Aunt Mae and Aunt
Mabel. Let the poor boy and girl alone. If they're meant for
each other, they'll find it out soon enough."

She didn't intend to meddle, but if the opportunity presented itself, she most certainly would help things along with
those two. They were both likeable people, and with women so

scarce, Jimmy couldn't find a better person to hitch up with. A smile tickled her lips. Now she was acting like Aunt Mae.

They spent the rest of the meal in small talk about family and friends. After she finished her dessert, Abigail opened her handbag to leave some money for the meal, but Daniel stilled her hand.

"It's on me today. You're bringing a lot of sunshine into this town, and I'm so glad you're here."

Abigail grinned and stood. "I accept your generosity, dear brother. Now I have to get back to the library before Miss Miller arrives with her students. Wouldn't do for the librarian to be late."

She left them still sitting at the table and headed back to her building. Five minutes after she reopened, Miss Miller and her students arrived. Abigail blinked twice when she saw them. A few of the boys were much bigger than she had thought, but their teacher seemed to have them in control.

Miss Miller introduced her students each by name. Abigail recognized a few of the last names and a few of the faces from church. The fifteen boys and girls ranged in age from twelve to sixteen. They stood in a semi-circle in front of Abigail as she explained the workings of the library and the procedures for checking out books.

"Your school is very fortunate to have the resources available here in the library. Places like this are just beginning to become a part of cities and towns across America. A man named Andrew Carnegie has donated thousands of dollars to establish libraries like this across our nation."

A boy raised his hand. "Miss Monroe, did he give you money for our library?"

She recognized him as Pete Davis from church. "No, Pete, he didn't. I'm very fortunate that my grandfather left me an inheritance, and I used it for our library here. Others have helped too, and you'll soon see their names on a plaque we'll hang in a prominent place."

Two boys, the Duncan twins she had seen about town, wore such bored expressions, she feared they might topple over any minute. She pointed to them. "I don't know which one of you is which, but tell me what you're interested in."

"Nuthin' this here old library has to offer," one answered. "Iffen you have books about horses, guns, and all that stuff, I might look at 'em."

Jessica stepped to his side. "Why, Bobby, I didn't know you had an interest in horses. I do believe Miss Monroe has some books like that. I'll be sure to put a few on the reading list."

Bobby didn't answer, and the bored look turned somewhat sullen. His brother, Billy, didn't look much happier either. They were quite a few inches taller than Miss Miller, and Abigail surmised the teacher must have her hands full taking care of those two.

Miss Miller moved to stand between the two boys until Abigail completed her talk. She then gave each one of them a permit form to fill out so they could check out books later. Three tables with six chairs each had been added in front of the shelves, so the students sat down and put their pens to work.

Pink tinged Jessica's face, and she spoke low so as not to attract the attention of her students. "I saw Mr. Lowell coming out of the library last Saturday. What kind of books did he check out?"

"He likes books about the history of our country. The one last week was about the Revolutionary War, and this week he took one with short biographies of our presidents." Maybe books would be the way she could bring Jessica and James Lowell together. "What types of books do you like?"

"I...I love the novels, but I read a lot of other things to keep ahead of my students. I'm so thankful for your generosity and that of others in town. The library is really going to make my work with the students much more pleasant."

The students finished their applications, and Abigail collected them. "If you'd like to check out a book today, you may look through our selections for one you might like. The signs on the end of each shelf tell you what is located there."

In less than fifteen minutes, several of them made selections and wrote the name of their books on the checkout sheet. Jessica gathered them in a group. "We all want to thank you, Miss Monroe, for the work you've done to bring a library to our town. I'm sure you will see us more often as we come in to check out books."

The students then filed out, and, except for the Duncan twins, the others thanked her as they left. However, she had taken note of the fact that Billy had checked out a book by James Fenimore Cooper. Abigail hid a smile. He'd like the story about Indians and the frontier.

After they left, the library became quiet and almost lonesome, but since Abigail loved books, she'd decided she'd never be lonely as long she had stories to read. She headed for the little storeroom in the back where new boxes of books waited to be labeled. After unpacking several stacks, she noticed the ones that had been stored in the room. They were on the top shelves, so she retrieved the ladder Frank had made for her in order to reach the higher ones.

If only she were taller she wouldn't have to climb so high to put things away or take things down here in the storeroom. The box she wanted was in her hands when she heard the jingle-jangle of the bell over the front door.

"Yoo-hoo, Abigail, where are you?" Rachel's voice sounded from the library.

"Back here in the storeroom." Abigail held the box with her right arm and stepped down. Her ankle twinged then gave way and she collapsed to the floor, hitting both her head and her left wrist on the way to the floor.

Pain shot through her wrist and pounded in her head. She shook it slightly to clear her vision.

"Oh, my goodness, Abigail, what happened?" Rachel knelt down beside Abigail and helped her sit up.

"I'm not sure." She held up her left wrist, which had started to swell and didn't look quite right. "I think it may be broken. I hit the edge of the shelf with it when I tried to grab hold, and then my head must have hit something because it hurts."

"You sit right there; I'm going for the doctor. I'll be back in no time."

Abigail nodded then the pain in her wrist shot up her arm. She clamped her teeth together and bit down hard. She had to keep still, or it would be worse. How could she have been so clumsy?

CHAPTER
ELEVEN

*E*LLIOT EXTRACTED INSTRUMENTS from the autoclave and placed them on clean towels. He heard the door slam then someone hollered his name. Somebody was in trouble. He dried his hands and ran to the waiting area.

Rachel Reed stood in the middle of the room with her hand to her chest. She gasped for breath and pointed across the street. "Doc Elliot, you have to come. Abigail fell, and I think she's broken her wrist, and she hit her head too."

Elliot grabbed his bag and called out to his uncle, who was in the examining room with a patient. "I'll be across the street seeing to Miss Monroe, Doc." What in the world had that young woman gotten herself into now? He'd warned her about doing too much after discarding those crutches.

He ran ahead of Rachel and burst through the door to the library, but he saw no one in the room. Maybe she had fallen between the shelves. Rachel hurried up behind him.

"She's in the storeroom." She nodded toward a door in the middle of the back wall. When he stepped over the threshold, he spotted Abigail immediately. Her eyes were closed in her ashen face, and she held her wrist at an odd angle.

He knelt beside her. "Where does it hurt besides your wrist?" He lifted the wrist with both hands to examine it. Definitely broken.

Her eyes opened slowly. "All over, well, actually just my head and wrist. I went to step down when I heard Rachel come into the building and lost my footing."

"I see." He glanced down at her feet peeking out from beneath her skirt. The injured ankle was encased in a lace-up shoe that looked somewhat tight to his discerning eye. "Are you sure that ankle didn't give you trouble?" His fingers ran over the bump now forming on the side of her head.

"No, I just…well, maybe it did. Oh, I don't know. One minute I was on the ladder, and the next I was on the floor."

Elliot shook his head. She shouldn't have been on that ladder in the first place, but knowing what he did of her, Abigail wasn't about to ask anyone for help. He decided not to scold her for that now because her pain was obvious. She bit her lip and squeezed her eyes shut as he placed a wrap around the wrist to hold it until he could get her across the street and into a room. He then unlaced her shoe and removed it.

"OK, now. I'm going to pick you up and carry you over to the infirmary so we can treat that wrist. Just hold on around my neck with your right arm." He scooped her up into his arms. How lightweight she was, almost like carrying a child.

Rachel scurried ahead to open the doors for him. Once inside the infirmary, Elliot placed Abigail on a bed in an examining room. "Now lie back and let's get a better look at that wrist." Just as he figured, the ulna had fractured just above the area where it joined the hand. At least the break was smooth and even. He gently manipulated the wrist while Abigail sobbed in pain.

"Looks like I'll need to put a hand and lower arm cast on so as to keep the bone aligned properly. I'll give you a bit of laudanum for the pain."

Kate rushed into the room. "I was with Doc Jensen when I heard Elliot bring you in. Rachel just told me what happened." She grabbed Abigail's right hand and held it. "I know you hurt something dreadful, but we'll fix you up." She turned to Elliot. "Do you want me to get the supplies ready for a cast?"

"Yes, if you would do that, I'll get her something for the pain." He strode to the medicine cabinet for the bottle of laudanum. First her ankle and now her wrist. Either Abigail was the clumsiest girl alive or one with the most bad luck. He had grown accustomed to seeing people in pain from injuries, but for some reason Abigail's scrunched-up face touched him in a way he didn't want to acknowledge.

After they finished applying the cast, Kate removed everything and began cleaning the area. Elliot inspected the cast that covered Abigail's hand to the first knuckles of her fingers and thumb then up to the midpoint of her forearm. "I think that'll about do it for now. I'm putting a sling around your neck for you to rest your arm because that cast, even as small as it is, will get heavy, and I don't want you letting your arm hang loose for long periods of time."

He turned to Kate. "Is Mrs. Reed still out in the waiting room?" Having her best friend present might give Abigail some encouragement.

"Yes, I'll go get her."

A moment later, Rachel stepped into the room and over to the bedside. "I'm so sorry I caused you to fall." She glanced down at the cast on Abigail's wrist. "Oh, dear, that's not going to help you get things done. I'm coming over every day and help. You are not to lift those books or climb any ladders."

Abigail shook her head. "It's my fault for trying to do so much on my ankle, and besides, you shouldn't be lifting and climbing either in your condition. Isn't that right, Doctor Jensen?"

Before he could answer, Rachel protested. "I'm fine and in the pink of health. It won't hurt me at all to help you."

Elliot suppressed his smile. Now he had two stubborn women to handle, and neither one would likely pay much attention to what he had to say anyway. "Rachel is fine, and you could do with some help with those books and boxes I saw in the storeroom. It wouldn't hurt to ask for assistance in lifting and carrying them to the other room if necessary."

Abigail looked down at her wrist. "I suppose you're right. Daniel isn't that far away at the courthouse, and he could come help me."

"Nathan can too since he's just down the block." Rachel turned to Elliot. "Don't worry. We'll be careful, I promise. I don't want anything to happen to my baby, and Abigail wants her wrist to get well."

Elliot had to smile at that. Mrs. Reed had a good head on her. "I believe you." He examined the cast again. "I suggest you go on back to the boardinghouse. It's almost closing time for the library anyway." He arranged a sling about her shoulder.

Kate held out her hand. "If you'll give me the key, I'll lock up the library for you. Rachel can walk with you down to

Aunt Mae's, and don't be surprised if she hovers over you like a mother hen. Two injuries in two weeks is going to bring out all mothering techniques for sure."

Abigail extracted the key from her skirt pocket and handed it to Kate. "I appreciate that, and it'll be nice to have Aunt Mae doting on me." Then she turned her brown eyes to Elliot. They glistened in the light from the overhead fixture. "And thank you, Doctor Jensen, for taking care of me again. I promise to follow your orders this time."

Elliot grinned and helped her from the table. "Call me Doc Elliot. Doc Jensen is my uncle."

Rachel grabbed Abigail's good arm. "Now let's get you back where you belong so you can rest before supper. When that laudanum wears off, you'll be hurting again." She stood a good five inches taller than Abigail and had no problem supporting her friend as they headed out.

When the door closed behind them, he turned to find Kate staring at him with a smile. "What's the matter now?"

"Oh, nothing. I was just thinking about how cute Abigail looks. She's such a tiny thing." Kate raised an eyebrow. "With all her energy and enthusiasm, she'd make some man a fine wife."

"Well, she'll have plenty of opportunities to find one around this town. I've already seen a few men giving her the eye." He picked up a tablet and headed out to his desk. He didn't care to discuss Abigail Monroe now or anytime except as his patient.

Kate followed him but said nothing more. However, he felt her gaze still on his back as he made notes to add to a file he'd begun for Abigail. Finally he turned around. "Can't you find something to do? I can't concentrate with you staring at me."

"Who's staring at you? I'm getting ready to leave." She untied her apron and tossed it into the basket to be taken to the laundry tomorrow. "I have to go over and lock up the library, and then I'll head on home."

"You aren't planning to cook Daniel a meal, are you?" He'd experienced firsthand some of Kate's cooking and didn't envy Daniel a bit in that area.

"No, I'm stopping by Aunt Mae's to pick up supper if it's any of your concern. And for your information, I am learning to cook. One of these nights I'll invite you over and show you."

"That will be cause for celebration for somebody, but I'll pass on that invitation."

Kate swatted his arm before heading for the door. "You'll be sorry, Doctor Elliot Jensen."

After she left, Elliot finished his charts. Doc must have left because all the exam rooms were now empty and he wasn't anywhere to be found. He'd probably already headed for a place to eat. Since Aunt Maggie was at her sister's, mealtime found Doc and him either at Annie's Kitchen or Aunt Mae's for supper. He preferred the boardinghouse over the new restaurant. Soon as he washed up, he'd head on over to Aunt Mae's. If anybody needed him or his uncle, they'd know where to look.

When Aunt Mae saw Abigail's cast, she made Abigail sit down to rest. "Now then, young lady, don't you move until supper's on the table." She planted her fists on her hips and asked, "All right, tell me, what in the world happened to you?"

Both Rachel and Abigail explained, and Aunt Mae shook

her head. "I don't know what we're going to do with you, honey. First your ankle and now your wrist. You keep having accidents like this, and we just might have to make a doctor your permanent keeper."

Rachel laughed. "I'll leave you two to discuss that. I'm going to meet Nathan so we can get on home."

Heat rose in Abigail's cheeks as Rachel departed. "I don't think either doctor would be interested in the job. Doc Elliot thinks I'm clumsy and stubborn, and not a very good patient. Doc Jensen's too busy for the likes of me, so it looks like it'll be up to you."

"Now that's a job I don't mind at all, but I figured someone younger, like Doc Elliot, would be more to your liking."

That would be nice, but as far as Abigail could tell, that young man had no interest at all in her as anything other than a patient. For a town full of eligible men, she'd seen precious few who had shown any real interest in her. Perhaps they were all too busy. Or maybe they were intimidated that she was a librarian. She shouldn't care, but she did. Was it more of a pride thing or just a normal girlish desire to have some attention?

"I see that look, and it means you're thinking about something, and I wager it has something to do with what I said. Come on, honey, out with it."

No getting anything past Aunt Mae's shrewd eyes and intuition. "It did, but the only two men I've had any interest in at all have shown none in me. Penelope Dawes told me that Philip has sent off for a mail-order bride for himself. Wonder if they have any mail-order grooms."

"Oh, pshaw, honey, you've been so busy with the library

that you haven't had time to think about the men in this town. Just you wait until the church has another social. I wager you'll have several asking you to dance at that."

"Maybe so, but I'm not really looking for a husband right now. I've got a library to take care of." That may be true, but it didn't sound very convincing even to her own ears. How would she take care of the library anyway with her arm in a cast? And as for a social life, who would want to risk dancing with someone with a weak ankle?

Aunt Mae hustled back to the kitchen, and in a few minutes the other residents joined her at the table for supper. Cory came up behind her and tapped her shoulder. He grinned and mischief danced in his eyes.

"Hear tell you had a little accident this afternoon."

His eyes held true concern, but it only served to emphasize the clumsiness she felt next to him. Heat filled her cheeks, and her heart raced. "I...I did." She felt like such a fool. First her ankle, and now this.

He eased into the chair beside her. "I'm sorry about that. Your ankle was just getting well too. Looks like the doc took care of you, though."

"He did, and I'm thankful it's my left wrist. At least I can still write and eat without a problem."

"But you might need help at the library. Maybe I can stop by and check to see if there's anything you need me to do...like climbing or reaching." His grin broadened and he winked.

Heat flooded Abigail's face again, and she bowed her head to escape those twinkling eyes. Her heart slowed, but the pounding remained in her ears. Cory may tease her, but it didn't annoy her like Daniel's teasing. In fact, she rather liked it.

When the prayer for the meal ended, Abigail cut her gaze to Cory and turned on what she hoped would be a brilliant smile. "You really would come to help me? I think I'd like that."

No sooner had she said the words than her gaze strayed to Elliot, who sat across the room. Why had she not noticed when he came in? The look he gave her didn't give a clue as to what he thought or felt, but for some reason, she was intrigued. She still wanted to get to know him better.

Cory spoke beside her, and her head jerked. Here he sat close enough to touch, and her thoughts had gone across the room. What was the matter with her? How could she have interest in both men? She was being as bad as Rachel when deciding between Nathan and that Edward fellow in Boston. It was time to get her head on straight.

CHAPTER
TWELVE

*T*HE NEXT WEEK flew past with Abigail able to carry out her responsibilities as librarian despite the cast on her wrist. Here it was on toward the end of September, and after just a few weeks, the library was a rousing success. She unpacked a new box of books she'd ordered and checked them against her list. Nathan and Daniel had both been such a big help in bringing over the goods as they arrived by train and putting them where she could easily reach them.

Rachel sat across from her making a list of overdue books. Abigail didn't worry much about the list. Most people returned their books on time, but a few of the ranchers and their families didn't always get them back. Perhaps she should allow them more time rather than imposing any type of fine. "You know, Rachel, I've been pleasantly surprised at the diverse reading interests of people here. They ask for classics as well as books about the history of our country and even books on cooking."

"With most of the people from somewhere else, like we are, that's bound to happen."

"I'm glad I decided to join Daniel out here, and I'm especially blessed that you and Nathan are here." Having her best friend close by had been one of the reasons the move to Texas had been appealing in the first place.

Abigail shelved a few books then returned to the front desk manned by Rachel. "It's so slow during the week. Only a few people come in, and of course the children after school. I wish we had more days like Saturdays. Then I'm busier than a bee in a hive."

Rachel stood and stretched. "Maybe those who live in town will start coming during the week to avoid the crowds on Saturday." She glanced at the watch pinned to her bodice. "Say, isn't it time for you to go to the doctor?"

Abigail jumped up. "Oh, my, yes, I clean forgot the time. Can you stay here and take care of this while I run over there? It shouldn't take long." With all the conversation Doc Elliot provided, she'd be back in less than ten minutes. If only she could get him to talk to her. He was a nut she'd like to crack open to see what he was like inside.

"Take your time. I'm perfectly content sitting her and sorting out these books."

Abigail nodded then headed across the street. Try as she might, nothing had worked in grabbing the attention of the doctor on the few visits since her broken wrist. On top of that, she never saw him anywhere except in the infirmary.

When she entered the waiting room, Doc Jensen greeted her. "Hello, Miss Monroe. Elliot is in the storeroom. You go on into that room over there, and he'll be right in. Kate's here, and she'll be out to see you too."

He disappeared through a door, so she made her way to the front examination room and stepped up on the little stool to sit on the examination table. Elliot appeared a few moments later with Kate right behind him. Kate said, "I told Doc Elliot that you'd been behaving yourself and taking good care of your wrist."

"Thank you, Kate. I don't want to make it worse since my...never mind." She held up her cast for Elliot to check. She wasn't about to tell them that her ankle still hurt some when she walked on it. She'd been foolish with that injury, but she'd be more careful this time.

"I'll leave you two to take care of business. I'm going down to the mercantile to pick up those drugs your uncle ordered." With that Kate swept from the room with her skirts rustling.

Elliot held her arm just above the cast and tested her fingers. It didn't hurt, so she kept quiet, but she liked the gentle way he probed and examined her hand. "You know, Elliot, God gave you an amazing talent. It's wonderful to see you using it to help people."

Startled eyes met hers, and the tips of his ears reddened. "I went to school to learn all I know. God didn't teach me."

What a strange reaction to a compliment. "But He gave you good hands and a caring heart. He's helped you develop your skills to be the doctor you are today. Some of what you do can't be learned in books. God gives the talent, then man makes use of it. I say you've done quite well in that area."

Darkness filled his eyes, and he let go of her hand. "It

looks good, Miss Monroe. Another four weeks or so and I'll remove the cast."

"That long?" She sighed and slumped her shoulders. "It doesn't hurt anymore, so I thought it might be well." Then she straightened up and smiled. "Does that mean I need to come every week to have it checked?"

"Not really. Unless something happens between now and then, you won't need to come back until the cast is ready to come off."

So now she had no excuse to come see him, and he kept to himself when he wasn't in the infirmary. She tilted her head and peered at him with her eyebrows knit together. "Why haven't I seen you at church? I've been here for over a month and haven't seen you there at all. Are you on duty every Sunday or something?"

Doc Elliot ducked his head and became busy with writing on a tablet. "I don't care much for church gatherings."

Abigail decided to keep pressing. "Oh, my, that's a shame. My friend, Reverend Winston, is a good preacher, even if I am a little biased in his favor from having grown up with him. You really ought to try it unless you don't believe in God or something." She stopped short. Now she sounded like an interfering busybody. That must be the reason for his response to her compliment, but if it was, she had to find a way to talk with him about spiritual matters without making him angry. The purpose was to help him find God, not to turn him away with her comments.

Before she could apologize, Elliot frowned. "Reverend Winston is very good. I heard him once after he first came to

Porterfield, but what he has to say has no bearing on my life or what happens in it."

"Doc Elliot, you can't mean that. God has every bearing on our lives. He brought me here to Porterfield once I'd prayed about it, and He made great provisions for all of us to come from Connecticut." This was going to be a much more difficult task than she first thought, but leading someone to find Jesus was too important just to leave hanging like this.

"That's fine for you to say. Believe whatever you want. I'm not interested." He stood and held out his hand to help her down from the exam table, clearly dismissing her.

Abigail blinked her eyes and reached for his hand. When his fingers grasped hers, a warm feeling flooded her arm up to the shoulder. What a sturdy, healing hand he had. He lifted his head, and their gazes locked. Neither said a word, but Abigail nearly gasped at the depth of pain reflected in his eyes. A lump formed in her throat, and she bit her lip. Something terrible had happened to this young man.

He jerked his head and looked away, and as quickly as it appeared, the pain was gone, replaced with an expression she couldn't quite determine. But that brief contact touched a spot deep within in Abigail, and she determined to find out all she could about Elliot and his past.

Elliot cleared his throat and let go of her hand. "Just remember what I told you about trying to lift anything very heavy with that wrist and hand before it has a chance to heal properly. You can still use your fingers, but don't grip too tightly with them."

"I understand." She hesitated a moment. If only she could think of something to let him know she cared about him and hadn't meant to pry. She wanted to help him as he had helped her. "Thank you for all you've done for me. You are a wonderful doctor, and Porterfield is very fortunate to have you. Do drop by the library sometime and see what all is there."

He walked with her to the waiting room. "I might do that." He stopped, and she proceeded on out the door.

On the boardwalk, she slowed her step. Something had happened in that examining room that had nothing at all to do with her injured wrist, but everything to do with a doctor who bore an ache in his soul. She prayed God would use her to help ease the pain.

Elliot stared at the closed door, his heart thudding much faster than normal. Every time he found himself near Abigail, something happened deep inside. She stirred longings he'd successfully buried over the past few years. He didn't want them to break through and resurface because he couldn't bear the hurt that would come with them.

He shook his head to clear it and turned to his desk. The door to his uncle's office where he held private consultations with his patients stood ajar. Doc's voice filtered through the air, followed by Kate's. He put his hand out to open the door to join them but jerked back when he heard Kate speak his name.

"Elliot is unhappy. I can see it in his eyes when he doesn't think anyone's looking, and I don't think it comes from feeling sorry for a patient."

What were they doing discussing him? His business was his own. If his uncle shared his secret, he'd leave Porterfield on the next train. The good people of the town didn't need to know he'd let a patient die back in Cleveland.

Then his uncle spoke. "I'm not at liberty to say what happened, but Elliot does have some issues he needs to work out."

Kate said, "I'll pray that whatever is bothering him will be resolved. He's a handsome young man and would make some lucky woman a good husband."

"And Daniel's sister may be just the one to help him. That's why I've made sure he's the one to treat her every time she comes in."

Bile rose in Elliot's throat. Who did they think they were? They were as bad as those meddling people back in Cleveland, the ones he'd run away from. He didn't need the frowns, whispers, or pointed fingers from the people here.

He started to barge in and let them know his life was none of their business but stopped short. He clenched his hands into fists at his side and turned to race up the stairs to the privacy of his own room.

Once there he collapsed on the bed. Every moment of that horrible night came rushing back to him in a wave that washed over him with despair and grief. If only he could go back and undo all that happened. If only he could have saved her.

Of course her parents blamed him. Elliot blamed himself. As her fiancé, he was supposed to take care of Angela and protect her, not let harm come to her. How could people believe in a loving God who took the lives of young people before they could have a chance to live? He'd seen mothers lose their babies during birth and babies who didn't live for many days or hours after birth. A loving God wouldn't do that. No matter how hard he prayed for Angela to live, God didn't answer and let her die.

Doctors were supposed to save lives, but that didn't happen with Angela. Despite the fact that he'd taken care of many others here in Porterfield with great success, guilt over Angela would forever be a part of his soul. God hadn't helped him when he needed it, so why would God help him now? He'd given up on ever having that happen. Elliot did just fine without Him these days.

He shoved the other memories back in the dark recesses of his mind. No need to think about such things now. What was done had been done, and he couldn't go back and change events no matter how much he wanted to, but he could control his future and make sure he didn't fall in love with another woman the way he'd loved Angela.

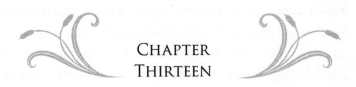

CHAPTER
THIRTEEN

*M*OVING DAY HAD finally arrived. They had scheduled it for the first Saturday in October, hoping the weather would be cooler, and it was. Not only that, but the house was finished and Aunt Maggie had everything packed and ready to go. Elliot stacked a few boxes in the waiting area of the infirmary. Donavan was coming into town to help move furniture along with Cory, Daniel, and Reverend Winston. The ladies were to help Aunt Maggie.

The door from outside opened, and he glanced up from his chore to find Rachel and Kate striding across the room.

Kate waved as they passed and headed up the stairs. "We're here to help your aunt. The men will be right behind us."

"We're here." Daniel and the others entered the room. All had their shirt sleeves rolled up and wore denim pants for working.

Elliot grinned and pointed up the stairs. "Doc is up there with Aunt Maggie. All the furniture is ready to move, as are these boxes."

Daniel headed for the stairway. "Then let's get going. We have two wagons to fill."

After greeting Elliot, the others followed Daniel upstairs for the larger pieces of furniture while Elliot moved the smaller boxes out to the boardwalk to be loaded on later.

Across the way Abigail hollered his name and waved. He breathed deeply and waved back. Just seeing her did things to his insides he couldn't control.

"You all excited about the move to your new house? I'll be coming by with some refreshments after I close the library for dinner."

He just grinned and waved again. That's all he needed. If she hung around for dinner, he'd never be able to keep his head straight. She should just stay home what with her wrist still in that cast. He headed back inside for more boxes. This was going to be a long day.

After the wagons were loaded, they all set off for the new house. Kate drove the ladies in the doc's surrey while the men rode on the wagons. Elliot perched himself on one of the boxes and held on as Daniel drove the horses down the street to the newly built house.

The new place had much more space than the rooms above the infirmary. With a larger kitchen, Aunt Maggie already talked about all the things she could do in the new one. If that meant more baked goodies, then Elliot heartily approved.

He leaned on his elbow and contemplated how far he'd come in the past few years. If not for his aunt and uncle, he'd probably be wallowing in some hole in Cleveland, completely cut off from everyone. He had much to thank them for.

An image of Abigail darted across his mind. Strange that

the one woman who had tapped into his wall of protection had a name so similar to Angela. Was this another of God's cruel jokes to set him up for disappointment once again?

Abigail's name wafted on the breeze back to him. Elliot's ears perked up, and he realized Cory and Daniel were talking about her. Cory laughed and said something about her independence and how he admired it in her.

Elliot narrowed his eyes and clamped his lips together. Of course the deputy would have a better chance with Abigail. He was with her so much of the time at the boardinghouse, and his sister being married to her brother didn't help matters.

His hands balled into fists. Who she preferred should make no difference to him, but it did. Unless he planned to let her fully into his life, he'd better repair that chink in the wall around his heart. He shook his head and clenched his teeth. Even if he did let down his guard and seek her favor, she'd much prefer the handsome deputy over a scrawny doctor.

The wagon slowed then stopped, and Elliot jumped down from the wagon. Henry Wilder sauntered up just as they began unloading furniture.

"I'm not sure I can be much help, but I would like to write up an article about the new house and the plans for the space you just vacated."

"That's a good idea, Henry. I'm sure Aunt Maggie will be happy to tell you all about it."

Cory swiped his head with his kerchief. "Hey, Henry, you've been missing a few meals at the boardinghouse. The newspaper got you that busy?"

Henry turned redder than the kerchief in Cory's hands. "Er, uh, um…Miss Annie invited me to have lunch in her little café. She wanted to treat me because of the story I wrote about her a few weeks back."

"That so? Well, it must have been a good lunch since you've missed a few noon dinners at the boardinghouse this past week or so."

"Oh, her cooking isn't as good as Aunt Mae's, but Annie and I found we have some things in common." He straightened up a bit. "Anyways, where I eat my noon meal is no concern of yours, Cory Muldoon." He tipped his hat. "Now if you'll excuse me, I'll go find Mrs. Jensen and learn more about this house."

Cory chuckled and shook his head. "Looks like another single man has found his mate. Yep, single women don't last long around here." He picked up a chair and strode toward the house.

Elliot snorted and picked up a table. He'd been just fine as a bachelor, and so had Cory for that matter. Of course, why Cory stayed single remained a mystery to Elliot. He knew his own reasons, but they grew weaker the longer he was around Abigail. As far as her favor for a person, he figured Cory already had a good head start on that.

Cory set a chair down by the fireplace in the parlor. Something must be eating at Elliot. He'd done nothing but scowl the whole morning. The young doc hadn't said a dozen words to any of them as they worked. He had to be happy for his aunt and uncle, so why the frowns? You'd think the boy had eaten green persimmons and had a bellyache. No business of his, so Cory worked alongside of Donavan and Daniel. Let Elliot do his work alone if that's what he preferred.

A rumble started deep in Cory's gut. Time to stop this heavy hauling and get some food into his stomach to restore the energy he'd lost this morning. If it hadn't been slightly cooler this October morning, they'd all be sweating and grunting even more than they were.

A flash of color caught his eye. He stopped and peered up the street. Abigail waved and hurried toward the new house. She held her hat with her good hand and carried a basket on the one with the cast. He grinned in spite of himself. That silly girl. She ought to be doing the opposite, but he wasn't going to be the one to tell her.

She ran up to him with her eyes sparkling and her cheeks rosy. "Aunt Mae sent some of her pound cake for everyone to enjoy. Sarah's bringing the fried chicken and a casserole, so looks like dinner will be all ready in a few minutes. Is there a table set up yet?"

Cory's blood raced through his veins. How pretty she looked in her dress the color of sunflowers. He blinked his eyes and grinned at her. "I think one's in the dining room. The ladies are stocking the kitchen, so you'll find them there."

That radiant smile of hers warmed him right to his toes, and the scent of rosewater floated in the air as she passed by on her way to the porch, stopping to chat with whoever happened to be along the way. Never had he let a girl get under his skin like he had Abigail.

Elliot greeted her at the door, and the smile she turned on him was even brighter than the one she'd given Cory. The deputy pushed his hat back on his head and stared at the couple who stood chatting as though they had all the time in the world. Green tendrils of jealousy began winding around his heart like English ivy on a stone wall. Elliot probably was more her style. What would she ever see in a cowboy lawman?

He yanked a box down from the wagon bed and lugged it into the house, not even caring about the strain on his muscles. He'd be sore tomorrow, but if it took his mind off Abigail for a few minutes, all the pain would be worth it.

Abigail left Elliot at the door and went to the kitchen. He had sure seemed happier when they talked just now. Maybe this move to a new house was just what he needed. Now if only she could get him to go to church, she'd be very happy.

Two so very handsome men, and neither of them had shown much interest in her. Cory had flirted with her and teased, but then her brother teased her, and she certainly didn't think of Cory like a brother. Elliot neither flirted nor teased, but he touched something in her heart, and she yearned to get to know him better.

Sometime in the next week or so she'd have to sit down and decide just what she expected from her relationships with those two. If she had to choose right now which one to turn her attention to as a possible mate for the future, she'd be hard pressed to make such a decision.

"A penny for your thoughts, Miss Abigail."

Abigail whirled around. "Oh, Sarah, I didn't realize you were so close behind me. And my thoughts aren't worth dirt, much less a penny." She hooked her free hand under Sarah's arm. "Come on, I hear the ladies chattering in the kitchen, and I think the men are about ready to eat."

The four women in the kitchen stopped their stocking

of the shelves when Abigail entered with Sarah. "Here's Aunt Mae's pound cake, and Sarah has the fried chicken and trimmings."

Mrs. Jensen took charge and in a few minutes had the dining table spread with a feast for the hungry crew. As was the custom, the women would wait until the men were well fed before eating themselves. It was a stupid custom as far as Abigail was concerned. At least Aunt Mae had cooked plenty.

The doctor's wife wiped her hands on a dish towel. "Doc should be here from the infirmary unless some unexpected emergency came up." She counted out silverware and napkins and laid them on the table. "Abigail, holler out there and tell the men to come on in before we eat it all."

Abigail laughed. Now *that* she'd like to do. On the porch she clapped her hands. "You out here and those inside ... dinner is ready in the dining room."

Even though the morning had been cool, the sun had warmed during the day, and all the men wiped perspiration from their foreheads before trooping up the steps and into the house. As they passed, the scent of the outdoors and hard labor filled Abigail's nose. Such an honest smell.

Cory winked and grinned at her when he passed. Heat burned in her cheeks. How forward of him to keep doing that, but she didn't intend to ask him to stop. She liked it too much.

She turned as Elliot descended the steps and stopped at the bottom. Abigail stared at him, and the admiration she saw in his face this time sent shock waves of delight to the tips of her feet. Then just as suddenly the admiration was gone, replaced by the familiar air of disinterest. He nodded at her and turned to go into the dining area.

Abigail stood with her hand reaching out for support from the highboy beside her. All her plans to be free and independent threatened to fly out the window. She'd better catch them and get them back in line. Unless God did a miracle in the next few days or weeks, she couldn't be thinking of Elliot as anything but a nice friend and a good doctor. She could never become involved with anyone who was not as sure of God as she was.

Then a smile played about her mouth. God was in the miracle business, and He wouldn't mind if she helped things along a little bit.

CHAPTER
FOURTEEN

*T*HE FOLLOWING WEEK passed without any opportunity for Abigail to make good on her vow. She didn't see Elliot except in passing, and unless he made himself more visible around town, most likely she wouldn't see him again until he removed the cast. Although his aunt and uncle attended church every Sunday, Elliot had yet to make an appearance. She'd only been able to pray for him since the day he'd revealed he had no use for God in his life.

Once again Abigail was invited to the Muldoon ranch for Sunday dinner. Afterward she joined the Muldoon women in the parlor while the men retired to Callum Muldoon's office to discuss business. Even Nathan and Daniel had joined them. The only one missing was Seth, who had stayed in town with his wife, Erin.

Abigail glanced down at the cast on her hand and wrist and grimaced. It itched worse than when she'd had poison ivy years ago as a child.

Ada wrapped her arm around Abigail's shoulders. "Are you in pain?"

"Not pain, but it itches something terrible, especially my palm."

"Hmm, I think I have just the thing for that." She scurried from the room and returned moments later with a long, thin wire.

"Here you are. When Callum injured his leg last year and had it all bandaged up, he used this to reach under the dressing to scratch." She proceeded to inch the wire under the cast and down to Abigail's palm. "Now scratch where the itch is."

Abigail moved the wire back and forth and sighed with relief. It really did help. "Thank you, Ada. That worked quite well."

"Then take it with you and use it when you need it."

Abigail laid the wire near her belongings to take it back to Porterfield with her. When she rejoined the circle of ladies, Sarah was speaking of Doc Elliot.

"We are so blessed to have him in our town. He shows such care and concern for me when I go in for my checkups."

Ada pursed her lips. "I liked the young man myself after the way he took care of Callum last year, but I still don't understand the need to go see him every month. We didn't do that in our day, did we, Mabel?" She glanced across at Aunt Mabel, who shook her head.

"We sure enough didn't. I think I may have seen my doctor twice during the entire time and then when it was time for delivery. Had my babies at home too, but now women are looking to hospitals for that. People say it's safer that way and more babies live, but seems to me that's God's choice whether you're in a hospital or at home."

Rachel, Kate, and Sarah all chimed in at once about the advantages of having a baby in a hospital rather than at home. Abigail listened with only a portion of her attention, as having babies certainly didn't interest her right now.

Her feet tip-tapped on the floor under her skirts as the voices droned on about her. She stood then wandered aimlessly to the window. Children played in the yard, and she spotted James Lowell playing with them. He must be telling them some tall tale as the children laughed and clapped at whatever he said.

Someday she would like to have children of her own, but first she would have to find the right man. Or he would have to find her! Right now it looked as though neither of her choices even wanted to find her.

A hand tapped her shoulder, and Abigail turned to find Cory behind her. He smiled and said, "I know all this talk is boring you. It's such a beautiful day outside, let's take a ride. You haven't really seen all of our ranch."

"That sounds delightful, but I'm not in any condition for horseback riding."

Cory laughed. "Of course not. We'll take the buggy. It's hitched and ready to go." He picked up his hat from a hall tree by the door and handed her the one she'd worn earlier. "The weather is perfect today for a drive."

Cory led Abigail out to where the family vehicles were hitched and unwound the tie on the one belonging to Kate and Daniel. Cory held her firmly about the waist as he lifted her up into the buggy. The touch of his hands burned through Abigail's dress.

She composed her thoughts as he climbed up beside her.

"Are your fall seasons always like this? I've never seen such beautiful weather in October."

"Your brother asked exactly the same thing last year. This is my favorite time of the year, when the weather is cool enough for a light jacket but not cold enough for a heavy coat. The colors are not as spectacular as those in your state, though, or so I've been told." He cut his gaze to Abigail and grinned.

Oh, that teasing smile again caused her to bubble over with laughter. "That would be my brother. Connecticut is alive with color now, but fall can also be cold and rainy. It's nothing like this."

Cory clicked the reins and pointed in the direction of a forest. "The pines are loblollies and grow to great heights. They're the ones the sawmill cuts down for timber. When the wind comes down from the north or up from the south, you can hear the singing in the trees. It has its own special music, or so Kate says."

"I never heard it described like that, but I love it. In fact, I've grown to love everything about this place." Being with him this afternoon made it even better.

Cory smiled. "I'm glad you like it."

He continued to point out spots of interest, including the types of cattle. To Abigail, they were ugly creatures with those horns sticking out of their heads. Cory called them longhorn cattle.

Her mind drifted to thoughts of Elliot Jensen. Kate worked with him, yet she didn't know much more about him than Abigail had learned on her own. As a doctor he was so caring and kind, but as a person he was withdrawn. Such a mystery she'd like to unravel.

Cory stopped the buggy. "Are you feeling ill? You've been very quiet."

Heat filled Abigail's cheeks. Here she sat next to one of the most handsome men in the area, and another man filled her thoughts. How rude she had been.

"I'm sorry. I guess I was thinking about this cast and when I'll be getting it off." She furrowed her brow. "Cory, do you have any idea at all what might be bothering Doc Elliot? He's such a good doctor, yet he can be so distant at times."

Something passed over Cory's face that she couldn't decipher. "He is a good doctor, and his patients all seem to like him. All I know is that something happened in Cleveland, and he nearly quit medicine altogether. I believe his uncle is the one who persuaded him to stick with it and come down to Texas."

"That was a good decision. I can't imagine Elliot being anything else but a doctor." She was grateful he had come. Although Doc Jensen was excellent, she preferred to have Elliot treat her.

Her right hand covered the one bound in the cast. His hands had been so gentle and sure when he took care of her wrist. Whatever had happened in his past couldn't have had to do with his medical skills. Something else must have caused him to want to quit. Her heart wouldn't rest until she learned the truth and helped Elliot put it behind him.

Then her mind snapped to attention. She had to forget the doctor and concentrate on the man beside her. He'd shown more interest in the past week or so than Elliot had in the entire time she'd been here. She turned to Cory and began to chat enthusiastically about her latest plans for the library.

The quietness of the new house touched a nerve in Elliot. They'd moved in only last week, but the solitude grated and left him bored and restless. His fingers drummed on his desk as he viewed what he could see of the town of Porterfield through his second-floor window.

Sunday afternoons meant empty streets and closed-up shops. Even the saloon closed down on the Sabbath day. The only places open for business were the hotel and the jail in the new courthouse. He turned from the window and grabbed his jacket from its hook near the door. With weather like today, a good walk about town might relieve the boredom as well as be good exercise. He descended the stairway as quietly as possible so as not to disturb his aunt and uncle, who indulged in their Sunday afternoon nap time.

Out on the sidewalk, he breathed deeply of the crisp fall air then strode out to the street. The boardinghouse, two houses down from the Jensen place, looked serene on this fall afternoon. As he passed, Miss Perth and Mrs. Barnett both waved to him from the porch.

Aunt Mae opened the door and stepped outside carrying a tray with a pitcher and glasses. She set it down then called to Elliot. "Yoo-hoo, Doc Elliot. Come on up and have some lemonade and cake."

He waved back and shook his head. "No, thank you. I'm taking a walk into town."

She shrugged and started pouring lemonade into the glasses. Elliot continued on his way and spotted children playing in yards down the street. Their laughter rang with joy through the afternoon air. Oh, to be young again with no more cares and worries than a child.

At one time he and Angela had planned on a large family, and seeing the boys and girls running about in fun brought back those old longings and dreams. If things had gone as they should, he and Angela might have been strolling the streets of Cleveland with their own baby in its carriage. But that was not to be.

The town park beckoned with its many benches offering a place to rest. Elliot sat and leaned back, his face tipped to the warmth of the sun. His mind whirled with all the plans he'd made with Angela that were never to be realized. Grief tingled in the back of his throat, and he fought the tears that threatened.

He stood and walked with a brisk pace back toward home. His thoughts jumped from Cleveland and the hospital there to the infirmary here in Porterfield. Neither resembled the other, but the smaller of the two had given him peace the past few years. He'd felt pride and a sense of accomplishment in Cleveland, but here the love of the people and their trust in him had come to mean more than all the accolades he'd ever received in Cleveland.

Elliot stopped and gasped. How had he arrived at the church? He hadn't been headed in that direction at all. *God, what are You doing to me?* Church was the last place he wanted to be. He turned to leave when he heard his name being called.

Reverend Winston hailed him from the porch of the parsonage next door. "Good afternoon, Doc Elliot. Wait a minute, I'd like a word with you."

He strode across the yard, and Elliot groaned. Now he'd

have to listen to another lecture about why he should be in church on Sundays. "Good afternoon, Reverend." Whatever the man had to say, Elliot wished for it to be quick.

"It's good to see you, Doc Elliot. I've been meaning to stop by the infirmary and thank you for the care you've given to Erin. This being our first child, we want everything to go perfectly."

Elliot had to smile. First-time fathers-to-be were always more worried and nervous than the mothers. "I understand that, and I can assure you we'll do our best to see that it is. With Erin's good health, she should have no problems at all."

"I'm glad to hear it. She's inside resting now. We were supposed to be out at the Muldoon ranch today, but she didn't feel up to the long ride out there."

"She's still about two months from delivery, but I'd say a rest is better than a carriage ride that distance any day. If that's all, I'll be on my way." He turned to leave. At least he'd escaped a lecture.

The reverend grabbed his arm. "No, there's something else I'd like to speak with you about."

Here it comes. No way would the reverend let him off without asking about church attendance.

"I've been concerned about you. I know you don't want to be in church, and you think you have no room for God in your life." He paused.

Elliot pressed his lips together. Reverend Winston was indeed right about that. Why couldn't he just leave well enough alone?

"Doc, don't you see that the real answer to whatever is bothering you is with God? Even if you think you have no room for Him, the Lord will find a place to dwell if you invite Him in." He held up his hand to quiet the protest on Elliot's lips.

"I'm not going to say anything else about it. I only want you to know that if you ever need anyone to talk to or confide in, I'm available. The doors to my office are always open, as are God's arms to welcome you back."

"Thank you, Reverend, but that won't be necessary. If you'll excuse me, I'll be on my way." He turned and hastened down the sidewalk in the opposite direction. The reverend's intentions were good, but he'd never understand why Elliot had no use for God or the church.

With a determined set to his mouth and his stride, Elliot headed home. Maybe he should quit taking Sunday afternoon walks. He always ended up talking with people who asked too many questions and wanted to know too much. He stopped on the house porch to observe the boardinghouse down the way. Its porch now sat empty and silent.

Abigail must be out at the ranch since she wasn't on the porch with the other ladies earlier. He shook his head. Where had that thought come from? He hadn't given her a thought all afternoon, and now here she was invading his territory again. Something had to be done about the situation, but he didn't have any idea what that might be. It became harder each time he saw her to resist her charm and warm personality, but then did he really want to resist? Of course he did, and he would.

CHAPTER
FIFTEEN

ANOTHER WEEK AND a half passed, and October blazed forth with all its glory. In Briar Ridge they would have already experienced a good frost or two, and the colors would be fading. In Texas the weather still offered mild days and cool nights. And Abigail had been told that snow most likely wouldn't come until January or February, if then.

Abigail breathed deeply, the fresh air invigorating her spirit. At least she'd managed to avoid more accidents. She eyed the cast on her wrist and grimaced. The itching started up again, and she reached for the wire Ada had given her. In a moment the itching eased, and Abigail sighed with relief. The cumbersome thing couldn't come off fast enough for her. She returned to her task of posting a flyer advertising the Fall Festival on the door to the library.

Even though it was still over a week away, signs for the Fall Festival appeared everywhere in town. The celebration commemorated not only the fall season but also the town's founding when Samuel Porterfield set up a trading post with the Caddo Indians in 1840. As more and more settlers came into the region, Porterfield grew into the town it had become today.

Abigail read the announcement about the festival again. A day full of events had been planned, and all the merchants in town were providing special merchandise for sale that day. Although the stores in general would be closed, most planned booths to sell their particular wares.

The bell over the door jingled to announce a patron. Abigail glanced up to see Erin Winston shutting the door behind her.

"Good morning, Erin. How's that little one doing?"

"I had an appointment with Doc Elliot for my monthly checkup." She placed a hand on her swollen belly. "This baby has begun somersaults these past few days. It must be a boy to be so active."

Abigail laughed. "That just means he's a healthy little one."

"I pray so. He's going to be a wonderful Christmas gift for Ma and Pa. With Rachel due in a few months and Sarah soon after, it looks like the Muldoon family will have its share of babies in the new year." She glanced at Abigail's hand. "When will you be getting rid of the cast?"

"Today, I hope. Doc Elliot is going to check it out, and if he's satisfied, it'll come off. Can't be too soon either. I'm anxious to get back full use of both hands." She picked up a book and examined its cover then peered up at Erin. "I've noticed that Doc Elliot doesn't attend church. Has Seth ever talked to him about it?"

"Yes, Seth has spoken to him several times, but then he decided to leave the doc alone for a while. Sometimes even a little pressure can be too much and drive a person farther away from God. Seth believes Elliot will come to church when he's made peace with God and himself."

"Oh, Erin, the last time I was in to see him a few weeks ago, I saw such sadness in his eyes for a brief moment, and it pained my heart. Something terrible must have happened to him." Perhaps if she could find out what it was, Abigail could help him.

"I've seen it too. The only thing we can do is pray for him every day. God will be with him."

"But shouldn't someone at least try to help?"

"If anyone could help Doc Elliot, it would be Doc Jensen. There's nothing we can do."

Abigail was a bit disappointed. Shouldn't a pastor do more than that? Prayer was all well and good, but weren't Christians supposed to do more to help the hurt and grieving? That made her decision to help Doc Elliot even more important to her, and she'd begin this afternoon when she saw him.

Erin pointed to the Fall Festival announcement. "I see you're advertising the big event. It's lots of fun."

"So I've heard. I'd participate in the church bake sale, but that's not my strong point. I can prepare simple things, but not cakes and pastries."

"We'll have plenty without you, so don't worry about it." She turned toward Abigail. "I came to invite you to Aunt Mabel's birthday. Sarah has invited all of us to come out to their place for a birthday dinner this Saturday evening."

"Oh, how wonderful. I don't want to miss that." Abigail reached behind the counter and pulled out some books. "Before I forget, the titles you requested came in. I've already checked them out under your name."

Erin picked up the books. "Oh, this is wonderful. I like to rest my feet in the afternoon and read a good book. Thank you, Abigail." She headed for the door and said over her shoulder, "Hope you get that cast off soon."

When she had left, Abigail stood at the window and stared over at the infirmary. So many things could happen in one's life to turn one away from God. Nathan Reed had overcome the tragedy of his past and returned to the Lord, and that could happen with Elliot. But how would anything ever change if no one talked to him about his past? Everyone seemed to dance around Elliot, not wanting to bother him or invade his privacy. Perhaps he needed a little disturbing.

A man strode across the street in her direction. What did Henry Wilder want now? When he spotted her through the window, he waved and a moment later entered the library.

"Hello, Mr. Wilder. What can I do for you today?"

"I'm not sure. I just came from Graysons' store, and I overheard a rumor that Allen's brother Philip had written off for a mail-order bride and she'd be here tomorrow. You're friends with Penelope. Has she mentioned it to you?"

Penelope had confided in her, and Abigail had promised not to say anything. Mr. Wilder could sometimes be too nosy for his own good. "Now, Mr. Wilder, I'm not one to repeat stories. Why don't you go ask Philip about it? He's sure to tell you what you need to know."

"Went there first, and he's on a freight run south of here and won't be back until Friday. Allen wasn't there either."

"Well, there now you have it. She can't be coming tomorrow if Philip is out of town. I'd be careful about those rumors." She picked up two books to return to the shelves. "Now, is there anything else I can help you with?"

"Hmm, no, I guess not." Then he grinned. "Had any more accidents lately?"

Heat rose in Abigail's face, and she forced politeness to her voice. "No, I've been most fortunate."

"Been seeing a lot of the young doc, I bet. Is he going to remove that cast soon?"

The nerve of this man. He tried to make everything into a news event. Well, he wouldn't this time. He could go find something more exciting. "I don't see that is any of your concern, Mr. Wilder. It will come off when the doctor says it is ready to come off." She stepped away. "Now if you'll excuse me, I have work to do."

"Well, I did have one—" The jangle of the bell above the door cut him off.

Maggie Jensen stepped through the door. "Hello, Abigail." Then she saw Mr. Wilder. "Oh, am I interrupting something?"

Abigail narrowed her eyes at Henry. "Good day, Mr. Wilder. It was nice talking to you." She then turned her attention to the doctor's wife. From the corner of her eye she saw Wilder staring at her. Then he shook his head and left.

Mrs. Jensen pursed her lips. "That's one nosy man. He won't leave Elliot alone."

"My sentiments exactly, and some of his questions are rather rude. I don't blame Doc Elliot for not answering. Now, how can I help you?"

"I'm going back over to my sister's home for a few days. She's been so terribly ill. Doc even looked at her, and both he and her doctor say not much can be done for her since her heart is failing. She's almost ten years older than I am and was like a mother to me." She blinked her eyes, which had grown moist. "Anyway, I want to check out a couple of books to take with me to read while I'm there. She likes for me to read aloud to her."

Abigail suggested a few books, and after Mrs. Jensen signed them out, she turned to leave. "Thank you, dear, and don't forget, you are to see Doc Elliot this afternoon."

"I won't, but thanks for the reminder." As if she could forget this cumbersome thing on her wrist. In the weeks since her fall, she had seen the doctor a few times, but their time together had been too short for her to engage him with any more questions. She tightened her lips. She'd make sure today was different.

She glanced at her watch and saw that it was only fifteen minutes until the time she normally closed for the noon meal. This would be a good time to walk over and see Elliot about her cast. No need to keep it on one minute longer than necessary. The first thing she planned to do when it came off was to scratch. Ah, wouldn't that be a relief.

Elliot raised his head from his paperwork to see Abigail at the door. He jumped up as she entered. "Abigail, I wasn't expecting you this early."

"It seemed to me that a few hours early wouldn't make that much difference, and I can't wait to get rid of this thing." She held up her hand wearing the cast and waved it in the air. "It's really a nuisance."

Elliot laughed. "Yes, casts do tend to get that way. Go on

into the examining room while I get your files." He couldn't take his eyes from her. She looked especially nice today in her dark yellow dress trimmed in brown. Her clothes were more fashionable than those usually worn by the women in Porterfield, but on Abigail, they didn't appear to be out of place. He shook off those thoughts and retrieved her files then strode toward the examining room.

Abigail perched on the edge of the examining table with her feet dangling. She hadn't worn a hat, and her hair hung in waves about her shoulders. A fringe of bangs dusted her fore-head, and her brown eyes glowed with anticipation.

"You really are ready to get that cast off. I can't say that I blame you." He examined the hand and tested the fingers. "Looks fine to me. I'll get my instruments, and we'll get this thing off."

A few minutes later her hand was free of the cast. She turned it back and forth, and a look of dismay filled her face. "It looks awful! It's all white and wrinkly and ugly."

Why hadn't he thought to warn her as to what her hand would look like? "That's common for tissue and skin that's been encased in plaster, like your hand and wrist were. It'll get back to normal soon enough."

She started scratching the palm and then the back of her hand. "Ahh, that feels so good. I almost went crazy with the itching."

Elliot laughed. "One of the more unpleasant side effects of a cast." He waited a moment for her to stop scratching. "Just be careful not to lift anything too heavy for a few more days or even a week. We want those bones knit tight and strong."

"I promise I'll be careful because I sure don't want any-thing like that back on it."

He reached for her right hand to help her down from the table. When his hand touched hers, once again a shock wave of warmth sped up his arm. His stomach clenched and his breath caught in his throat. Her smile filled him with a longing he'd long since denied.

"You can let go now, Doc. I'm steady on my feet."

He looked down at their hands, still clasped. He dropped it like a hot coal. "Oh, sorry."

"For a moment there you seemed to be thinking about something else."

Elliot cleared his throat. "Um, no, I wanted to be sure you were all right."

"How do you like living in the new house?"

"It's fine." Why didn't she just leave?

"It's much closer to the church. Maybe now you can find time to attend with your aunt and uncle. It's always nice to see a family worshiping together."

He fought to keep the ice from his words. "I don't think that will happen. I have other things to do on Sunday."

"Why, Doc Elliot, it seems to me that nothing is more important than being in God's house on Sunday."

That may be what she believed, but it didn't hold true for him. "I have to disagree, Miss Monroe."

She blinked her eyes and then tilted her head to the side. "I'm sorry. Something really terrible must have happened to cause you to feel that way about the Lord's day and His house. No matter what it was, though, God can fix it."

Now she'd done it. Harsh laughter spilled from him. "Now

that's a good one, and none of your business." He turned away and walked toward the door. He may be rude, but he'd had enough of her probing.

Red now tinged Abigail's cheeks. "I'm sorry. I didn't mean to sound nosy. Guess I'll be going now." With that she strode through the door with her back straight and her head held high.

Elliot groaned and slapped his palm to his forehead. His uncle walked in, drying his hands on a towel. "What was that all about?"

"I was rude to Miss Monroe, and I shouldn't have been. She was getting a little too personal with her interest in my past, and I'm afraid I offended her." Abigail Monroe managed to get under his skin and into his mind no matter what he did to prevent it.

"I'm sure she understands." Then he grinned. "Have you thought of asking her to the Fall Festival? That might smooth things over."

Elliot almost snorted. "Not hardly. I plan to spend the day here in case of an emergency." Who did Doc think he was fooling? He more than anyone knew that Angela was the only one for him, and now she was gone. Besides, he wanted no more of Abigail's talk about church and God.

"Suit yourself, young man, but you'll be missing out on a lot of fun." Doc disappeared up the back stairway.

Elliot busied himself with finishing up reports about the patients he'd seen today. When he picked up Abigail's, he stopped. Something about that girl drew him to her like a moth to a flame. He had to be extra careful in the days ahead to keep his mind from going places he'd sworn to never visit again.

Just then Henry Wilder burst through the door. "Come quick, Doc Elliot. Annie's been hurt!"

CHAPTER
SIXTEEN

*E*LLIOT GRABBED HIS bag and followed Henry. What had happened now? Just when one thing healed, something else happened. Wilder ran so fast ahead of him that Elliot had no time to question the reporter further.

One block from the infirmary Elliot found Annie lying in the middle of the street. A man stood nearby trying to control his horse hitched to a buggy. Aunt Mae, Mr. Fuller, and several others stood around her with Mrs. Bennett kneeling at Annie's side.

"Let me see to her." He shoved aside Mr. Fuller and crouched beside her while the others stood back. Annie's pale face stared back at him, her eyes closed. He ran his hands over her head with as gentle a movement as possible and discovered a knot at the base of the skull and then spotted a bruise above her left temple.

He glanced up at the crowd. "How did this happen?"

Aunt Mae said, "I...I don't know. Please help her, Elliot. She looks so pale."

Henry leaned over Elliot. "I saw it happen. I was going to meet her, and she stepped off the boardwalk into the street just as that man came around the corner in his buggy. She screamed and frightened the horse."

Mrs. Bennett wrung her hands together. "I had come out of my shop and was walking a ways behind her. I could tell she wasn't looking and hollered at her. That's when she stopped and looked up to see the horse."

The man driving the buggy wrapped the reins around the hitching post and hurried over to the scene. "I didn't see her until it was too late to stop. Please tell me she'll be all right."

Elliot continued to check Annie as he listened to explanations. He breathed in relief when he found no broken bones. Blood on a rock in the road explained the cut and knot on the back of the head. Her pulse was thready and her breathing shallow. He needed to get her inside where he could examine her further. Satisfied that nothing was broken, he scooped her up in his arms and headed for the infirmary without waiting to send someone for a stretcher. He didn't want to waste any more time.

Henry trailed behind him. "Is she gonna be all right, Doc Elliot?"

"As right as I can make her, Henry." Looked like there was more to Henry's feelings for Miss Annie than anyone had thought. The only wound to give her trouble might be the cut on her head.

As he entered the building, he hollered for his uncle to come down then headed for the examination room and laid her on the table. Aunt Mae, Mrs. Bennett, and Henry Wilder gathered in the waiting area.

Doc rushed in, followed by Kate. He washed his hands and peered at Elliot. "What do we have here, son?"

"She was hit by a horse." Elliot wiped at the blood on her head. "This is what concerned me, but with the blood washed away, it doesn't appear to be so bad. The knot on the back of her head could be the cause for her unconsciousness."

Kate donned an apron and came around to stand across from the doctors. "What do I need to do?"

Elliot cleansed the remaining blood from the back of her head with gentle strokes. "We'll take care of this first. Doesn't look like it'll need stitches because the cut is superficial. After that, we'll step outside and let you loosen her clothing, and then we'll put her in one of the rooms." Scalp wounds tended to bleed more even when they were as minor as this one. Her not waking up concerned him more than the cut.

After the cut had been treated, Elliot and his uncle left to join those waiting. Henry grabbed Elliot's arm again. "She's going to be all right, isn't she?"

"She has a cut on the back of her head, along with a bump that knocked her unconscious. We'll keep a close eye on her here."

Suddenly images from the hospital in Cleveland flooded his mind. He turned and headed into his office and closed the door. Cold sweat covered his forehead, and his hands shook. This couldn't be happening again. All the horror of that night washed over him. He couldn't do this.

The door opened and closed behind him, then an arm circled his shoulders. "I know what you're thinking, Elliot. This isn't like Angela at all. Annie will wake up soon and be fine."

When Elliot didn't respond, his uncle turned him around

to be face-to-face. "It's time to forget what happened and move ahead. Annie will be fine." Elliot didn't want to look ahead, but he couldn't deny Annie proper treatment. He slipped from his uncle's grasp. "I need to get back and check on her. She should wake up soon. It won't be good if she goes into a coma." Elliot strode from his office and back across the waiting area. No one stopped him with questions, but the crowd had grown considerably. She may not have been in town long, but in that time Annie had sure made many friends.

At the same time he reached for the doorknob, Kate opened it from the other side. A grin split her face. "She's awake. Groggy, but awake."

Thank You, Lord. Elliot shook his head. Where had that come from? He hadn't been praying. No matter. She was awake, and that was good news.

Annie turned confused eyes in his direction. "Kate says I was hit by a horse." She rubbed her forehead. "Feels more like a raging bull to me, but I remember that horse and buggy now."

The laughter from those around her brought relief to Elliot's soul. "I'm not surprised, but you should be fine now.

Annie lifted her hands to her head. "My head hurts, but then it always does after I've fainted. That horse scared the living daylights out of me."

"That's to be expected at first, but it should go away."

Annie bit her lip and frowned. "Does that mean I have to stay here in the infirmary? I have the café to take care of."

"No, you'll be able to leave as soon as you can stand and not be dizzy. Kate will finish up with the bandage here, and then we'll see."

"But what about my kitchen? We're serving the noon meal now, and I gotta be there."

Aunt Mae threw her hands in the air then grabbed her apron. "Land sakes, I clean forgot. We have people waiting at the boardinghouse for their meal." She raced from the room and almost knocked over Abigail at the door.

Elliot shook his head. The infirmary was more like a train station with all the comings and goings. Abigail stepped into the room, and his hand shook like a schoolboy reciting a poem for the first time. He shoved it into his pocket.

Kate patted Annie's arm. "I'll send someone to check on things there. You have two people helping to serve and a good extra cook, so it should be OK for one meal."

Abigail stood beside Kate. "Annie, I just heard about your accident. I'll go check on the café for you. Don't you worry about it. Let the doctors take care of you first."

Annie blinked her eyes as a tear slipped down her cheek. "I can't believe how people step in and help others in this town. I've only been here a month or so, and everyone's been so kind."

Kate grinned. "That's Porterfield for you. Now let me help you get settled and comfortable since you're going to be here for a little while longer."

Elliot left the room to let Kate take care of Annie. Abigail grabbed Henry's arm. "You come with me. We can help Annie more at the café than we can here."

Elliot's gaze followed Abigail out the door. Everything about her was good and kind, just as Angela had been.

He spotted his uncle in the corner. He wore a grin that niggled its way under Elliot's skin. No matter what ideas Doc might hatch, Abigail was not the girl of his future.

Abigail marched down to Annie's Kitchen with Henry in tow. What he could do she wasn't sure, but she'd find some way to put him to use. She remembered the one time she'd fallen and hit her head back in Connecticut. Annie would have a stupendous headache and be dizzy for a while, but she'd be back in her kitchen before most folks missed her.

When she entered the café, several people asked about Annie and if what they'd heard was true. Abigail assured them that Annie would be fine and headed for the kitchen. There she found a burly man in an apron removing cornbread and rolls from the oven. Delicious odors of cooked food filled the air.

The man turned when he set the breads on the counter. "What happened to Miss Annie? She did all the cooking this morning and then went to meet Mr. Wilder and hasn't come back."

Abigail grabbed an apron and tied it on, all the while explaining about Annie's accident. "She'll be fine, but she has to rest awhile to make sure she's really all right. I've come to help."

"I'm glad to hear she'll be back." He reached for a pot of stew and began filling two bowls. "My name's Buster, and I'm Annie's brother. She and I grew up cooking together. The food's all done, but the girls need help with serving it."

"I can do that." She turned on her heel and went in search of the two women who usually served the meals. All the tables were full, and the women hustled back and forth trying to take care of them all. "Hi, what can I do to help?"

The older of the two brushed her hair back with her wrist. "Take those tables over there by the wall. See what they want, then go to the kitchen and order it. That's all." She turned to pour iced tea into a diner's glass.

That was all? It couldn't be too hard to do that. The younger woman smirked and handed Abigail a pad and pencil. She recognized the woman as Buster's wife. She'd been in to the library once or twice.

She headed for the tables in the corner with a smile on her face. This would be fun.

After she wrote down her first order, a man at another table called to her. Undecided about whether to take the order to the kitchen or answer the man, Abigail stood there until Lorraine Bradley, Buster's wife, jerked her head toward the customer. That must mean to take care of him first.

On her return trip with glasses of water and sweet tea on a tray, she stumbled and almost dropped the tray. One glass did tip over and spilled right into a man's lap. He jumped up and began brushing at his clothes with his napkin.

"Clumsy woman! See what you've done!"

Abigail's cheeks burned as she mopped up the water after setting the other glasses on a table. The heat of the man's glare bore down on her back. At least it'd been cold water and not hot coffee.

She stood and looked down at the man. "I'm truly sorry, and for my clumsiness, your meal is on the house." Paying for his meal was the least she could do for the inconvenience she had caused.

After what Abigail believed must be umpteen million trips back and forth from the tables to the kitchen, her ideas about this job changed completely. Her feet ached to the bone, as did her back, but at least she hadn't dropped any food on people.

She stared at the other two waitresses and marveled at the fact they could still scurry around as fast as they did. How did those two do this every day? She'd be finding a new line of work right away.

Abigail plopped down in a chair and fanned her face with her apron. "Now that was a job. I'm so tired I can hardly move."

Henry jumped up. "Now's the time I can help. You stay right there, and I'll take care of cleaning off these tables."

Buster leaned on the door frame leading to the kitchen. "You did better than I thought you would, missy. My wife says you worked as hard as they did. We do thank you for that and for paying for Hugh Daley's meal."

"You're welcome, and I sure have more appreciation for what it takes to run a café." Annie's closed after lunch every day and didn't open again until the next morning for breakfast, but that was still a lot of work. She much preferred library work, that was for sure.

Abigail studied her wrist while the others cleared the tables. Thankfully it hadn't bothered her at all while she worked. But then she'd been too busy to really notice.

She sat up straight. No more daydreaming. She had work to do and couldn't afford to waste time building castles in the air.

Henry finished his duties at the kitchen and hurried back toward the infirmary to check on Annie. That woman meant more to him then he'd ever admit to anyone but God. He'd never figured on finding love at his age, but then Annie had moved into town with her brother and his wife and opened up that café. One meal there, and Henry was hooked. To have a woman like Annie cooking for him and taking care of him the rest of his life had more appeal than he could ever have imagined.

He remembered the look in Doc Elliot's eyes when he talked with Abigail in the infirmary a little while ago. His eyes showed much more interest than a friend. Something was going on between the doc and Miss Monroe. She'd had two injuries Elliot had treated, and the two had been together rather frequently because of them. There might be a story there. After all, women were not that numerous, and anytime a man and woman in Porterfield came together, a love story had to be in the making.

Then he stopped and lifted his head in laughter. Wasn't he making one of those love stories now? He and Annie would be the talk of the town, but he didn't care. He was falling in love, and *that* was better than getting the scoop on any story, no matter how big.

Then his thoughts sobered to what his editor wanted. He'd told Henry to keep digging and get the facts behind Doc Elliot's move to Porterfield. Successful doctors in a large city didn't usually move to a small town without a good reason, and it was up to Henry to find that reason and write the story. So far, his contacts in Cleveland had given him only the bit of information that Dr. Elliot Jensen had been an up-and-coming doctor at a major hospital then suddenly had quit and moved away.

Abigail's story had been interesting but not headline news. She came from a family who loved her and provided well for her means. She had followed her brother to Texas and spent her inheritance from her grandparents to open a library for the town. That was the only thing to make her story worth noting, and it had endeared her to the people of Porterfield.

He'd taken note of the way the deputy treated Abigail as well as the way Doc Elliot looked at her. Now there lay a good story. It'd be most interesting to see which one of the gentlemen would finally win the lovely Miss Monroe's hand.

CHAPTER
SEVENTEEN

ABIGAIL STUDIED HER wrist again. It'd been only three days since Elliot removed the cast, and the skin had returned to its normal color. She flexed it and moved it in circles. Perfect. No pain and no ache. The party this evening out at Sarah and Donavan's ranch should be fun, as she'd be able to dance and take part much better than the last social event she'd attended.

When Daniel arrived to pick her up, he wore denim pants and a striped shirt like most of the other men in town. He had slipped right into the role of a Texas lawyer, and except for his ever-present Yankee accent, one wouldn't know he wasn't a native.

"I stopped by to let you know Cory is coming to get you and take you on out to Sarah's. Doc Jensen needs Kate at the infirmary, so we'll be going out a little later."

Abigail's heart jumped. "Oh, I'm sorry. I mean, I'm sorry that Kate has to stay, not that Cory is taking me."

Daniel only grinned and then flicked the brim of his hat.

She had to be more careful around her brother, or he'd really start getting ideas about her and Cory.

Five minutes later she sat on the front porch and spotted Cory coming down the street on his horse. Was he expecting her to ride out to Sarah's on a horse too? Not in this dress she wouldn't.

Cory swung down from his horse. "Let me take him into the barn and unsaddle him, then I'll bring the buggy around. Daniel said he'd hitch up Danny Boy for me." He disappeared around the side of the house.

Well, that settled one question. She decided to stroll out to the barn and meet him instead of waiting for him to come back. She stood to the side while he tended his horse.

"I'm glad Annie is able to take care of feeding the boarders for Aunt Mae," Abigail commented.

"Do you think she's really up to it? That was a nasty spill she had the other day." Cory headed her way with Danny Boy in tow.

"Horsefeathers, you know she is. You make a bump on the head sound like a major incident. Besides, Annie's healthy as your horse."

Cory's laugh rang out. "Listen to you. You've picked up Texas vocabulary quicker than your brother did." He reached for her hand. "Your buggy awaits, Miss Monroe." Again he grinned and winked at her.

What was she going to do with him? All that teasing and nary a word about courting her. Men in Texas sure had some strange ways of showing women they cared, that is, if Cory did. She let him assist her up onto the seat, and her heart did a flutter step when he came around and joined her on the seat.

Cory clicked the reins, and they headed out. She prayed Cory didn't see her as just some clumsy Eastern girl he could tease. She valued her independence, but it seemed like ever since she'd been here, things had happened to make her dependent on others for help, and that didn't sit well with her at all. Her main reason for coming in the first place had been to prove she could make a life on her own. If she'd wanted others to look after her and take care of her needs, she'd be Mrs. Wentworth now and living in Boston.

She turned her head to stare at Cory. What a handsome profile. "Did you see the look on Mr. Fuller's face at noon today when Aunt Mae invited him to the party tonight?" The picture of the man tickled her soul. A slight scar graced his head where Elliot had taken stitches in it a few months ago. The fringe of hair encircling his bald head sported more gray than dark brown, but his blue eyes sparkled with enthusiasm at Aunt Mae's invitation.

"Yes, I did, and Aunt Mae's face showed more happiness in it than I've seen in a long time. I think those two may have been made for each other."

A sigh escaped Abigail's lips. Everyone in town lately was pairing up. Even Philip Dawes's mail-order bride was due to arrive soon. Annie and Henry and Aunt Mae and Mr. Fuller proved that love knew no age boundaries. She had begun to wish such love would happen to her.

Cory turned to look her in the eye, and heat filled her face. She hadn't realized she still stared at him.

"Was that a sigh? I'm sure Mrs. Newton wants only happy people at her party, and not sad ones."

"Who said I was sad? And besides, what's that Mrs.

Newton thing? Didn't she ask you to call her Aunt Mabel like the rest of us?"

"Yes, but it does feel strange since she's my sister-in-law's mother and not my aunt."

"What does that have to do with anything? Aunt Mae isn't mine either, but that's what I call her."

"That's because everyone in Porterfield calls her that. I'd wager that a great many of them don't even remember her name is Sullivan."

That was most likely true. Mae Sullivan was everyone's aunt, and she loved playing the role. How nice to be so well regarded by the community.

She gazed at the scenery around them and almost groaned. Here she'd sat beside Cory for this entire ride and talked about other people, and not a romantic word passed between them the entire time. What a wasted opportunity.

The carriage slowed as it drew closer to the sprawling one-story house set back from the road. Buggies and carriages as well as horses belonging to other Muldoon family members and guests filled the yard where some of the older Muldoon children raced and played.

After Cory helped her down from the carriage, she turned toward the house where Sarah waited to greet them on the porch. Then another figure appeared behind Sarah. Abigail's breath hitched in her throat when her gaze locked with Elliot Jensen's.

What was he doing here? And why wasn't he back helping Doc and Kate so they could come on to the party?

Abigail stood frozen in her tracks. This was the last thing she'd expected this afternoon.

Elliot stood transfixed for a minute and simply stared at Abigail. Why had he let Doc and Aunt Maggie talk him into coming here in Doc's place? They all knew Abigail would be here, but Doc had convinced Elliot that he should be the one to accompany his aunt to the party while Doc remained behind to take care of the emergency with Kate. He'd be out later.

The way Cory had helped her down from the buggy grated on Elliot. She looked light as a feather, and his hands itched to circle that tiny waist and help her down. He swallowed hard and turned away.

Why had he really come? Had it been because deep down he wanted to see her again—and not as a patient?

Before he went through the door, a hand touched his shoulder. Abigail.

"Good evening, Doc Elliot. I didn't expect to see you here."

"I...I didn't expect to be here, but Mrs. Boatwright didn't want anyone treating her except my uncle, so here I am in his place." His tongue became thick as corn chowder. He had to get away from her charms and let Cory have her. "If you'll excuse me, I want to speak with Mr. Muldoon." How could he keep his distance from her when all he wanted to do was sit by her side?

He spun on his heel and went into the house in search of something cold to drink. He needed to cool the thoughts that had come creeping in when he spoke with Abigail. Where was all that protection he'd had around his heart for the past few years? He must remember his vow to not get involved with another woman.

He didn't really need to speak with Muldoon, but that had been a good excuse for getting away. Elliot searched the room for his aunt. Perhaps if he stood by her, he'd be better off. Then he spotted Reverend Winston headed his way. Elliot's gaze darted about the room, seeking a way of escape, but found none except to turn around and risk running into Abigail, who had remained on the porch with Sarah.

Facing the preacher became the better of the two choices, so Elliot smiled and nodded as the young man drew near. "A fine party Sarah and Donnie have planned for Mrs. Newton."

"Yes, it is, and she's thrilled that so many have come to pay their respects. She was always in the middle of things socially in Boston, so this is good for her."

"Yes, she does appear to be having a grand time. But tell me, how is Erin? Is she taking those pills I gave her?"

"Oh, yes. She plans to do everything you've told her. She says that between God's providence and your skills, she'll have a very healthy baby."

He wasn't sure God would have anything to do with it, but his own knowledge would help. "As I've assured you before, she's in good health, so I foresee no problems at all."

"That's what I like to hear." The reverend grinned broadly and clapped Elliot on the shoulder. "And that reminds me. Erin is usually very involved with the Fall Festival, and I want to make sure you think it's OK for her to help out with it this year."

"I don't see any reason for her not to, as long as she doesn't plan to climb ladders or race horses."

"That won't happen." Reverend Winston tilted his head to

one side. "Tell me, are you planning on escorting someone to the festivities?"

"No, and why would you ask that?"

"No reason. I just thought you might be taking Abigail Monroe. She's one of the few single girls in town, and a very pretty one at that. Since she's been around the infirmary so much, I thought maybe you two had struck up a friendship."

"Not hardly. She's a patient and nothing more." This gave him another reason for avoiding the reverend. Not only did he press Elliot about religion, but he had taken an interest in Elliot's personal life. If only people would leave him and his personal life alone, he'd be much happier.

"Whatever you say, Doc, whatever you say, but I think you protest a little too much. Now if you'll excuse me, I'll join Erin for some of that food Ma Muldoon is setting on the table."

Elliot watched his departure and blew out his breath in relief. Movement to his side caught his eyes. Abigail Monroe arranged her skirts about her as she sat across the way. Before he could think about what he was doing, his feet carried him to her side.

"Miss Monroe, may I get you anything from the food table?" All his plans for avoiding her evaporated like morning mist in the sun when she gazed up at him and smiled.

"That would be lovely, but please, remember to call me Abigail. Miss Monroe makes me sound ancient."

"Abigail it is." He turned and hurried over to where Sarah and Mrs. Muldoon had filled two tables with meats, vegetables, breads, and all types of accompaniments. He filled two plates with slices of roast beef, a piece of chicken, wedges of potatoes, fresh bread, and corn. If he planned to take a meal to her, then he must stay and eat or be seen as being impolite.

"Here you are, Miss…I mean Abigail. I hope this is sufficient." He handed her a plate and napkin then pulled up a straight-back cane-bottomed chair to sit beside her.

After they ate a few bites in silence, Elliot said, "Abigail, would you allow me to escort you to the Fall Festival?" His heart jumped. Those were not the words he'd intended to say, but he had no way of retrieving them now.

Again her smile pierced his heart. "I'd be delighted to go with you. How sweet of you to ask."

She may think it was sweet, but it had become a bitter pill for him to swallow. Somehow he had to get his head and his heart in line with each other and prevent such mistakes in the future. For whatever reason the invitation had burst forth, he'd follow through. One afternoon with Abigail wouldn't undo the hardness he'd allowed in his heart since Angela's death.

"Didn't I see you come in with Cory Muldoon?" Elliot didn't see the deputy anywhere around. How could he have left Abigail alone?

"He did bring me, but that was only because Daniel had to stay behind to wait for Kate. He's probably off discussing law with Nathan Reed or checking up on family members."

That meant Elliot could have her to himself for a while. He sat beside her and balanced his plate on his knee. "Tell me, Abigail, what the town of Briar Ridge was like."

"It's quite nice, a little larger than Porterfield, and quite a bit older. It's beautiful country, and even when it's too cold to be outside, the snow is so gorgeous. Of course, many people hate the snow and fuss about it all winter. I loved it. When we were all younger, Rachel, Seth, Daniel, and I had our own sleds and went down a hill not far from my home for our rides. We had a skating pond too."

She stopped abruptly. "I'm sorry, I've been babbling on like a creek in spring thaw."

"It's quite all right. I've enjoyed listening to you." And he had. He could imagine her flying down a hill on a sled with her hair flying out in a stream behind her.

She leaned toward him, almost like she wanted to tell him a secret.

"Doc Elliot, I really admire the way you took care of Annie. She was so worried about her café."

"Until you stepped in to take over and help her out. That must have been hard." He tried to picture her with trays of food and a big white apron, but he couldn't quite make it appear.

Abigail's laughter rang like music of the greatest symphony in his ears. Spending the afternoon with her at the festival would not be a hardship.

"I tell you one thing, I wouldn't have that job full-time no matter how much it paid. My feet have never hurt like that."

Such pretty feet too. He'd noticed them right off when he had treated her ankle. Soft, smooth skin with no calluses or corns or bunions was a beautiful sight after some he'd examined. He took in a deep breath. That was not the direction his thoughts should be headed.

"Have you thought any more about coming to church with your aunt and uncle? Seth's sermons this month have been on the Book of John and some of Jesus's miracles. I always marvel at how Jesus worked among the people, much like you do here in Porterfield. It takes special skills to be a doctor, and you learned well in Cleveland."

She may as well have thrown ice water over his head. Cleveland was the last place he wanted on his mind tonight.

"What hospital did you work in there?"

His lips tightened. "Cleveland General."

"Why, that's a wonderful hospital with a great reputation. Why on earth would you leave there and come down to Texas and this small infirmary?"

Now she'd gone to meddling again, stepping into places she shouldn't enter. "Let's just say things were not running smoothly." He picked up his glass. "I think I need a refill." He had to get away.

When he looked in on her later, she was busy chatting with friends. She wouldn't miss him, and neither would anyone else. He thanked Donavan for the invitation to the party and slipped out when no one was looking.

CHAPTER
EIGHTEEN

*E*LLIOT FACED HIMSELF in the mirror and grimaced. He still didn't understand what had prompted him to ask Abigail to attend Fall Festival with him. He'd only seen her once this week since the party at the Muldoon place, and that had been to check on a medical book Doc had wanted Abigail to order for him. He'd found himself wandering up to the window and gazing across at the library several times this past week. No matter what else he did, his thoughts kept turning to Abigail. Just yesterday he'd seen her with a group of young students at the library, and her enthusiasm and excitement had been visible from his vantage point at the infirmary window.

Aunt Maggie had been thrilled when she found out he planned to be with Abigail today. She'd even cut short her visit with her sister to return for the festival. He'd have to be very careful today, or his aunt would be reading more into it than was really there.

Nothing he could do about that now as it was time to

meet her and join in the fun that could be heard even here on the outskirts of town in the new home.

At a few minutes before noon, he stopped at the open door to the library. Several patrons walked out with books in their arms and greeted Elliot. Maybe Abigail would choose not to close the library with so many people there. Then he wouldn't have to worry about escorting her around town.

He had no such luck. Abigail spotted him and waved. He stepped inside as she rang a bell and announced that the library was now closed. Patrons scurried about either to leave or to get their selections checked out. With each one, she had a few words and a smile.

In less than five minutes the building had cleared and Abigail had donned her hat. She met him at the door. "Just let me lock up and we can be on our way." She used a key from a ring in her hand then dropped the keys into the handbag on her wrist. "Now we're all set. Where to first?"

Elliot hadn't thought that far ahead. "Why don't we walk over to town hall and check out the schedule posted there?"

"That sounds like a good idea." She hooked her hand into the bend of his arm and tilted her head to peer at him. "I'm surprised the weather is so nice. It's a beautiful day for the celebration."

As they headed down the boardwalk toward town hall, several people greeted them with smiles and knowing looks, which meant he and Abigail would be the topic of a number of conversations later in the day. He could do nothing about their talk, but he could keep it light between Abigail and him. "With our climate, we have many sunny, mild days on into December and January. It makes the hot, humid, summer days much more bearable." Talk about weather bored him, but it was safer than others he could think of.

"We have a founder's day celebration at home, but it's in February and usually accompanied by very cold weather. Everything has to be indoors. I love being able to have outdoor activities even this late in the fall season."

Another safe topic. Elliot grinned. "Tell me more about what you did for fun." As long as he kept the conversation light, the afternoon would be just fine.

"We have booths like you have here, but they are in the school building where they have a big gymnasium blocked off. The speeches and such are all indoors at our city hall where they have a big dinner at night. That's followed by a dance, and I must say it's nothing like the dances you have here."

"You have a full day of fun activities." They arrived at the entrance to town hall and stopped to read the announcements.

Abigail squealed. "A real shoot-out and horse race! Oh my, that's exciting."

Elliot laughed. "I would imagine that just about every town in Texas has competitions just like this. Some even have calf-roping and bronco riding."

"Bronco riding? What's that?"

"Men ride untamed horses, and whoever stays on the longest wins a prize." He'd tried it once then decided falling off of a bucking horse was not his idea of fun.

"Now that sounds dangerous, but exciting to watch." She leaned in for a closer look at the schedule. "The shoot-out is at three thirty and the race is at four. That gives us time to eat, check a few of the booths, and see the contest as well."

He didn't have the heart to tell her that Donnie and Cory

Muldoon usually ended up as the last two competitors, and one of them always won. He'd rather she enjoy it for the first time without knowing who always won. As for the horse race, it would be much more interesting this year since several newcomers had posted their names.

Elliot placed his hand over Abigail's hand, still on his arm. "Shall we investigate the food wares? I understand they have a new concoction called a 'red hot.' Sam over at the bakery is making them."

"Oh, yes, I heard him talking about them. It'll be interesting to see what they taste like."

They walked up toward the food booths set up around the county courthouse lawn. Elliot had no trouble spotting the red and white bunting adorning the baker's wares. Not only did he have the sausages in a bun, but he also displayed fancy cakes and pastries that tempted the senses.

Abigail stopped to investigate. "These look delicious and smell heavenly."

Sam grinned at them from behind the counter. "Ready to try my new sausage in a roll?" He picked up a bun about five inches long and placed a hot sausage in it then doused it with mustard.

"That looks good. I'll have two for me and one for the lady." Elliot turned to her. "That is unless you would like two."

"No, one is fine for me." She eyed them with wariness. "I'd like two of those chocolate frosted pastries though." Abigail grinned and pointed to the pastry tray.

Sam prepared the meat and rolls and placed them on squares of paper. "I predict that these are going to be very popular in the coming years. Many people who had one have come back for more."

Elliot had no doubts about that. The spicy aroma of the sausage already made his taste buds ready for the first bite. Sam handed them the rolls then wrapped the two pastries in paper and handed them to Abigail. Elliot paid the man then led Abigail to an empty park bench.

At the first bite, he savored the taste on his tongue before swallowing. "Ahh, they do live up to his predictions."

Abigail's eyes opened wide. She finished chewing then swallowed her morsel. "That is quite good. Sam may have something there. I heard about these from a friend who had one in Baltimore a few years ago, but they didn't sound very appetizing then."

They continued to eat in silence with Elliot enjoying every bite. The volunteer town band set about their playing and provided a rousing background to accompany their meal. The men who played brass instruments had been practicing for weeks, and the sounds coming from the music stand filled the air with delightful music.

After they finished eating, Elliot disposed of their trash in one of the receptacles. "Would you like to visit the booths?"

"Yes, let's do." She gazed around. "There's such a big crowd, and I see a lot of strangers. Do all these people live here?"

They began strolling toward the other merchant booths. "We have visitors from all over this area, including adjoining counties. People everywhere like to have fun." The large crowds had surprised him the first year too, but then he realized everyone flocked to these types of festivities all over East Texas.

Elliot observed Abigail as she exclaimed and commented on all the different wares exhibited in the booths. Her enthusiasm sparkled when she talked with merchants to learn more about them. For a petite woman, Abigail had more energy than anyone else he'd seen except Kate Monroe, and it had begun to affect him.

Normally he didn't care for all the hoopla of events like the one today. They reminded him too much of the fun he and Angela had exploring the city of Cleveland. Yet here he stood, watching a young woman so different from Angela and finding himself beginning to care about her more than he could ever admit to anyone, including himself.

Abigail couldn't remember when she'd had this much fun. Even the celebrations in Briar Ridge paled in comparison to all the activities and events of this day. After visiting several booths, she strolled over with Elliot to watch the shoot-out. Targets had been set up, and two men at a time competed. The one having the best time and most accurate shots with one round of bullets after several bouts was proclaimed the winner.

She covered her ears and shuddered when the first two contestants started and the guns went off. Elliot laughed. "I should have warned you. We can go move to the back so you won't be so close to the noise."

Abigail shook her head. "No, I want to be able to see what they do. I was just startled, that's all." She'd seen the Muldoon men had all entered, and she wanted to see if one of them was the best shot. Her money would go to Cory if she'd been a woman given to wagering. His being a deputy meant he had to be really good at handling a gun.

Then the pairings of the contestants went up, and Cory wasn't among them. Elliot shook his head. "I don't see Cory's name anywhere. He's won without any problem the past few years. I wonder what happened."

"My winning is what happened."

Abigail turned to see Cory standing behind her and Elliot, and her heart skipped a beat. Heat rose in her cheeks. "What do you mean by that?"

"Sheriff Rutherford and I discussed it, and seems how since a lawman needs to be good shot, it isn't fair to the other participants for me to keep entering each year. So I dropped out."

Elliot laughed. "That's a good one. A Muldoon giving up a sure thing, but I admire you for it. I see Donnie is still in the running, so a Muldoon may still take the prize."

"I don't know about that. I hear one of the new guys hired on at the Gibson spread is pretty handy with a gun. Might do Donnie some good to be beaten by somebody besides me."

Abigail listened to their banter and grinned. How much more fun it was living in Texas than in Connecticut. Real-live cowboys competing in a shoot-out and horse races later on whetted her appetite for more events.

While the two men talked, she studied the contrast between them. Both were tall, but Cory's broad shoulders and chest outdid the lanky Doc Elliot. At least Cory had made the doc laugh, a rare occurrence in the time she'd known him.

Being a Muldoon would carry weight in this town, but he was still a cowboy and a bit rough around the edges. He wasn't at all as refined and sophisticated as Elliot. Of course that could be because Elliot was so quiet.

Cory said his good-byes and sauntered over to where the contestants in the shoot-out were gathered. The first round had concluded, and Donnie Muldoon was on the list. Elliot nodded toward the men. "Do you want to stay and see if Donnie wins? They have two more rounds to go. Eight started out, and now they're down to four. After the next round they'll have the final two contestants."

"It is loud, but I want to see who wins. I hope it is Donnie. He and Sarah can probably use the money with a new baby coming."

"Then we'll stay, but I suggest moving back just a ways. You can still see, but the noise won't be quite as bad."

Once again he covered her hand with his and sent a shiver of delight through her arm. She gazed up at him as they walked. He had asked her to this festival and seemed to be enjoying her company. Could this be the beginning of a new phase in their friendship? She began to hope so.

CHAPTER
NINETEEN

*O*VER A WEEK had passed since the festival, and Elliot
had not made any further attempts to escort Abigail anywhere. She glanced across the way to the infirmary and sighed.
Against her own better judgment, she'd begun to let Elliot into
her heart. It would be best for all concerned if she closed it up
again and went on about the business of running the library.
However, that was much easier to say than to actually do.

The bell over the door jangled, and Penelope Dawes shut
the door against the wind, which had grown colder. "Brr, I
think that norther Allen talked about has blown in."

Abigail laughed. "I was beginning to wonder if we ever had
cold weather around here. It feels good to me."

"I know, rather reminds me of Illinois now. But weather
discussion is not why I came in to see you. Philip has finally
heard from the young lady he's been writing to, and she's
coming to Porterfield to meet him."

A smile curved the corner of Abigail's lips. "I'm glad to

hear it. I haven't told anyone except Aunt Mae, but all sorts of rumors have been floating around. Do you know her?"

"No, but her name is Sophia Langston, and she's from Cleveland, just like Doc Elliot. He may know her, but I haven't had the chance to ask him about it."

"When is she expected to arrive, and where will she stay?" Philip still lived with Penelope and Allen, so she couldn't stay there, and the boardinghouse only had vacant rooms on the men's floor.

"She's coming on the afternoon train from Dallas. She had to go there from St. Louis and then come to Porterfield. Aunt Mae and Philip are working out living arrangements right now. He's planning to move into the boardinghouse, and then Miss Langston will stay with us while they court. Philip's already made arrangements for a house on the lot next door to where Doc and Mrs. Jensen live."

"That makes perfect sense. Philip couldn't live in the same house with her." Penelope would take good care of the young woman. If things went well, they may have a Christmas wedding as well as several Christmas babies. "That's why I came to town. I want to make sure she's greeted properly." Her blue eyes sparkled with excitement. "And that's where you come in. I'd like for you to be there to meet her too. It'd be nice for her to meet more women at first."

Before Abigail could answer, Frank Cahoon stepped into the library. "Howdy, Miss Monroe, Mrs. Dawes. I hear a bride for Philip is arriving this afternoon, and she's from Ohio. That's where my Suzanne's from, and I thought she might know her."

Abigail peered up at Frank. At four inches above six feet in height, he towered over her and the equally petite Penelope

Dawes. Penelope took two steps back so she wouldn't have to crane her neck so much to speak to the blacksmith.

"She's from Ohio, and I know Suzanne is too, but it's a big state, so most likely they don't know each other. I'd still be happy for her to join us at the station to greet Miss Langston."

"Thank you, Mrs. Dawes. I'll tell Suzanne." As soon as he exited the doorway, he shoved his hat back on his head and sprinted off in the direction of the house he'd built for his bride.

"Looks like she'll get a warm reception. Let me finish up a few things here, and I'll go with you to the depot."

After checking in two books and securing the cash drawer, Abigail grabbed her wrap from its hook and joined Penelope at the door. When she opened it, a blast of cold air greeted her and reminded her of home. Most likely she'd not see any snow this year, but the cooler weather well above freezing suited her just fine. She wrapped the shawl about her shoulders and tied the strings to her hat under her chin to keep the wind from whisking it away.

Allen and Philip met them in the middle of the street. Philip's mouth twitched and his hands shook. He jammed them into his trouser pockets. "I hope she's as nice as you are, Penelope. Her letters sounded real sweet."

Penelope grasped Allen's arm as they walked. "I'm sure she'll be every bit as nice as you'd expect from her writing."

Abigail hid her smile. She'd never seen Philip so nervous. Usually he was the picture of calm while his brother did the fretting and stewing about their business. Philip had always been quiet and reserved when he came into the library, but now he was nervous as a cat in a roomful of rocking chairs.

She supposed she would be too if she was meeting for the first time the man she hoped to marry.

The blast from the train approaching the town split the air, and Philip took off into a run. Allen chuckled. "Guess he doesn't want to be late."

Frank and Suzanne already stood on the platform, as did Henry Wilder. Abigail shook her head. That man. Everything was newsworthy to him, and a new mail-order bride would certainly be fodder for an article in the *Porterfield Gazette*. Editor McBurney was lucky to have such a go-getter to supply news for the biweekly newspaper.

The train rolled to a stop with steam hissing and spewing from the engine. Abigail covered her ears against the screech of the wheels braking on the rails, and her jaws clenched at the grating of metal against metal.

Mostly men disembarked, but then a willowy brunette stepped down to the platform in one fluid movement. Although not beautiful by most standards, she had an air about her that spoke of a refined background. What in the world was a woman like her doing in Porterfield, Texas, as a mail-order bride? Perhaps Henry Wilder would have a good story after all.

Philip stood with his mouth hanging open and his eyes bugging from his head. He held his hat in his hands with a clutch that crushed the brim to a wrinkled mess. Allen slapped him on the back and extended a hand to Miss Langston. "Welcome to Porterfield, Miss Langston. I'm Allen Dawes, and this poor fellow here is my brother, Philip."

Philip's Adam's apple bobbed up and down before he managed to squeak out a greeting. "Hello, Miss Langston."

She smiled, and sunshine lit her face. Abigail couldn't take her eyes off the young woman. If Sophia hadn't already been promised to Philip, every man in town would be vying for her attention simply because of that smile.

Philip introduced her to those gathered around. She smiled and acknowledged each one, and when she laughed, it was like the sound of tinkling chimes. Abigail sighed. Philip was one lucky fellow.

When the introductions were complete, Miss Langston gazed at the group. "Please call me Sophia. Since this is going to be my home, I would like to be friends with everyone."

Abigail held no doubts that would soon happen. She already liked the young woman from Ohio and hoped to get to know her better in the next few days.

The couple strolled to the baggage cart where Frank and Allen made quick work of loading Sophia's things on the wagon Philip had brought for that purpose. After the two climbed up onto the wagon seat, Sophia waved, and Philip headed the wagon toward the Dawes home, where a reception would be held for Sophia to mingle with the people she'd just met.

Henry Wilder watched the couple as they drove down Main Street. That Philip Dawes was one lucky man. If Henry ever sent off for a mail-order bride, he'd probably end up with one as plain as a slice of white bread. Not that a plain girl would be bad. Even though she wasn't beautiful, Miss Langston drew people to her like bees to nectar.

His first order of business would be to question her to see if she had known Elliot Jensen in Cleveland. Of course, in a city that size, they may never have come into contact with each other, but it never hurt to try.

He waited until the couple arrived at the Daweses' house before making his way there. Many people would be coming to welcome them, so his presence would not be questioned. Besides, Henry was known to interview all newcomers to Porterfield.

Frank and Suzanne Cahoon, Abigail Monroe, and Reverend and Mrs. Winston joined Allen and Penelope at the house. Henry made his way across the street and up to the porch. Penelope opened the door and greeted him with a smile.

"Hello, Mr. Wilder. I suppose you've come to meet Miss Langston too. Come on in. She's in the parlor with Philip and the others."

Henry made his way to join the guests. Penelope Dawes had set up a table with coffee and pastries for refreshment in the dining room, but the guests congregated in the parlor. Miss Langston made one pretty picture standing beside Philip, who looked more like a love-struck schoolboy than an adult business man.

The smattering of conversation around him always interested Henry, and he listened with a reporter's ear to glean any information he could use from the tidbits. Finally a lull arrived as guests began partaking of the refreshments. Henry made his way to Sophia's side.

"Hello, Miss Langston. I'm Henry Wilder from the *Porterfield Gazette*. Sometime soon I'd like to interview you for an article in our paper. I've written about every other newcomer to our town because it helps people get to know you."

Her eyes sparkled and crinkled at the corners when she

smiled. "That would be lovely. Just let me know when. I'll be staying here with Penelope and Allen."

"That's what I understand. I'll be in touch." He turned to leave and then addressed her again. "I say, we have a doctor in town who came here from Cleveland. His name is Elliot Jensen. Perhaps you knew him there."

Her smile dimmed just a fraction, and her eyes opened wide. Henry noted a tinge of pink in her cheeks. "Cleveland is a large city, Mr. Wilder. I'm not familiar with that name." She then glanced over his shoulder. "Philip is beckoning. Good day, Mr. Wilder. You may contact me later about an interview."

Henry nodded and observed her as she joined Philip then glanced back at him for a brief second before turning away. That shift in her smile and the look in her eyes led him to believe Miss Langston wasn't being entirely truthful. Another piece of the Jensen puzzle presented itself, and now Henry's curiosity grew even greater.

Elliot busied himself with removing instruments from the autoclave and wrapping them in sterile towels for later use, an everyday occurrence around here now that they were expanding and adding beds. The morning had been slow, and his uncle had retired to his office to look over the medical records of some of his patients.

The only two Elliot had seen today were Erin Winston and Sarah Muldoon. Both ladies were in good health and progressing right along with their pregnancies. He figured Erin had about another five weeks or so before the arrival of her baby, putting her due date at right around Christmas. Of course with first-time deliveries, that date could go either way and be shorter or longer than he predicted.

Henry Wilder walked through the door. "Good afternoon, Doc Elliot. I see the good citizens of Porterfield don't need a doctor today."

"Yes, it looks that way. What can I do for you?" Elliot continued to wrap instruments. Anytime Henry came by, it usually didn't bode well for him.

"Oh, I just came from the Daweses' place. I met Philip's mail-order bride, and she's one nice woman."

"He's might lucky then. Some of those mail-order brides aren't all they make themselves up to be." Elliot would never understand why a man would send off for a woman and then seek her hand in marriage before ever laying eyes on her.

"This one is."

Henry didn't speak for a few minutes, and Elliot's patience with the man wore thin. "Is there anything else you wish to let me know?"

"Not really. I'll let you get back to sorting those instruments." He turned and sauntered toward the door.

Elliot reached for another set to wrap just as Henry made a last comment. "Oh, and by the way, she's from your hometown of Cleveland. Sophia Langston's her name."

The instruments fell to the floor with a clatter. Elliot bent to retrieve them, his breath coming short and fast. He glanced over his shoulder, but Henry Wilder had disappeared. Elliot slumped against the table and struggled to control his breathing. Sophia Langston in Porterfield? It was impossible. Her father would never have allowed it. It had to be a mistake.

Everything he'd hope to flee from in Cleveland had

followed him. His only goal had been to escape the accusations and begin a new life here. Now Sophia threatened to undo all his hopes and plans for a new beginning. He had to get away before everyone knew his secret, that he had as good as killed Angela with his negligence.

CHAPTER
TWENTY

SEVERAL DAYS PASSED, followed by the weekend, but Elliot's indecision froze in his heart. After all his uncle and aunt had done for him, he couldn't just up and leave without explanation. So he kept his head down and kept working even as he grappled with his dilemma.

Monday morning when Elliot stepped out onto the board-walk with one of his patients, a carriage with two women drove past. One was Penelope Dawes. The dark-haired one turned her head in his direction, and Elliot gasped. It was Sophia Langston, just like Henry had said. Their eyes locked for a moment, and although he couldn't see her eyes, she did recognize him.

He bid his patient a hasty good-bye and stepped back into the infirmary.

Elliot gasped for breath and gripped the edge of a chair with white-knuckled hands. He should have left as his first instinct dictated, but now it was too late. Sophia would most likely let everyone know his part in the death of her best friend.

He couldn't hide from her forever, and the only way to deal with the problem was to face her and let her make her accusations and get it all out in the open between them.

Once again God had proved his cruelty in Elliot's life. If He was a loving, forgiving God, He would never have sent Sophia to Porterfield. Now he'd have to listen again to all the grief he'd caused Angela's parents and friends.

An arm slipped across his shoulders. "I hear that Sophia Langston is in town. You have to talk with her." His uncle's voice caused even more turmoil.

"I know, but it means hearing again how I failed Angela and being accused of causing her death."

"You don't know that. Things may have changed. She may not feel any anger against you at all."

"How could she not? She was Angela's best friend and was helping her plan the wedding. She shunned me at the funeral. It was almost as if she resented my being there."

"Maybe she did then, but you still have to acknowledge her. Why not take the afternoon off and think about what you need to do and how you can handle it. God hasn't left you, and this may be His way of getting you to face your guilty feelings and resolve them."

Elliot's heart hardened, and he clenched his teeth. He'd faced his guilt and still believed God should have helped him save Angela. No one could take the blame for her death but him. "There's nothing to be done, but if you don't mind, I will take the rest of the afternoon off."

He turned on his heel and strode from the infirmary, slamming through the door and almost knocking down Henry Wilder in his haste. Elliot steadied Henry with his hands. "Sorry, but I'm in a hurry." He let go, but Henry grabbed his sleeve.

"Wait a minute. I'd like to talk with you about Miss Langston. Since you're from Cleveland, I figured you two might know each other."

Elliot's heart lurched. He had to get away from the reporter before everything fell apart. "Cleveland's a large city, not like Porterfield. I don't know everyone from there." He narrowed his eyes. "And if you don't leave me alone and quit asking about my past, I'm going to tell your boss that you're harassing me and I don't appreciate it."

Henry stepped back. "I'm sorry, Doc Elliot. Curiosity is the way of the reporter. We can't find good stories if we're not curious about others and what they do. If it's that important to you, I won't bother you anymore. Besides, right now, Miss Langston makes for a really good story."

He tipped his hat and strolled off toward the newspaper. Elliot slumped against the wall of the infirmary. All would be exposed, and his reputation in Porterfield would be ruined.

Elliot pushed away from the wall and headed toward home. He pulled his coat tight about his chest in the chill wind, which matched the frost forming around his heart. What was he going to do? Where could he go? The world didn't seem big enough to flee his past.

A bell jingled over the doorway, and Abigail glanced up from the fabric she held to see Sophia and Penelope enter Mrs. Burnett's shop. "Good morning; you're out early today."

Sophia glanced around the shop. "We're here so I can

pick out fabric for my wedding dress. Penelope tells me Mrs. Burnett does beautiful work. I must say she does have beautiful fabrics."

Abigail brightened. Apparently all had gone well between the couple over the weekend, and a wedding was now definitely in the works. "Indeed she does. I was just selecting fabric for a few winter skirts. I'm afraid the ones I brought from home are really too heavy for wearing down here all the time."

"I didn't bring much with me for that very reason, but I wasn't sure what women wore for their weddings in Texas, so I waited." Sophia paused, then said, "Would you like to help me choose a fabric? It's ever so much more fun to shop with friends."

Abigail smiled. "I'd be honored to help."

Mrs. Burnett bustled in from the back room with her arms filled with bolts of fabric. "Good morning, Mrs. Dawes, Miss Langston. I have several samples here for you to look at." She laid the bolts on a table, and Abigail followed the others to see them too.

It didn't take long for Sophia to decide on a color and style. "I know white is becoming more and more popular for weddings in the East and North, but it seems impractical for living here. The royal blue silk taffeta will be fine trimmed in cream lace and with a cream insert in the front bodice. What do you think, Penelope?"

"I agree. I chose a pale pink for my gown, and now I wear it to church and for special occasions."

Abigail fingered the delicate lace. Would she ever wear something like that for her wedding? Not anytime in the near future, for sure. "That would be my choice too."

Mrs. Bennett nodded and rolled out the bolt of fabric. "This will be lovely with your eyes and coloring, Miss Langston."

Abigail waited while Sophia chose a pattern for the dress before handing Mrs. Burnett two bolts of fabric. "I have to be getting back to the library, but I want those two skirts we discussed in this dark blue and in this deep shade of green. No need to hurry since I know you want to get Sophia's dress made."

Mrs. Bennett escorted her to the door. "I'll have them ready for you soon as her dress is done. Thank you for coming in."

"My pleasure, Mrs. Bennett." She waved to Penelope and Sophia. "Stop by the library if you have time. I'll have a pot of tea brewing and a few sweets from the bakery."

Sophia's face lit up with a smile. "That would be lovely. We do have time, don't we, Penelope?"

"Of course. We'll be there shortly."

Abigail hurried down the boardwalk toward the bakery. Sam made wonderful muffins and had a great selection of cookies, and she loved his sugar and cinnamon ones. They'd be perfect with a spot of tea.

Maybe she could learn more about Miss Langston and if she had known Elliot in Cleveland. Of course it was a big city, but it wouldn't hurt to ask.

Forty-five minutes later Abigail waved and closed the door behind her guests. Well, that had been of no use. Sophia had neither claimed to know Elliot nor denied it. She was as good at skirting answers as Elliot had been, but not as rude. The visit had been pleasant, but she knew no more about Sophia and Elliot as she had this morning when she left home.

She hung the "Closed" sign on the door then locked it. Her stomach rumbled in anticipation of the noon meal. She turned just in time to see Elliot hurry away from the infirmary. The position of his body and his hands over his eyes communicated a great sadness, and Abigail's heart ached for the young man. He had barely spoken to her since the Fall Festival over two weeks ago, and she felt instinctively that something was troubling him even more than usual. She had to find a way to help Elliot find peace with the Lord. It would not be an easy task, but since when had Abigail ever backed down from something difficult? But in this case, it may be not only difficult but also impossible.

A cold gust of wind whipped her coat open, and she hugged herself against it. Then a smile crossed her face. Didn't the Bible say that all things were possible with God? And she still believed in miracles. With renewed determination, she hurried the distance to the boardinghouse and a hot meal.

Once again Henry was absent from dinner. Cory sat beside Abigail and whispered, "Annie's really captured old Henry. He'd never pass up one of Aunt Mae's meals otherwise."

Abigail smiled and reached for the bread. "You should have seen the way he pitched in and helped clean up that day Annie was hurt. Wouldn't surprise me any if we heard wedding bells for those two in the future."

Cory nodded and dug into his chicken fried steak. She'd never seen a man eat with such gusto. Cory was as big as life in everything, and one couldn't help but notice when he entered a room. Being married to him would keep her in the spotlight as well. Married? Now where had that idea come from? He hadn't even indicated any interest in her in that way.

She sighed and stirred her fork in the mashed potatoes. Lately it seemed she'd been doing a lot of sighing and contemplating two men. A lot of good it had done her. Maybe it was time to use another tactic.

"Cory, I worry about Doc Elliot. He hasn't been to church once since I arrived in town. He told me he had no use for God or religion. Have you ever talked with him about such things?"

He looked at her like she had gravy on her face or something. Was that so hard a question?

"No, I haven't. I leave those sort of things to Seth and his preaching. I figure each man's relationship to God is his own business."

"But God told us to witness to people and make sure everyone knows about the grace, love, and forgiveness of God. Sometimes we're the only Bible or sermon a person might hear." Not talking to others about God was not the way she and Rachel had been brought up. Why, it was the very boldness of Rachel speaking to Nathan that brought him to the Lord.

"It's just not something I'm comfortable doing. My job is to capture bad men and put them in jail. Saving their souls is a job for Seth."

Abigail shook her head in disbelief. This was certainly something she never expected from Cory. Maybe Cory wouldn't be such a good match after all.

A scream from the kitchen had both Abigail and Cory bolting from their chairs to investigate. In the kitchen they found Aunt Mae holding a towel around Miss Perth's hand.

"She was slicing up an apple when the knife slipped and cut her thumb. Somebody go get the doctor...quick."

Cory turned on his heel. "I'll do it. They'll be at the house eating, so it'll only take a few minutes to get one of them."

Abigail wished Kate were there, but Aunt Mae looked like she had things under control. The pinched look on Miss Perth's face let Abigail know the woman was in great pain. She stepped over and hugged the elderly school teacher. "I'm so sorry. The doctor will be here in just a minute and will take care of you."

Tears rolled down Miss Perth's cheeks. "But who's going to take care of my babies this afternoon? They'll all be coming back from lunch soon."

"I imagine Miss Miller can handle them." Jessica had always been the sort who could corral a bunch of older kids, so she should be able to see to twelve extra children.

Someone burst through the back door, and Abigail looked up and into the eyes of Elliot. He started at the sight of her, then his professional side took over and he hurried to Miss Perth.

Cory must have gone back to the sheriff's office since Elliot came in alone. Although nearly the same height, Elliot's presence didn't command the attention Cory did. Elliot was quiet and efficient whereas Cory, although good at his job, was loud and teasing. Right now she preferred the quiet, calm assurance of the doctor who was treating Miss Perth. But did he welcome *her* presence?

CHAPTER
TWENTY-ONE

*E*LLIOT KEPT HIS eye trained on Miss Perth and the wound as he pressed the towel against it once again. Still, he was very much aware of Abigail standing nearby. Her rosewater scent filled his nose again.

Miss Perth bit her lip. "Doc Elliot, it's not serious, is it?"

"No, but it's a deep slice to your thumb. I can bandage it so it won't need stitches. Unless the pain worsens, you can probably go on back to the school. It just might be a little clumsy using that hand."

Miss Perth brightened considerably. "Thank you. It hardly hurts at all now. Just a dull throb." She held her hand still while Elliot wrapped it with the supplies from his bag. From the corner of his eye, the light brown of Abigail's skirt filled the space.

He worked and worried at the same time. Miss Perth would be fine, but would his life be fine with Sophia here in town? If Abigail knew how he'd neglected to use the one treatment that could have saved Angela, would she have the same high opinion of him as a doctor? Most likely not.

Until he knew exactly what Sophia would do or tell people, he had to keep up his guard against the charm of Abigail and concentrate on preserving his privacy.

He sat back in his chair. "There now. You'll be fine, Miss Perth. Drop by the infirmary tomorrow, and I'll take another look at it."

Miss Perth reached over and hugged the doctor. "Thank you. You're wonderful." With that she hurried back to get her hat and coat to return to school.

"You were wonderful, you know."

Abigail's soft voice froze him in place. How could he resist the charms of one so lovely as her? He didn't know, but he had to try. "Not a serious cut, just bled a lot." He stood. "If you'll excuse me, I must get back to the infirmary." That wasn't completely true, but it would get him out of the same room with her. He refused to meet her eye as he brushed past her. He headed out the door and down the street to the infirmary.

When he entered the waiting area he stopped short, his heart slamming into his chest. Sophia Langston sat on one of the benches. He swallowed hard and closed the door.

She jumped up and hurried to him. "Elliot Jensen, it is you. Remember me? Sophia Langston, Angela's friend."

As if he could he ever forget the young woman Angela talked about constantly. "Yes, I remember you. It's been awhile." Trapped like a rabbit in a snare, he chose to be polite rather than rude. Perhaps she'd leave him alone if he simply acknowledged their acquaintance.

She grasped his hands and forced him to look at her

face-to-face. "Elliot, everyone has been so worried about you, and none of us knew where you had gone. I didn't even know you had an uncle in Texas."

"He came here when the town was still new and raw. He and my father are brothers."

"I gathered that...about the brothers part, but you left so suddenly and without any good-byes, so we were all curious."

"Curious as to where I was or curious to know how I could have let Angela die?" Sophia had survived the blaze that claimed Angela, and seeing her now brought back all the old pain that now stabbed at his gut with the same intensity it had only two years earlier.

"We all wanted to know where you'd gone. After the funeral you disappeared completely."

"Did you ever stop to think about why I had to leave? I couldn't face Angela's parents knowing I had let them down." Their devastated faces at the service told him more than any words. He was a doctor and supposed to save people...not let them die. He tried to pull his hands from Sophia's grasp, but she held on even tighter.

"No one, not me, not the Petersons, not any of our friends accused you of anything. It was just a horrible accident where I happened to be at the right place at the right time and was spared."

"But if I had been there and not on duty, I could have helped her get out of that place, and then she wouldn't have been on that table in the emergency room."

"I don't think you could have. There was so much confusion, and the smoke so thick that everyone panicked. If I had been more careful to make sure she was behind me, we both would have made it out. As it was…" Her voice trailed off to silence.

"That doesn't matter. I had my chance at the hospital, but nothing we did kept her from dying. She never even regained consciousness so I could say good-bye." He looked away. The grief he'd bottled so successfully in the past few years now threatened to rise to the surface and overcome him.

"That's it, Elliot. You did everything you and the other doctor could, but it was simply her time. I know that sounds so trite, but the Bible says that our days are numbered even before our birth. You ought to read Psalm 139. It can make a real difference. I know, because that's the only way I got through losing two of my best friends."

That was the same psalm his uncle wanted him to read. He didn't see how it would make any difference to him. God had deserted him at the time of greatest need, so there was no reason to make an effort to find comfort in the Bible or anything religious now.

"So I suppose now you'll let everyone in town know what happened to you and what I did in Cleveland." His heart pounded against his ribs. He couldn't bear the thought of people staring and whispering about their doctor. All the trust he'd built with his patients would be wiped out.

Sophia squeezed his hands, and her strength made him gasp. "No, Elliot. I wouldn't and won't say anything. It's your secret to reveal when and where you choose. I'm just someone who knew of you in Cleveland, and that's all. I promise."

He wanted to believe her, but his mind couldn't grasp the idea that she'd keep quiet. "If that's true, then you'll leave me alone. I'll nod or speak when we happen to meet on the street, but no more visits like this."

"All right, but if and when you're ready to talk more, I'll be available." She finally released her hold, and Elliot shook his hands to return the circulation.

"You do have a strong grip. My fingers are numb."

Sophia's smile lit up her face just as it had so many years ago. She and Angela had loved having fun and laughed a lot. "I'm sorry, but that comes with having to defend myself against three brothers."

"Which reminds me. What are you doing here as a mail-order bride? I can't imagine your father letting you do something so wild."

Now her face clouded with pain. She bit her lip then sat down. "You'd better sit with me. It's a long and painful story."

Elliot sat across from her and listened as she spoke. "Papa was making so much money that Mama and I never gave much thought to what he was doing with it. As long as we had enough to shop and do what we wanted, we didn't worry. Then last year it all began to change. Suddenly all the money was gone, and we had nothing."

"Oh, Sophia, I'm so sorry. I had no idea." No wonder she had shown such pain, and it still filled her eyes.

"Papa made some bad investments and lost it all. We had to let all the servants go, sell all but one horse and one carriage. Then we had to sell the house and move in with one of my brothers who still lived in Cleveland. That was awful since he really didn't have that much room."

Elliot could only imagine the humiliation her father must

have suffered. His heart ached for the family. "So how did you wind up out here?"

"My sister-in-law Emily told me about a cousin, Suzanne, who had come to Texas as a mail-order bride and loved it. I didn't think much about it at the time. But then Mama and Papa were both killed in a carriage accident and left me without anything at all."

"Sophia! How tragic." He reached over and squeezed her hands. It reminded him of the loss of his own parents when he'd been a young boy. He'd have been lost if it had not been for his aunt and uncle.

She wiped away a tear and continued. "Since I have no skills, I had to find a way to support myself. I couldn't live with my brother and his family the rest of my days, and all my friends had deserted me. None of the men in our circle would even speak to me."

Elliot's heart went out to Sophia. Instead of avoiding her, he must make every effort to let her know he would still be her friend.

"Anyway, I thought about Suzanne and found an ad from Philip Dawes looking for a bride. It was in the same town as Suzanne, so I took a chance and wrote to Mr. Dawes. His letters impressed me, and I can see now he is the same good man in person as he was in his letters. So now I'm here, and I've never felt so blessed in my whole life. The people here are wonderful and accept me for who and what I am."

She patted her cheeks with a handkerchief. "I mustn't take up any more of your time. Just remember what I said. You know where to find me if you need me."

Elliot stared after her departing form. With all that had

happened to Sophia, she still showed concern for him and his situation. What a good friend she would be. Maybe her coming to Porterfield wasn't such a terrible thing after all. He wasn't the only one in the world with troubles and tragedy in life, and he wouldn't be the last. It would do him well to remember that, but if Sophia's old friends had deserted her in time of need, what would the people here do if they learned the truth about him? All he could do now was to believe she'd keep her word, and his secret would be safe.

Abigail stood by the window of the library and spotted Sophia leaving the infirmary. She'd been in there awhile. She hoped Sophia hadn't taken ill after being here such a short time. From what she had seen between the two of them, they shared something from the past, and it must have to do with why Elliot had left Cleveland, but neither one seemed to want to acknowledge knowing each other.

She turned away from the window when a patron called her over to check out a book. Being so late in the afternoon now, even the children had left to go home for supper. When this one left, she'd be alone.

After the man left, the bell jingled again, signaling someone's arrival. Abigail's eyes opened wide. What was Sophia doing here?

"Good afternoon, Sophia. How can I help you?"

"I just thought I'd drop by for a visit since I was in town. Philip is out on a run with Allen, and so I came in to purchase some things from the general store."

"I just saw you come out of the infirmary. Are you ill?"

Well, how was that for being nosy. When would she learn to keep her mouth shut? "Oh, no. I just stopped in to visit with Elliot. We're old friends, and we haven't had a chance to visit."

At last she admitted to a friendship. Now if only she'd share what she knew about Elliot. "I thought you might be, seeing as how you're from the same city."

Sophia narrowed her eyes and studied Abigail for a minute. "So there is interest in our physician?"

How much should she admit? Perhaps the truth would bring more information than evasion. "I suppose there is," she confided. "Although I didn't come to Porterfield looking for a man, there's something about Elliot that draws me. The sadness I see in his eyes makes me want to know him better and take away some of that pain and help him to see how much God loves him too."

Sophia smiled warmly. "If anyone could do that for Elliot, I believe you're the one who could accomplish it. How could he resist your charm?"

Abigail shrugged. "He's done a pretty fair job of doing just that so far. Although he did ask me to attend the Fall Festival with him, and we had a delightful time." But he'd mostly ignored her since then.

"I knew Elliot in Cleveland, and he had a rough time there. I can't go into details because I promised him I wouldn't, but suffice it to say he needs encouragement and friendship more than anything else. Keep praying for him to see God's love in those around him. He feels pretty much alone and abandoned by God at the moment."

Abigail sighed and nodded. "I figured as much. He's a wonderful doctor. Kate, his nurse, has told me about some of the things he has done to help people here in Porterfield. They all respect Elliot and his uncle." And she was beginning to care more about him than she really wanted to admit. Only the matter of his religious beliefs stood in the way of her falling for him completely. And the fact that he didn't pursue her.

"I can see that you care a great deal about Elliot, and I want to do everything I can to help you. I'm expecting a letter from some friends in Cleveland that might help, but your friendship and encouragement should go a long way."

Abigail's eyes glistened with tears. "Oh, I pray so, Sophia. I do pray so."

"Then we'll both be praying for the best outcome." She turned toward the door as the bell rang. "I see you have someone needing assistance, so I'll leave and hope we will have another conversation very soon."

Abigail turned her attention to the new patron, but her mind still dwelled on Elliot and what she could do to show him how much God loved him. What could she do that would heal the pain in his past? She had no idea. But she prayed that the anticipated letter would do some good.

CHAPTER
TWENTY-TWO

*E*LLIOT MADE A few notations on Erin Winston's chart. She had just left from having her checkup for the baby, and he had told her that it was now only a matter of weeks. He dropped his pen on the desk and rubbed his temples.

Over the last week Sophia had kept her word and not said anything to anyone about Angela, but it gave him little comfort. A knock sounded on the door frame, and he glanced up to see his uncle.

"About finished up here? It's getting close to noon, so I'm heading home to eat. Thought you might want to walk with me."

Elliot grabbed his coat and hat from the rack beside his desk. "I think I'll do just that. My stomach is letting me know it's time for food." He shoved his arms into his coat and turned his head so his uncle wouldn't detect the worry he bore.

They stepped outside to bright sunshine and another mild fall day. The air had enough chill to warrant a coat, but the sunshine kept the temperature up to a comfortable level. His uncle kept silent for the first few blocks, but as they crossed the street near the boardinghouse, Doc cleared his throat.

"Are you planning to attend the big party Kate and Daniel are giving for Sophia and Philip? Their wedding is only a week away."

"I hadn't thought much about it. I heard it is to be a pounding so they will have their kitchen stocked in their new home."

"That's right. The ladies plan to make sure the couple has plenty of flour, sugar, meal, and staples like that." He paused a moment then stopped in the middle of the walkway. "Have you spoken to Sophia?"

A vise tightened about Elliot's chest. "Yes, and she has kept her word about not telling others what happened, but she strongly advised me to do so and to quit blaming myself. After hearing her story, I do realize I'm not the only one with problems."

Doc resumed walking. "She's right, you know. You do need to quit feeling so much guilt and be willing to forgive yourself."

It wasn't going to happen. No matter what they said, he couldn't get past the fact that if he'd used available medical knowledge, he could have saved Angela.

They entered the house, and wonderful aromas of home-made soup, cornbread, and apple pie wafted from the kitchen. Elliot breathed in deeply and removed his coat. Nothing like a good bowl of hot soup on a cool fall day to help a body forget his troubles.

Aunt Maggie greeted them and nodded toward the table. "It's all ready for you. Wash up and have a seat."

A few minutes later Doc had said the blessing, and Elliot sliced off a chunk of cornbread. His mind churned with all the events of the past days since Sophia's arrival. When he first came to town, he'd managed to push thoughts of Angela into the background, but Abigail's arrival and then Sophia's had planted it squarely in his life once again.

He'd taken the blame for so long, that now thinking about letting it go seemed all but impossible. Abigail stirred up long buried and forgotten emotions, but he didn't want to explore them now that Sophia was here. If only he could put the past behind him. He almost choked on his soup. Isn't that exactly what people had been telling him to do?

"Are you all right, Elliot?"

His aunt calling his name jerked him back to the present. "What was that, Aunt Maggie?"

"I asked if you're all right. What has your mind so troubled today?"

Elliot clenched his teeth trying to find the answer when his uncle spoke. "He's probably thinking about Sophia Langston."

His aunt pursed her lips. "Oh. I see. Brings back a lot of bad memories, I'm sure, but having her here could be a very good thing."

How that would be possible, Elliot couldn't see. He kept waiting for the worst scenario of his secret being exposed even though Sophia had promised to keep quiet. What had happened to Sophia when her family was ruined could very well be the same for him once people found out he'd been negligent with a patient. They would lose all their trust in him as a physician.

"Son, I know you're tired of hearing it, but you have to move ahead in life. Holding on to the tragedy of the past keeps you from doing that. Doc and I have worried about you, and as we both have said so many times, it wasn't your fault. You have to quit blaming yourself."

Easy for her to say but not for him to do. He'd wrestled with it often and came to the same conclusion each time. He should have been able to save Angela. Even though, as a doctor, he understood death could be inevitable in many cases, it shouldn't have been in this one. Concealing the story had become burdensome, but it was a burden he wasn't ready to lay down.

Doc took off his glasses and polished them with his napkin. "Just what are you afraid of with Sophia?"

"That she'll let Henry Wilder get the story he wants from her. He knows we were acquainted in Cleveland, and knowing him, he won't let go of this until he has it all out in the open. My patients would never trust me again if they knew I'd let someone die."

"Horsefeathers." Aunt Maggie's eyebrows raised and her eyes sparked fire. "That's the most ridiculous thing I've heard you say yet. People here love you and respect you. They know people die. Why, Doc here has lost a few patients himself, and as hard as it is, it's a part of life, and those of us on the frontier know that better than most folks."

Doc chimed in. "She's right. Nobody has any guarantees in life. You could walk out of here and be run over by a carriage or drop dead of a heart attack. Only God knows the time and place of each person's death. When the time comes, the time comes."

"That's one reason I'm so angry about it. Angela and I were ready to begin our life together. What good did God think would come of ending her life before we had our chance at love and marriage?"

Aunt Maggie reached over and covered his hand with hers. "Elliot, dear, we don't understand the way God works, but the Bible tells us that even when tragedy strikes, He always uses it for good. We have to trust Him and His plans for our lives. What is planned for us is not always what we plan for ourselves."

Death was certainly not what he had planned with Angela, but God apparently did, and that Elliot could not accept. He could see no possible good that her death might bring. It had only brought heartache and sadness to so many people. Where was the good in that? And even if something good eventually came of it, he could not imagine it being worth all the suffering that preceded it.

He didn't care to hear any more, so he dropped his napkin on the table and stood. "I'll be at the infirmary. Thank you for the lunch. The soup was delicious."

Elliot headed for the door and grabbed his coat and hat on the way out. Clouds now blocked the sun, and the dreary day matched the mood that fell on him during the meal. He pulled the collar of his coat tighter about his neck. Thanksgiving was next week, but again this year he could not find anything for which he wanted to give thanks.

Abigail walked back with Mr. Fuller to the bank, where she planned to deposit another check from her grandfather's trust to add to her funds. She listened with half her mind as Mr. Fuller went on about Aunt Mae and her cooking. Why he hadn't asked Aunt Mae to marry him remained a mystery to Abigail as well as to Kate and her family. Of course, Aunt Mae's independent spirit may have something to do with it.

When they passed by the infirmary, she noticed Elliot unlocking the door and going inside. Ever since Miss Langston arrived, he seemed to have isolated himself even more. After hearing Sophia's explanation, she understood a little better, but why did it keep him from visiting her? She'd just have to make more effort to see him.

Mr. Fuller spoke her name. "Miss Monroe, we are so pleased to have you as a customer at the bank. Mr. Weygandt said just the other day that having a library in town has certainly been an asset."

Abigail pulled her gaze from the infirmary and back to the bank teller. "Thank you, Mr. Fuller. It's been quite exciting to see the response from everyone."

They reached the bank entrance, and Abigail noticed four riders headed into town from the direction of the courthouse. At this time of day, only light traffic filled the streets. These men must be ranchers coming in to deposit their pay. Usually a large number of them came in on Friday nights and spent most of what they'd earned on women and hard drink. They rode easily in their saddles like cowboys, so she turned her head back to the bank and followed Mr. Fuller inside.

She waved at Mr. Weygandt, the bank president, and stood at the teller window. Mr. Fuller pulled a dark blue visor over his forehead and opened up. She finished her transaction and turned to leave. But two men stood blocking the door.

They were two of the cowboys she'd spotted riding into

town, but this time their neckerchiefs were pulled up to cover their faces. Abigail choked back a cry and attempted to pass by. One of them grabbed her arm then pointed a gun toward Mr. Fuller. The other man drew his gun and headed toward Mr. Weygandt.

Abigail wanted to scream, but her throat closed and her heart pounded. No sound came from her mouth. The man's hold tightened on her arm when she tried to jerk away.

"Don't try anything, miss. Keep still." He tossed a bag at Mr. Fuller then pointed a gun at the teller. "Fill it up with all your cash."

Mr. Fuller's hands shook as he stacked bills and shoved them into the bag. Then he swept the coins off the counter into the bag. All the time the other robber held Mr. Weygandt at gunpoint and pushed him toward the vault.

He handed another bag to the president. "Get the cash from the vault."

Abigail opened her mouth in an attempt to scream again, but only a squeak emerged. This was enough to anger the man beside her. He released his hold long enough to slap his palm across her cheek. "Do that again, and I'll make sure you don't make any noise."

From the corner of her eye she spotted Mr. Fuller reaching under his counter. The gunman squeezed her arm then strode the few steps to the window, pulling her with him. He brought his gun down on the teller's head, and Mr. Fuller slumped to the floor, blood oozing from the wound. The robber holstered his gun and gathered up the sack of money with his free hand.

Mr. Weygandt finished stuffing the money from the vault into the other robber's bag and stepped forward to see about Mr. Fuller. That's when the gunman at the vault shot the banker. The one holding Abigail cursed a blue streak and dragged her with him, kicking and yelling, out to the rear of the bank where two other men waited with the horses. She opened her mouth to scream louder, but something smashed into her face and her brain exploded in a rainbow of color before blackness enveloped her.

A gunshot rang out from the bank, followed by the screams of a woman standing on the boardwalk outside the bank. Cory ran toward the bank, yelling for the others to get out of the way. If the bank was being robbed, he didn't want to chance anyone else getting in the way.

He slammed through the bank doors to find Mr. Weygandt bleeding on the floor and an unconscious Mr. Fuller nearby. Sheriff Rutherford slid to a stop behind Cory. "I heard a shot…" He took one look and yelled over his shoulder, "Get the doc, quick."

Mr. Weygandt waved his hand toward the back. "They went out that way, and they have Abigail Monroe with them."

Cory's heart jumped to his throat. Abigail? How did she get mixed up in this? Visions of what the outlaws could do to her caused his stomach to turn. They had to rescue her.

The sheriff went outside then returned with two men. "Stay here until Doc arrives. We have to go after them."

Cory snapped back to his duty and raced out to where his horse was hitched and swung up into the saddle. He and Rutherford were of the same mind. He heard his name and turned to see Daniel running toward him.

"Cory, is it true the bank was robbed and they took Abigail with them?"

"Yes, and we're going after them now."

"I'm coming too. She's my sister."

Sheriff Rutherford held out his hand to stop Daniel. "No, stay here and let us handle it. I'm leaving you in charge here again." He pointed to three others, including Frank Cahoon and an Indian Scout named Hawkeye. "You, you, and you get saddled. I'm deputizing you to ride with us."

They nodded and mounted their horses. A man on the street called to the sheriff. "I saw them head that way, and they had a woman with them."

"Thanks, Clem." Rutherford wheeled his horse around, and the others followed.

Cory dug his heels into his horse's flank and sped away in a cloud of dust with the sheriff. The sheriff had chosen his men well. Frank was big but fast both on foot and on horseback. Hawkeye was the best tracker in area. If any man could keep on the trail of the robbers, Hawkeye Ramey could. Abigail's life depended on it.

CHAPTER
TWENTY-THREE

*E*LLIOT AND DOC raced into the bank and found Mr. Weygandt being treated by one of the townspeople. He had stopped the bleeding with pressure on the wound but gladly relinquished his hold to Elliot while Doc checked on Mr. Fuller.

Daniel stood at the door and kept people away while Elliot worked on the bank president. The sheriff must have left Daniel in charge judging by the badge now pinned to his coat. Elliot glanced up at the man who had helped the banker. "What happened here?"

"I don't know. I heard one gunshot and someone yelling about the bank being robbed. I came running because I know a little about bullet wounds. I was a soldier once and saw lots of 'em on the battlefield."

"You did a good job and most likely saved his life." The bleeding had stopped, and Elliot applied a bandage over it.

"Uh, something else happened, Doc Elliot. They took that librarian girl with them."

Elliot's heart skipped a beat. "They took Abigail Monroe?"

"Yes, that's what they did. I heard her scream, but then she stopped."

Before Elliot had the chance to digest the news, Kate hurried into the bank with two men carrying a stretcher. "We have only the one, so who needs it?"

Elliot staggered to his feet and pointed to the bank president. "Kate, they have Abigail."

Kate whirled around, her mouth agape. "They have what?" She looked over his shoulder and hollered to her husband. "Daniel, they have Abigail."

He rushed to Kate's side and enveloped her in his arms. "Yes, I know. Cory and the sheriff took a posse to go after them."

All the breath escaped from Elliot, and he grabbed the teller's counter for support. Cory had gone after her. He cared about Abigail and wouldn't come back without her.

Kate trembled in Daniel's arms. "They have to find her. She's not big enough to fight them off like I would. They'll squash her like a fly."

Elliot gasped for breath. He had to get out. He clutched his throat and ran outside and gulped in as much fresh air as he could. His stomach roiled. It was happening all over again. Someone he cared about was in danger, and he could do nothing to save her.

Mr. Weygandt had been loaded onto the stretcher, and the two men headed for the infirmary. Elliot slumped against the wall as Doc came out of the bank followed by a man carrying Mr. Fuller.

His uncle grabbed his arm. "Come, Elliot, we have

wounded to take care of. The posse will find Abigail and bring her back safe."

How could he be sure of that? Nothing was certain where outlaws and guns were involved. What if she was badly injured and Cory couldn't save her either? No, he wouldn't think about such a thing. He pushed off from the brick wall of the bank and hurried after Doc.

Keeping busy with patient care would help keep his hands busy, but his mind strayed to thinking and worrying about Abigail. *Lord, if You remember me, hear my prayer and keep Abigail safe.* Why he prayed he had no idea, but it seemed to be the logical thing to do. It probably went no higher than the rooftop, but he had to utter the words. If this prayer went unanswered, then Elliot would know God was sending more punishment.

Inside the infirmary, he took over the care of Mr. Weygandt from his uncle and examined the wound more closely. The bullet remained in the man's flesh, but Elliot could see that it had hit mostly fatty tissue and missed any major organs.

"Mr. Weygandt, I'm going to give you ether to put you to sleep so I can remove this bullet. You've lost some blood, but you'll be fine once I get it out and sew you up." He motioned to Kate to come help.

"What do I need to do?"

"Give him some ether while I wash up good. We need to get that bullet out of his side."

Kate began her task, and Elliot scrubbed his hands up to the elbows at the basin. Lucky for him, Mr. Weygandt had substantial girth, and the bullet had lodged in fat first. This was something he could handle without thinking, but he wanted no slipups.

"If he's under, go wash so you can assist me." He unwrapped a towel of instruments then turned to the banker. Kate had removed his shirt to expose the wound more clearly and wiped it with alcohol.

He breathed deeply then probed in the hole with small forceps. It took only a minute or two until he clamped on something hard. He pulled out the bullet. Sweat beaded on his brow and dripped to his nose despite the coolness of the air.

Kate immediately sponged the excess blood so Elliot would have a clear field of vision for the sutures. Ten minutes later he and Kate both removed their bloody aprons and washed their hands.

"Soon as we can get someone to help us, we'll move him to one of the beds." He nodded toward the closed door to the waiting area. "Didn't I hear his wife talking to Doc?"

"Yes, and I'll go tell her he's going to be OK." She pushed through the doors, and he heard Mrs. Weygandt asking about her husband. This time they had good news for the family. Elliot savored the few moments of victory before thoughts of Abigail intruded again.

How he wished to be riding with the men trailing her, but his first responsibility lay with those who needed treatment. But then Abigail could be badly injured herself and need a doctor when they found her. He cursed inwardly. Why did his profession always keep him from saving those he really cared about? His medical skills served the general public. But they doomed the one he loved.

He could no longer deny the feelings growing in his heart

for Abigail. If he didn't have so much trouble of his own, perhaps he'd have a chance with her. After today, that likely
wouldn't happen. If Cory saved her and brought her back, he'd
be her hero, not Elliot. Jealousy reared its head once again, but
this time he did nothing to squelch it.

Cory kept a keen eye toward the ground and spotted the marks
almost as soon as Hawkeye did. Horseshoe prints here, bent
twigs there, a broken limb ahead all pointed to the robbers
having gone this way. From what he could see, there had to be
at least four men.

He rode up alongside Hawkeye. "Looks for certain that
they came this way."

Hawkeye's dark brown, almost black eyes, looked ahead.
"Yes, and I count four different sets of prints. The young
woman must be riding with one of them. See how those prints
are a little deeper in the dirt there? That most likely indicates
extra weight on that horse."

With no rain for several months, dirt tracks were all they
had. A good rain with marshy ground would have given clear
prints to follow, but the dust was deep enough for the shoes to
leave their marks. Hawkeye spoke again and spurred his horse
onward. "They're not riding hard, but they'll get ahead of us if
we don't get going."

A noise broke through the brush and trees to the right
of Cory. He drew his gun and waited in a clump of bushes.
Marshal Slade rode into view. He spotted Cory and rode
toward him. Cory slipped his gun back into its holster. "How
did you find out about the robbery?"

"I got into town a little after you left and followed. They told me the men have a hostage."

"Yes, it's Abigail Monroe, the librarian and Daniel's sister. Hawkeye says there are four of them, and one of them is carrying Abigail on his horse."

They rode up ahead to join the others. Sheriff Rutherford pulled up his horse. "Glad to see you, Marshal. We can use all the help we can get. Any news about the two bankers?"

"Yeah, they'll be OK. I told Daniel we'd find his sister, so let's get to it."

Cory's heart lightened knowing the lawman would be with them. He'd made a promise to Daniel and Kate, and he planned to keep it. Who was he fooling? It was a promise to himself too.

Abigail's head throbbed with pain much worse than when she'd been clipped by a horse at home. She opened her eyes a slit, but images were hazy. Something covered her mouth so she couldn't speak. Where was she? Angry voices argued across the room. One of them cursed and asked why they had brought the woman with them.

The woman would be her, and the memory of the bank robbery, the shooting, and then being hit in the face came back in a rush of color and sound. She moved slightly and realized both her feet and hands were bound. Her teeth clamped down on a gag that tasted of dirt and sweat and sent her stomach into turmoil.

A chair scraped on the floor, and footsteps came close. She lay as still as possible, hoping he'd think she was still unconscious. A voice she recognized from the bank laughed. "I know you're awake. Don't try to pretend." The toe of his boot poked at shoulder.

Despite her desire to keep quiet, she winced in pain and a moan escaped her throat. "Now we have to decide what to do with you." His footsteps faded, and once again the chair scraped.

The haze cleared enough for her to see four men at a table. Two she recognized from the bank, and the other two must be the others she saw coming into town before the robbery. The skinny one with the mean look in his eye had shot Mr. Weygandt. She closed her eyes and tried to erase the memory of his blood-stained shirt. Something had happened to Mr. Fuller too. Her whole body ached to the point she couldn't think straight. She didn't have the strength to fight any one of them, much less four.

One of the men started talking, but his voice didn't carry to Abigail. She strained to hear even one word to give her a clue as to her whereabouts. Her fate lay in the hands of these men, and from what she'd seen, they'd shoot her and leave her here if she made a move. Determination and anger coursed their way through her blood, but no amount of pulling and tugging loosened her bindings.

Death was not an option she'd accept. She had too much life yet to live and too much work to be done. She twisted her hands behind her again in an attempt to free them, but the cord or rope or whatever it was only bit into her wrists and caused more pain. Abigail clenched her teeth against the rag and almost retched at the foul taste.

She waited for her stomach to settle again and went back

to twisting her hands. Pain she could endure if it meant loosening whatever bound her. One of the men turned and glared at her. The evil in his eyes slammed into Abigail's chest. These men would never leave her alive.

Cold air blew through cracks in the walls, and Abigail shivered. Somewhere along the way she'd lost her shawl. She drew her knees up to her chest and rested her forehead on them. The voices and arguing continued, and she could make out only a few words about what to do with her, how much money they had, and how soon they had to get out of here— wherever here was.

Cory and the sheriff must be on their way to find her by now. All she had to do was be quiet and wait, unless the men decided to leave now and kill her. Abigail shuddered at the idea of her body being found by Cory. Daniel and Kate would be heartbroken, but one thing for certain, if these men did kill her, Daniel wouldn't rest until they were found and hanged.

Once again footsteps drew near. "Not as spunky as ya were, are ya? All the fight gone out of ya?" He yanked her to her feet. "You're going with us. Sweet little thing like you oughta bring us a pretty penny from a pa or a brother or even the sheriff."

The other three laughed, and the sound sent more chills through Abigail. Somehow she had to get away. Where was that posse? What if they couldn't find the trail? Then if they did catch up, how were they going to negotiate with these men? She didn't trust them one bit.

"We'll be leaving soon, so jest make yourself comfortable." He shoved her back into the corner against the rough boards.

He returned to the others, and she gazed around the room. The room was small and had only one door. This must be one of those shacks she'd heard the cowboys talking about. No light shone through the window, so it must be late in the evening. She'd been unconscious since it all began around noon. How long and how far had they traveled?

A kerosene lantern flickered on the table giving eerie shadows to the faces of the robbers. Abigail hunched over in an effort to warm her body. *Please, God, help Cory and Sheriff Rutherford find me. Protect me from these horrible men.*

God was her only hope now. He'd guide Cory and the sheriff to her. She had to believe that and hang on to it with all her strength.

CHAPTER
TWENTY-FOUR

*A*s dawn painted the sky, Cory and the posse approached an abandoned shack. A few miles back they had found the shawl Abigail had worn yesterday, and the trail led here. The robbers would have had to stop for the night just as the posse had, and this was the most likely place for them to hide.

No signs of life arose around the cabin, but the sheriff still approached it with caution. The cabin was one room with one door and one window, so if they were in there, they'd have to come out that door. Marshall Slade positioned the men in the trees facing the door.

The sheriff kicked in the door then turned and shook his head. "No one's here, but it looks like they were. Must have left just before we arrived."

Cory's heart sank. Where to now? They had to find the men and get Abigail away from them. He held her shawl up to his face and let the rosewater scent wash over him. Her bright eyes and warm smile danced behind his closed eyes. *Please, God, we have to find her.*

The sheriff mounted his horse. "Which way, Hawkeye?"

The former Indian scout studied the ground around the cabin then pointed east. "That way. Four horses."

Marshall Slade spurred his horse. "They're headed for Louisiana. We gotta get them before they reach the river. "

The posse moved, following Hawkeye to the east and the Sabine River. If the men got across and into Louisiana, their trail would be more difficult to pick up. Cory remembered the river being low this time of year because of the lack of rain in the summer. If the gang stayed in the river before exiting the other side and heading to Louisiana, the posse could waste valuable time trying to find where the exit might be.

Carthage lay to the east, but the men would most likely skirt around the town. Whether north or south of it became the question. Hawkeye pulled his reins and held up his hand. "They came through here, but it's getting harder to follow. Looks like they went south."

Sheriff Rutherford scanned the area. "That makes sense. The river flows into the state line there. Just keep looking for marks."

The others agreed, and Cory fell in line to follow them. If the gang didn't stop at all, they'd be at the river by tomorrow. This reminded him of when they chased the rustlers last year, but caught up to them before they crossed the cattle over the Sabine. His father had been hurt, but by a steer and not a gunman. He prayed this trip would have no injuries.

The sun rose higher in the sky with low-hanging clouds partially blocking its rays. The air smelled of approaching winter. The temperatures hadn't dropped considerably in the past few weeks, and the area was due for a good blast of cold air from the north. Cory hoped that wouldn't happen until they had Abigail safe at home.

Kate and Sarah must be worried sick by this time. It would soon be twenty-four hours since the abduction. How he wished he could ride back into town right now with Abigail safe in his arms. She had spunk and wouldn't go without a fight, but as Kate had reminded him, Abigail wasn't big enough to overpower one man, much less four.

Hawkeye stopped up ahead and waved to the sheriff and marshal. Cory followed them The scout pointed to the ground. "Looks like they came this way and stopped. See the prints here, and then the prints of a man and a woman. They go a little beyond the trees here."

A smaller footprint was definitely that of a woman, and from the imprint, she wasn't heavy and didn't need help. It could only be Abigail. He dismounted and followed the prints to the trees. He found a fragment of cloth clinging to a branch. He snatched it off and gripped it in his palm. It was the same color and material as the skirt Abigail had worn yesterday. His heart pounded in his chest as he scanned the area for more clues. Nothing there. Time to get on with the hunt.

He climbed back on his horse and rejoined the men. He handed the piece of cloth to Hawkeye. Maybe she had done that on purpose and would do it again later on the trail.

Hawkeye had also dismounted to study the area for prints. He glanced at the cloth then back to the ground. "Tracks indicate they're headed down river to that shallow section. They're

almost an hour ahead of us." He remounted and turned south
to set out again.

Cory turned his horse to follow. If the gang stayed south
before crossing over, the chances of catching them were slim to
none. If it weren't for the density of the trees in the area, they
could move faster, but the same trees slowed down the robbers.
Still, they needed to make up the distance between them.

Abigail kicked and squirmed until she was slapped again.
These men had no respect for a woman, and would do worse
the next time they stopped if she didn't be still. She whim-
pered and said, "I...I must stop a minute. Please."

The outlaw helped her down and followed her to a larger
tree then stood watch while she tended to her personal needs.
She bit her lip and tore off a another scrap of her skirt to leave
behind. She prayed the posse would find her clues.

The leer on her guard's face sent icy chills down her spine
and added to the discomfort of being cold and using the forest
ground as a privy. He yanked her up and pulled her back to his
horse. When she was in the saddle, he climbed up behind her
and wrapped his arms about her body.

She cringed at his touch and tried to shrink into herself,
but his hold only grew tighter. His hot breath warmed her neck
and at the same time caused her stomach to recoil in disgust.
She squeezed her eyes shut and tried to think of her family.

Then the breath became damp as his lips touched her skin.
She jerked away, but he only laughed.

Where were Cory and the sheriff? They had to be coming
to get her. She'd rather die than go on with these men to the

river. Maybe they planned to stop there and wait for the posse then make a deal or something for her release. But she'd also heard tales of what happened to women who had been kidnapped by men like this, and it caused her throat to fill with bile. With one great heave, she leaned over and expelled the contents of her stomach.

His hand grabbed her. "Now see what you've done! Made a stinkin' mess on yourself and me. We'll just have to stop and clean you up at the river. Won't be long now." One gloved hand came up to caress her cheek.

It may as well have been a snake for the revulsion filling her. What had happened to that courage and bravado she'd always had? It had to be buried down deep somewhere. For the first time ever, she realized there was nothing she could do. She could only pray. Would that be enough?

Elliot spent a sleepless night wrestling with his memories and images of Abigail. He cared for her, and now her disappearance filled him dread. What if she was hurt, and he couldn't save her? What if she was already dead?

He skipped breakfast and headed for the sheriff's office in the courthouse where Daniel watched over the town. Aunt Maggie had called after him, but he'd ignored her and saddled his horse.

Daniel sat at the sheriff's desk and jerked his head up when Elliot burst through the door. "Have you heard anything yet?"

"No, most likely won't until they come back either with the thieves or alone." His voice choked on the last words.

Elliot grimaced and gripped the brim of his hat with his

hands. Abigail was Daniel's sister. Of course he would be worried and concerned. "I'm sorry, Daniel. I know if anything had happened, you'd have let us know. I'm so worried about Abigail, but the good news is that Weygandt and Fuller will be OK."

"If we could only say that about Abigail. She's a fighter, but I don't want to even think about what they might do to her." He slapped his palms on the desk and stood. "I should be out there with them hunting her and not in this office."

Elliot understood that because he'd thought the same thing last night, but his uncle had tried to convince him that a doctor in town was more important. "I want to go too. What if she's hurt and needs a doctor? No telling how far away they are or what they'll need when they find her."

Daniel's breath came out in whoosh as he sat down. "So glad you said *when* and not *if*. Don't think I could stand it if you'd said *if* like several others have."

Elliot said nothing more to keep from revealing his growing concern for Abigail. His heart had already let her in, and now all he could do was wait for someone to bring her home.

He turned toward the door to get away from Daniel's now probing eyes. "Let us know when you hear anything. I'm heading back to the infirmary to give Doc a hand. He stayed the night with our patients. We'll most likely let them go home today." He strode through the door and swung up onto his horse.

Up and down Main Street the citizens of Porterfield went about their daily business except at the bank. Those doors remained closed and locked. Someone was on their way from the government to check into how much damage had been done. Several men and women stood at the bank doors reading the notice Daniel had posted.

After a few murmurs and comments, they shook their heads and went on with their errands. Elliot trotted on past them and headed for the infirmary to relieve Doc, although his uncle most likely wouldn't leave.

When he entered, Kate met him. "Has Daniel heard anything at all?"

He recognized the fear and concern in her eyes. He'd seen it before in family members of patients he'd treated, and it always sent tremors of guilt when he had to deliver bad news. He shook his head. "No, but he'll let us know as soon as he knows anything. Cory and the sheriff will find her. After all, Hawkeye is the best tracker in these parts."

Kate sniffed and blinked her eyes. "I know. I've heard Cory talk about him enough. But Abigail is not as strong or tall as most women, and from what I've heard, those men are big and mean."

That he had seen from the damage done to the president and teller in the bank. His uncle came out of Mr. Fuller's room. Before the door closed, Elliot spotted Aunt Mae in the room. A brief smile crossed his mouth. At least they wouldn't have to worry about Mr. Fuller and Mr. Weygandt getting good care. Mrs. Weygandt had spent the night in her husband's room.

Doc stepped to Kate's side and wrapped his arm around her shoulders. "These two are good enough to go home today, so now we can concentrate on what to do for Abigail."

What that could be Elliot had no idea, but he'd be willing to do anything to see her home safe and secure. Doc reached for his hand. and Elliot let his uncle grasp it. Then Doc bowed his head and began praying. Elliot stiffened, but Kate slipped her hand into his, and for some reason he began to relax as his uncle's words filled the room.

"Dear God and Father in heaven, hear our plea for Abigail. Keep her safe in Your arms. Protect her under Your wings of mercy. Watch over the men trying to find her, and lead them in the right direction to find her soon. Amen."

Elliot glanced up to see Kate's eyes filled with tears. Prayer hadn't helped him when he'd needed it before, so why should it help now? If it gave any solace to Doc or Kate, then he'd keep quiet and let them pray as they wanted. Still, he'd put more money on the tracking skills of Hawkeye right now than he would any of their prayers.

Abigail's kidnapping made a mockery of the Thanksgiving holiday coming next week. Who would want to give thanks as long as she was missing?

CHAPTER
TWENTY-FIVE

*T*HE ONE THE others called McGraw yanked Abigail down from his horse and landed her with a thud on the hard-packed dirt. Pain shot through the ankle she had injured weeks earlier, and she clenched her teeth to keep from crying out. He shoved her against a tree and pushed her down. The skinny one leered at her, and she squeezed her eyes shut.

His voice filled with all the evil she could imagine. "C'mon, McGraw, ain't nobody out here but us. We can use her to keep warm."

She heard flesh hit bone, and every muscle in her body tensed as tight as her bindings. "No, I said we're going to use her to get what we want. If that posse catches up to us, she's our guarantee they'll be careful. Once we cross the river and get into Louisiana, we let her go. Until then she's our ace up the sleeve. You lay a hand on her, and it's the last thing you'll ever touch."

Abigail held back a sob. They'd let her go across the river.

For the first time, hope that she'd get out of this alive and unhurt built in her heart. God was taking care of her.

Something fell over her head. "Here, you might need a blanket to keep warm tonight."

Abigail reached up and pulled it off and glared at him. After much effort, she finally managed to arrange the blanket over her body. She curled up with her knees tucked to her stomach and fell asleep.

The next morning she awakened just as the sky became gray with the light of dawn. Today had to be Sunday, but with the dense cloud cover, she had no way of knowing the time.

Three men still had not stirred, and the fourth stood watch with only the lower part of his face visible under his hat's brim. Abigail tried to move around a bit, but her bound hands and feet made that difficult. Snores emanated from the three still hunkered under blankets.

She kicked her feet forward, wishing her target could be the head of one of the men. The blanket tangled about her feet with the effort, and she tried to sit up. Her hands, now in front of her, were bound with her wrists crossed one over the other, which made doing anything, even eating, more difficult. Finally she made it to a sitting position and rearranged her skirt the best she could.

"Feel better now?" The sentry leered at her with eyes so evil they made her skin crawl.

She said nothing but glared back at him and pulled the blanket up to her chin to ward off some of the chill and to shield her body from the smoldering glance of the gunman. He wore a long dark duster like she'd seen on many of the cowboys from the ranches. A black leather gun belt with silver studs and a hefty-looking handgun circled his body just below the waist. She'd seen that last night when he'd removed the long coat. This morning he sat with a rifle cradled in his arms, ready to shoot whatever or whoever got in his way.

None of the men had shaved recently, which made their faces even more sinister, even in sleep. McGraw, apparently the leader, cursed the other men if they didn't do as he said. She didn't understand exactly why he protected her against the others, but she wouldn't question it and would accept it as grace from God.

McGraw yawned, stretched, and hopped up in a second. He turned his gaze to Abigail and towered over her. Dressed in all black from his boots to his hat, his height and the width of his shoulders gave him the appearance of a giant. It was no wonder he'd been able to fling her up on his saddle like she'd been a rag doll. Not to be intimidated, she sat up straight and lifted her head.

"Sorry we don't have room service, Missy, but we don't take time for luxuries." His lips curled to a snarl, and he kicked the rear ends of the two still sleeping. "Time to get movin' if we're to stay ahead of that posse. Two minutes to get your gear and get on your horses."

In that time the four men erased all signs of their camp. Abigail pulled back from McGraw's grasp. "I must relieve myself before we go."

McGraw snarled then shoved her toward the trees. He nodded to the one who had watched her earlier. "Take her, and make sure she hurries."

The man picked her up at the waist then deposited her behind a tree. He untied her hands, but kept one anchored to a tree limb then loosened the bindings at her ankles. With one hand she managed her skirts, her cheeks aflame with humiliation and anger. She ripped off another piece of cloth from her damaged skirt and concealed it in her hand.

When she had finished and stood up, she turned away to straighten her petticoats and skirt. With the scrap now secure in her waistband, she held out her hand to be bound to the other again. At the edge of the clearing, she grabbed the scrap then dropped it to the ground, praying the men wouldn't notice.

McGraw slung her up onto the saddle, and she landed with a thump that jarred her already sore bones and rattled her teeth. She sat with her feet, once again securely bound, hanging on one side. She clutched the saddle horn to keep from falling while McGraw mounted to sit behind her. His arms encircled her again as she flinched and tried to move away. Once again he bent his head so that his warm breath feathered her neck. She cringed at his touch, but he only laughed and jerked the reins.

The Lord was her light and salvation, and she would not be afraid. Cory and the sheriff would be here soon, and then it would all be over. She clung to that hope as the horses began moving through the trees.

Elliot waited until his aunt and uncle had left for church before he dressed and followed after them. A longing for fellowship with others gathered to worship God had worked its way into his heart. Long ago church had brought peace and solace, and he sorely needed both now. God had to be there somewhere.

He arrived after the services had begun and slipped into

a seat in the back row near the door. Reverend Winston led the congregation in prayer. Elliot listened to the words. Would God listen and bring Abigail home?

The prayer ended, and sniffles and nose blowing filled the air as Reverend Winston began his message. He talked about God being in control and God protecting Abigail through this ordeal. When he mentioned a scripture, Elliot grabbed a Bible from the rack on the pew and turned to Philippians 4. "Be careful for nothing; but in every thing by prayer and supplication with thanksgiving let your requests be made known unto God."

Reverend Winston explained that Paul meant we are not to worry about what may or may not happen but to trust God fully to take care of Abigail. "May we offer up our prayers for her and be thankful not for the situation, but that in the midst of it we can thank God for being there with her."

Elliot pondered those words. If God was protecting Abigail, why hadn't He been there to protect Angela? Did God pick and choose whom He saved and didn't save? Once again the doubts and fears from the past few years threatened his peace of mind.

When the service ended, members crowded around Reverend Winston, but Elliot dashed out the door before anyone could speak to him. He made it only as far as the road before Sophia ran up to him.

"Elliot, you did come this morning. I'm so glad you did. I remember how happy you were going to church with Angela and how much you both loved the Lord." She grasped at his arm. "Elliot, only God can bring the peace we need after a tragedy. I learned that after Mama and Papa died and all my friends abandoned me. God is the only one to stay true and never leave us."

The same old argument, but today it didn't irritate him quite as much. "Sophia, don't you understand that I knew what needed to be done for Angela, but I did it too late?"

"Ask God to help you understand. Ask Him for the wisdom to accept what happened and handle the grief that still fills you."

"I don't think I'll ever understand why, but I have to deal with it my own way. If you'll excuse me, I have to go now." He strode away, and Sophia didn't attempt to stop him. He turned to look back at her. She stared at him for another second or two then spun around and headed back to the church.

Elliot slowed his walk home. The anger he'd built up against God for these past few years didn't seem to burn with as much fire today. Reverend Winston's prayer and his sermon had touched a long buried yearning he'd once had for God's Word. The decision now before him was whether to let it grow or to once again shove it deep to a place where it would die.

Elliot trudged up the steps to the house. Worry for Abigail filled his mind, but once again he had no control over what was happening. How could he have let her into his heart?

He hung his coat on the hall tree then slumped on the sofa in the parlor. His thoughts again turned to Abigail. Her warm smile, vivacious spirit, and optimistic attitude had succeeded in doing what no others since Angela had accomplished. How could he have let it happen? He wanted to shake his fist at God, a God so cruel that He brought another woman into Elliot's life then snatched her away again as soon as he began to care about her. The punishment for his inadequacy in Cleveland would never end.

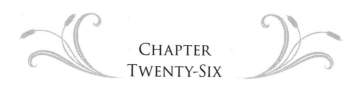

CHAPTER
TWENTY-SIX

*C*ORY AND HAWKEYE rode at the front of the posse with the tracker examining every bit of the trail. The sheriff had pulled them out of their camp before daylight in order to shorten the distance between them and the outlaws. A short time ago they'd passed the last place the gang had stopped. Even though they'd tried to erase all evidence, Hawkeye's skills spotted the scrap of cloth then pointed out two dainty prints left behind.

Cory's heart filled with more admiration for Abigail. She'd left another clue for them to know they were on the right track. Smart thinking.

Marshal Slade was ready to take them in for robbing the bank as well as shooting the two bankers. And if anything happened to Abigail, Cory himself would have a hard time keeping his hand off his gun.

The feisty little librarian had worked her way into his heart, and that was something he'd fought for too many years to count. Whether he wanted to admit it or not, she was one young woman who could make him willing to give up his single life. The men most likely wouldn't kill her, but the alternatives sent tremors of fury through Cory. If any one of those men had laid a hand on Abigail, he just might kill him on the spot. He let his anger boil for a time then remembered who he was. He swallowed hard and prayed.

Dear Jesus, help me to hold my temper and let Rutherford and Slade do their jobs. Protect Abigail. Keep her safe.

Talking with the Lord calmed his spirit but not his determination. He held his rifle loosely in his arms, ready to fire it at a moment's notice. They stopped, but Rutherford sent Hawkeye on ahead. The half-breed Caddo moved in silence and disappeared into the dense growth.

Rutherford pulled up beside Cory. "We're getting near the river, and I feel we're getting closer to them. Hawkeye will find them and let us know where to go next."

"If they just cross the river and come out even with where they went in, it'll be easy to follow, but what if they decide to go upriver or downriver then make it to the other side? Won't that keep us from finding them as quick?"

Rutherford scratched the stubble on his chin. "Might and might not. Depends on what Hawkeye finds. Most likely they'll be in a hurry, and that haste will leave clues for him to find."

He waved his hand to call the other men to join him. When the others reined in, Frank Cahoon said, "We better catch these men today. I don't like the idea of Miss Abigail being in their clutches one more night."

"Me neither, but we have to be careful." Rutherford nodded to Marshal Slade. "Got any ideas on where to go from here?"

Slade leaned on his saddle horn and gazed at each man. "I can see this gal means a lot to each of you, which means you have to control your feelings for her and concentrate on getting the men. Now, there's six of us and four of them, and we've determined they're part of the McGraw gang. With Hawkeye up front leading the way, I figure we can surround them and take them with minimum gunfire. If they're this side of the river, we can sneak up on them. If they've already crossed over, we don't want to attract their attention with our movements. We'll plan our next move when Hawkeye returns."

If McGraw hadn't stopped for food, that meant they'd been without for nearly two days. Cory grimaced at the thought of Abigail with no food for that time. Sheriff Rutherford had gone into Carthage and picked up supplies for the posse, which gave them an edge over McGraw's men.

After what seemed an eternity, but in reality was only half an hour, Hawkeye returned. "Found 'em at the river getting ready to cross. The girl's bound hand and foot but appears to be OK. I don't think they'll try to go north or south on the river, so they'll probably cut straight across. It's not as shallow here, and the current's rather swift for this time of year, but they should make it across OK."

Slade dug his heels into his horse's flank. "No sense waiting any longer. Let's go."

Cory followed, as did the others, with Hawkeye leading the way. The river curved like a slithering snake in this area. When they reached the woods overhanging the river, they were able to creep close because of the density of the trees. They dismounted and followed Hawkeye's lead. Cory wanted to shout when he spotted the four men still on this side.

Slade raised his hand to stop them. "Here's the plan. We spread out so that Hawkeye and you, Cory, go down to those trees and rocks and get close as you can. Each of us will take one man from this angle. I'll aim at McGraw. Be mindful of the girl. I want each of you to give a signal when you're ready. Cory, once you're close, be ready to snatch her soon as the outlaws are down. Don't shoot to kill, but wound them enough they can't fight back. I want these men alive to take back to Porterfield."

They nodded in agreement and began to spread through the trees. Cory slipped among them as he had as a child playing hide-and-seek with his brothers. Just when he got close enough to hear their voices and see their faces, a series of birdcalls echoed through the air. All the men must be in place. Now it was up to him to keep his eyes open and run in for Abigail.

Then shots rang out, and two of the men went down. One held his knee with one hand and reached for his gun with the other. The other two spun around and snatched their guns from their holsters, firing in the posse's direction. Cory took aim and shot the gun out of the hand of the one with the knee injury. The largest man grabbed Abigail from the saddle and threw her to the sandy shore, using her as a shield.

Cory growled. That no-good coward. Then the other two men were down and lay still. The one with the wounded leg nursed both his hand and his leg. The only one left was the big one holding Abigail.

Clanton called out, "McGraw, let the girl go. You're surrounded with no way out."

"You let me go, and I'll let her go; otherwise I'll shoot her right here." He shoved the gun up under her throat.

Cory fumed. With his back to the river, McGraw effectively protected himself with Abigail. He scooted over behind a boulder, dragging Abigail with him. Cory turned and headed downriver to where a curve hid him from view. He crawled across the sand and into the water. If he could creep up from behind, he'd have a shot at McGraw. He could only pray the others would spot him and realize his intentions.

Marshal Slade's voice reached Cory's ears. "We don't have all day, McGraw. Throw down your weapon and give up the girl."

McGraw answered with two more shots toward the trees. "Not unless you let me cross the river and go free."

Cory was almost even with the outlaw, who concentrated on the trees and not the river behind him. Holding his gun just out of the water, Cory managed to bend down and draw closer. Another shot rang out, and McGraw ducked and turned his head. At the same time he spotted Cory and swung his gun around to shoot.

Abigail screamed, and Cory aimed from where he was and hit McGraw in the shoulder holding the gun. He grasped the wound with his left hand and fired with his right. Abigail screamed again and rolled away from McGraw. The bullet hit the water inches in front of Cory, who dove to safety. Slade raced from the trees, gun drawn, and managed to subdue McGraw.

Slade yanked the outlaw to his feet and handcuffed him. He hollered at Rutherford and the others. "Check those other two there and take care of the leg wound." He turned to Cory. "You all right?"

"Yeah, he missed me by a foot or two." Cory slushed

through the water to shore and grabbed Abigail to help her stand up. He untied her hands, and she threw her arms about his neck.

"I knew you'd come. I knew you would." A floodgate of tears washed down her cheeks and onto his shoulder.

Cory wrapped his arms around her tight. Thankfulness filled his soul, and he fought back his own tears. He kissed her hair and whispered in her ear. "You've been out here long enough. Now let's get you home."

He flinched at the sight of the bruises to her face and neck as well as the scratches on her arms. He prayed those were her only injuries. First stop at home would be the infirmary for Doc Jensen to give her a good going-over.

Slade, Rutherford, and Frank secured the outlaws to their horses and were ready to head back to Porterfield. Cory set Abigail on his saddle and swung up behind her. He wrapped his arms around her to grasp the reins. She leaned back against his chest and closed her eyes. The warmth of her body took some of the chill out of his, and it took all the strength he had left not to lean over and kiss her right there.

He tapped his horse's sides with the heel of his boots, and the group headed west through the trees. They were going home.

Early Tuesday morning the bedraggled group rode into Porterfield. Elliot and his uncle had walked down to the infirmary to open up and spotted the posse coming down the street. Elliot's heart jumped with fear mixed with joy at the sight of Abigail with Cory. The sheriff and the marshal turned off and went to the jail with their prisoners, but Cory headed straight for the doctors.

Kate rounded the corner, and when she saw her brother, she ran toward him. "Cory, Cory, you found her!"

Abigail slumped against Cory's chest with her eyes closed. A pang of jealousy shot through Elliot at the sight. Cory had rescued her and he was the hero, not Elliot.

Cory handed Abigail down to Elliot and his uncle. She stirred but didn't open her eyes. "She's worn out and hasn't had much to eat since she was taken. Sheriff Rutherford stopped in Carthage and brought some food back to the camp, but she only ate a little."

The concern in Cory's voice and the emotion in his eyes plunged a knife into Elliot's heart. Cory loved her, and he'd saved her life. What chance would a doctor have against a real live cowboy hero? With his uncle's help he carried Abigail into the infirmary, his heart bleeding with the pain of knowing she couldn't be his. Once again he'd lost.

Henry Wilder arrived just as Elliot laid Abigail on a bed. Of course he would be here. This was a big story for the *Porterfield Gazette*. Elliot hung back as his uncle began an examination of the bruises and cuts on Abigail's face and arms. Elliot's hands itched to care for her himself, but he couldn't bring himself to do it with Cory standing by. He slumped against the wall. Kate raised her eyebrows as she passed him to get the supplies Doc needed.

Questions were bound to come, but Elliot left the building and headed back to his home. Abigail was in good hands, and if he stayed any longer, the feelings he'd repressed for the past week would surface and ruin everything. Better to stay out of sight and away from her. She'd want Cory to be by her side now.

He passed the church and paused, tempted to go in. Had it been God who led them to Abigail or Hawkeye's experienced tracking abilities? Elliot fought the emotions rising within him and picked up his pace to go home. The Monroe and Muldoon families would have a happy Thanksgiving after all.

When he entered the house, he headed straight up to his room and closed the door. His breath came in short spurts and his heart raced. The full realization of what could have happened with Abigail hit him in the chest like a sledgehammer, and he slumped into his chair. Why couldn't he have rescued Abigail instead of Cory? This newfound love for her poured through his soul like a balm. Why had he waited so long to admit it was there? Would it have been different if he'd admitted it to her? Now he wanted her to love him. But it was too late. Cory had not only rescued her, but he'd undoubtedly also captured her heart.

A lump rose in his throat, and he fought the tears welling in his eyes. Then he finally let it all go, and sobs shook his body in release of all the grief and despair he'd stored up for the past two years.

CHAPTER
TWENTY-SEVEN

*J*OY FILLED THE Muldoon home on Thanksgiving Day. Though still somewhat tired and sore from her ordeal, Abigail basked in their love as they all gathered to celebrate. The physical wounds would heal quickly, but it would take the love of God and this family to heal her heart and soul.

Laughter rang out around her as she soaked up the camaraderie of this loud, fun-loving group. They treated her like a princess today, and all she had to do was sit back and enjoy it.

The only dark note on the entire day was the fact that Elliot had not spoken to her or even been to see her since her return. When she had awakened in the infirmary on Tuesday, he'd been nowhere to be found, and Doc Jensen treated her.

Kate sat down beside her. "Everything's all cleaned up, and the younger ones are down for a nap, so we have time to talk and visit." Kate tilted her head and peered at Abigail. "I sense there's something not quite right for you. Did something happen out there that you haven't told us about?"

Abigail shook her head. "Oh, no, it would have if the posse

hadn't caught up to us, but other than getting banged up and bruised, I'm OK."

"Then could it be the two men who care so much about you?"

Abigail's mouth dropped open. Two men? How could that be? Neither Cory nor Elliot had given that impression. "What do you mean by that?"

"I've seen the way Cory stares at you and the look on his face when he brought you into the infirmary. Elliot saw it too, and he wilted on the spot. I thought it was because of your injuries, but now that I've had a chance to think about it, I believe it was Elliot seeing you in Cory's arms and how Cory looked at you. They both care a great deal about you."

"But neither of them has shown any indication of that." Abigail bit her lip. That wasn't exactly true. Cory had been paying her more attention and had shown great relief and concern when he rescued her. She'd been paying so much attention to Elliot that she'd completely missed the depth of Cory's feelings.

"If I've seen it, others have. So you need to make a decision. I'd love for it to be Cory, but you must follow your own heart."

What Kate said made sense, and she did have to decide. She did love Cory, but it wasn't the love on which she could build a life. How much should she tell Kate? The truth was usually the best way, so she'd go that route now. "The plain fact of the matter is I've come to care about Elliot, and I'm disappointed he wasn't there at the infirmary to treat me."

"I figured as much. When you came in, a look of such desperation came into his eyes that it almost frightened me. He was in no condition to treat you or anyone else, although I believe he did go over to the jail later to treat those men who'd been shot."

"But he didn't come back to the infirmary the whole time I was there. It was like he was doing everything possible to avoid me." Cory had stayed around until he was sure she was all right, but Elliot's absence hadn't meant anything to her then.

"Most likely he was. I think he's hiding something from his past, and it must be about someone he cared for. I guess he hasn't put it behind him yet, and you reminded him of it when you were injured."

Guilt clutched Abigail's heart. "Oh, dear, I've made it worse for him. I really care about him, and I've tried to help, but nothing seems to get through to him."

"Something happened to cause him to isolate himself and to lose faith. But I want you to know that the Sunday you were missing, he did come to church. He sat in the back and didn't talk to anyone, but just his being there says something is going on in his heart."

Kate placed her hand on Abigail's shoulder. "I think the shock of your disappearance and then the way you looked when Cory brought you in was too much of a reminder of whatever it was that happened in his past." She paused then said, "If you care that much for Elliot, you must be prepared to let Cory know."

Kate stood. "I have to go help Ma with the table."

Abigail squeezed her eyes shut. Two men she cared about a great deal, but only one of them could she love with all her heart and soul.

Cory waited until Kate left Abigail sitting alone before going to sit beside her. "It doesn't look right for you to be alone."

Abigail looked at him with a dazed expression filling her eyes. He must have interrupted something. "I'm sorry, you look like you were thinking about something far away from here."

Her eyes opened wide, and the depth of emotion in those liquid brown pools caused his heart to thump. She gestured to him. "I'm sorry, and don't go. I guess I do need your company right now. I've never truly thanked you for your bravery in rescuing me. I was never so glad to see anyone as I was you and that posse."

He reached for her hand and clasped it in his. "And I was never so scared for someone else as I was you in that man's clutches. I was determined we were going to find you and bring you back before you could get to Louisiana."

"I know, and I'm so thankful to be back home and safe." She covered their clasped hands with her free one.

Her touch burned like a branding iron, and his heart beat a faster. He took a deep breath and decided to speak. "Abigail, that adventure and the thought of losing you made me realize that I cared more about you than I could have imagined before. I love you, Abigail."

Her eyes opened wide, and she pulled her hand from his. "I...I love your family and the way they've taken me in and made me feel like a part of it, but—"

Now his heart sank. "But" was not a good word coming from a girl he had opened his heart to. He swallowed hard and waited for her to finish. The hollow place in his gut rolled with hunger, but it stormed even more in fear of what he was about to hear.

"I do love you, Cory, but it's not the kind of love on which we can build a relationship. You're a wonderful person, and someday you'll find a girl worthy of your love and attention."

There it was. The rejection, but the pain he'd expected didn't come right away. "I see." But he didn't. He should have guessed she'd choose Elliot over a cowboy lawman. He steeled his heart against whatever might come next. He stood. "I think Ma is about ready to call us into dinner."

They entered the dining room together, but Cory sat away from Abigail. He had to think about what had just happened, and he couldn't do it sitting beside her. If he could do so with a legitimate reason, he would leave the house and ride back to town.

After a dinner of turkey, cornbread dressing, sweet potatoes, and pumpkin pie, Elliot helped Aunt Maggie with the dishes. She'd spent so much time preparing the meal, she deserved some help with the cleanup.

Someone knocked on the door, and Aunt Maggie left to answer it.

"Sophia and Philip. How nice to see you. Come in. Do you need Doc for something?"

Elliot dropped the towel he was holding and grabbed the plate he was drying. What was she doing here? It couldn't be good. His stomach churned with the meal he'd just eaten threatening to come back up.

"Actually I need to speak with Elliot. Please don't let him refuse."

"I...I'll do my best. Go in and have a seat, and I'll get him."

Elliot wanted to hide, but the only way upstairs was through the hallway where they'd be sure to see him. He eyed the back door, but he was too late. Aunt Maggie returned.

"I suppose you'd rather not see them, but it might be best for you to find out what she wants."

After a few minutes Elliot all but stormed into the room "What do you want, Sophia? Why is he with you?"

Sophia stood and reached into her handbag. "I wanted to bring this to you." She handed him the letter. "It's from Mr. and Mrs. Dupree, and I think you need to read it."

When he refused to take it, she hastened to add, "No, I didn't read it, but I got one from them too, and they told me what they were going to tell you."

Elliot grasped the letter but didn't look at it and let his hand fall to his side. "Was there anything else?"

"Please read the letter, Elliot. It can make a difference."

Philip stepped over and placed his hand on Elliot's shoulder. "Listen to her. This young woman has more wisdom and goodness in her than I could ever deserve. God has seen fit to bring her to Porterfield to marry me, but I sense a far greater reason for her being here. Talk to God about it, and you will find the answers you need."

Elliot said nothing, but his jaw tightened and the veins in his neck throbbed.

Sophia came closer, her gaze calm but determined. "That's all I have to say. The rest is up to you. If you ever want to have peace, you must resolve this issue with Angela. When you do, you'll be amazed at the doors God will open for you." She grasped Philip's arm. "Come, it's time for us to leave."

Elliot crushed the letter with his fingers and turned to march up the stairs to his room. What nerve Sophia had to write to Angela's parents and tell them where he was. He never wanted to see or hear from them again. Their attitude at the funeral had been all he needed to know that they'd forever blame him for the death of their daughter.

He entered his room and all but slammed the door behind him. Tears of rage and heartache filled his eyes. Elliot swallowed hard and clenched his teeth. He would not give in to weakness and cry again. He tossed the crumpled letter onto his desk and sat on the edge of his bed. His hands hung between his knees as he stared at the paisley-patterned rug on the floor.

Life had become as complicated as the swirls and whirls of the design that swam before his eyes in a blur. All he thought he'd escaped by leaving Cleveland had come back in a tide he couldn't stem. First Abigail with all her accidents had begun to work her way into his life despite his efforts to lock away his heart. Then Sophia had come, and with her all the memories and horror of that one night.

Once again he questioned how a loving God could be so cruel as to allow the events of the past to happen in the first place. Then, just when he'd begun to think maybe the future could be good, He'd sent a reminder of how tragedy could strike at any moment, destroying happiness in one blow. Elliot slammed his fist against the mattress. God had punished him two years ago, and now He was at it again. Would it never end?

A knock sounded on the door, followed by his uncle's voice. "May I come in?"

Elliot's first impulse was to say no. All Doc would do was tell Elliot how wrong he was and how he had to get over it, but then he realized his uncle always meant well. "Come on in."

Doc entered and sat in the chair at the desk. He spotted the balled-up letter on the desk and picked it up to smooth it out. "So this is what Sophia had for you." He stared at the envelope a few minutes.

Finally Elliot responded. "Yes, it is, but I don't care to read more accusations and blame from Mr. and Mrs. Dupree."

"You seem sure of what's in it. Maybe you should see what it says instead of imagining the words." He stood. "I just wanted to check on you, but I see you have a great deal of thinking to do, so I'll leave you alone. Your aunt has a blackberry cobbler waiting if you decide you want some."

After he'd left, Elliot continued to sit, but his mind began to clear.

He eyed the letter lying on his desk in a crumpled heap. He reached for it, and its touch stung his fingers with a heat that went straight to his heart and laced his soul with fear. He raised his arm to toss it into the waste can near the desk but stopped.

If he didn't read it now, he'd never know what they had to say. He'd heard it all before and during the funeral, but Sophia had said this was different. Better to go ahead and find out. He had to end the agony, but would this help? He smoothed out the envelope then slid his fingers under the lap and unsealed it. Unfolding it with trembling hands, he swallowed hard as the words swam before his eyes.

After he focused on them, he began to read.

Dear Elliot,

Sophia told us she'd found you there in Porterfield. We've always wondered where you had gone. We've missed you. Please know that we've prayed for you to find peace with God as we have. Do not blame yourself for Angela's death. As difficult as it is to accept, this was God's will for her life. Yes, He took her too soon for our liking, but in it all He had a purpose and a plan.

We pray that you have found His purpose for you in your life there in Porterfield. Listen to His voice, and follow His will for you. We pray that you will reclaim the joy you once had in the Lord and will find the happiness you deserve. Please don't feel guilty if you find another young woman to love. Our hope is that you do, because Angela would want you to be happy and go on with your life.

With our best regards,
Caleb and Alice Dupree

The paper shook in Elliot's hand, and the writing on the paper blurred even further. How could they ask him to go on with his life? His whole life had been Angela. Then he reread the last line. Could it be possible to find happiness and go ahead into the future without her? He laid aside the letter. This was one thing that would take much thought and consideration in the days ahead.

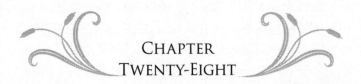

CHAPTER
TWENTY-EIGHT

Abigail slipped into the pew beside Daniel and Kate just as the organist began to play the prelude for Sophia and Philip's wedding ceremony. When Daniel knit his brows and frowned, she shrugged. "Sorry I'm late, but I had some last-minute things to take care of."

Ever since her return on Tuesday, Daniel had been so protective. Abigail wanted to tell him to leave her alone, but his concern did touch her. Now, after four days of his hovering, she was ready for him to back away and give her room to breathe.

She had opened the library for the first time this morning so books could be returned and she could straighten out records for the days she'd been out, and he'd complained about it being too early. Maybe in his eyes, but the sooner she put that nightmare of an ordeal behind her, the sooner she could get on with her life.

From the corner of her eye Abigail spotted Penelope walking down the aisle. The wedding had started. Then everyone stood and watched as Sophia made her way down the aisle on the arm of Philip's brother, Allen. She looked radiant.

Since they were facing the aisle, she used that brief moment to scan the room for Elliot. Just before the congregation turned to be seated, she spotted him near the back. Several times this morning she had glanced over at the infirmary, but it remained empty. With no patients on the premises, Doc and Elliot had no cause to be there.

She tried to listen to the ceremony and the vows, but her mind wouldn't stay put. The past four days had been filled with visitors and well-wishers who were glad she was home. The only one who mattered, Elliot, hadn't visited or said a word to her. She supposed he avoided her because of Cory or because of his own hurts. How could she let him know that Cory meant nothing to her? And how could she ever heal him from the pain of his past?

Then Seth's words broke through her meandering thoughts. She leaned slightly forward to hear them. He quoted from Psalm 139 then explained. "Before you were even born, Sophia and Philip, God had planned this day for you. God knows the days each of you has remaining on this earth. No one can take that time away from you. The love you proclaim here today will last for a lifetime if the foundation of your marriage is based on our Lord Jesus Christ and if you follow Him all the days of your life."

Abigail's heart swelled with her love of God. He had been with her every moment she had been held captive by McGraw. As the psalm said, she'd never be able to get away from that loving Spirit. When she had called on Him, He had answered.

Tears filled her eyes as Sophia and Philip repeated the vows that would bind them together in God's love for a lifetime.

From the corner of her eye she noticed Daniel reach over and squeeze Kate's hand. No words needed to be spoken as love and understanding flowed between them. Daniel had a special kind of love for Kate, and Abigail truly wished for a love like that. Would she ever find it?

The ceremony ended, and everyone applauded when Philip kissed his bride. Abigail smiled and clapped as hard as any of the others. This was truly a day of celebration.

A short time later the guests greeted the couple then headed for the big party at the town hall. All the gifts that were supposed to have been delivered last Saturday now waited for the happy couple there.

Abigail climbed up into the surrey behind Daniel and Kate. She once again scanned the crowd searching for Elliot. She finally spotted him heading back to his own home. Her spirits fell at the realization that he didn't plan to attend the party at all.

Kate must have seen him too. She turned and reached out to Abigail. "He has a lot on his mind, dear. Let him be for today. Reverend Winston is planning to talk with him again. Keep praying, and God will hear."

"I know, but it's so hard to see him walk away like that. What have I done that has made him not even want to speak to me?" Abigail faced back front, and Daniel pulled out onto the road leading into town.

"You haven't done anything. Now cheer up and plan to have some fun this evening. Penelope says they have enough food to feed everyone in town, and I think just about everyone in town will be there."

Abigail smiled and nodded her head. She would have a good time. This was a joyous occasion for the new Mr. and Mrs. Dawes, and she wasn't about to ruin it with her gloomy thoughts.

When they reached the town hall, buggies, wagons, and surreys filled the streets. The weather had cooperated and the sun shone down on them as if God too celebrated the marriage. People milled about the room inside.

"Abigail, it's so good to see you out and about after what you went through. Frank told me some about how they tracked you and then the rescue." Suzanne Cahoon pressed her lips together and shook her head. "I don't know what I would have done in your place."

"You'd have stayed strong just like I did." Never had she been so glad to see two men as she had been to see Cory coming out of that water with his gun blazing and Frank swooping down to tie up her captors. "I was scared, but I knew Cory and the sheriff would find me."

"Well, I, for one, am glad they did. This town wouldn't be the same without you." She waved at someone. "Frank wants me. Maybe we can visit some more later."

Abigail watched Suzanne join her husband. A deep sigh welled up inside and then escaped in a puff of air. Every female here had a husband or suitor on her arm. Even Aunt Mae had Mr. Fuller, who still sported a bandage on his head from his injury during the holdup. Her kidnapping had made her realize just how alone and unprotected she was. But instead of making her fear men, her experience had made her long for someone to love her and protect her. So why did she sense that Cory was not the one for her? Had she turned him down too soon?

She wished Elliot had come, but if he had, he wouldn't pay her any attention. Maybe if she had another accident, he'd have to treat her and talk to her then. No, that wouldn't do any good. He'd just have his uncle take care of her. Short of whacking him on the head, she could think of no way to draw his attention.

Elliot sat at his desk staring at the Duprees' letter. He should never have gone to the wedding. It had brought back all the memories of the plans he and Angela had made for their own wedding. Only a few weeks and their lives would have been joined just as Sophia's and Philip's had.

Abigail had been there. He had stared at her profile when everyone stood for the bride's entrance. When her head turned slightly toward him, he'd dropped his gaze to keep from looking into her eyes. Guilt washed through him like waves upon a shore. He hadn't even been to see her to let her know how relieved he was that she was all right. If he had, he might not have been able to hide his feelings for her. Besides, he would have ended up embarrassing them both if Cory was with her. Better that she be free to enjoy the attentions of Cory, who had earned her love in a way he never could.

Further guilt washed over him. Over the past few days Angela had begun to slip further back into his memory. How could he have let his feelings for Abigail replace his memories of Angela?

Doc would probably have an answer, and it would be all about how God ordained the things that happened in our lives. Reverend Winston had even said as much in his message to the bride and groom. But Elliot couldn't understand why God would bring two people together when He knew full well the love would never be completed. That didn't make sense to him and only proved to him that God didn't really care how hurt people might be by what happened.

He looked again at the letter before him. The more he thought about it, the more he realized Mr. and Mrs. Dupree had truly forgiven him for the mistake. To them it was a tragic accident. But how was it that they could forgive him when he hadn't been able to forgive himself? It didn't make any sense. The walls of his room closed in on him, and he could barely breathe. He needed fresh air and space.

A few minutes later he roamed up the street with no destination in mind, but his feet took him to town. He stopped across from town hall and surveyed the area. A lot of people had come to wish Sophia and Philip well. He should do the same, but he didn't have the heart for it.

A woman exited the building. She glanced across the street, and when her gaze landed on him, she strode across in his direction.

Kate Muldoon had purpose written all over her face. Elliot had no place to hide, and from the look of her, he was about to get an earful about not being at the party.

"Elliot, I didn't think you'd show up here today. I saw you headed home after the ceremony."

Her soft voice and non-accusing words set him back a step. Where was the anger he'd been sure she would spout in his presence? "I did go home, but it was too quiet, so I came out for a walk and ended up here."

She stood close enough for him to reach out and touch her. Her eyes held a sympathy that did not speak of pity but of concern. "Elliot, I know something terrible happened in Cleveland, and I want to help you. It hurts me to see you enjoying yourself one minute and then see you filled with sadness the next."

Pain and guilt washed over Elliot with such a flood that if he didn't get them out in the open, he'd drown. Kate knew him better than anyone except Doc and Aunt Maggie. Somehow, somewhere, something had to give, and it may as well be here and now with Kate. He grasped her arm. "Come with me to the infirmary. I'll tell you exactly what happened."

Kate only nodded and followed him to the infirmary. Once inside, he lit one of the lamps and gestured for her to have a seat.

He paced back and forth in front of her. "I'm not sure where to begin, so I will just tell you my way. I was deeply in love with a woman named Angela. We were engaged to be married and looked forward to our wedding. Her parents were so proud of her and of me being a doctor. My parents passed when I was a young boy, so Doc and Aunt Maggie have always taken care of me. Mr. Dupree treated me like a son too, and I couldn't have been happier."

The memories rained down in a deluge of color and sounds from the hospital that fateful night. He swallowed hard before continuing his story. "As a first year out of medical school doctor, I was on call whenever the hospital decided I was needed. That night I was supposed to pick Angela up from a party her friends were giving at a popular restaurant. At the last minute I had to take care of an emergency and couldn't pick her up. When I didn't show, she decided to stay longer with the party."

He stopped. Now came the hard part, but he had to go on. "A fire broke out in the kitchen of the restaurant and quickly spread to the dining area. Of course the patrons panicked and ran over each other trying to get out. Sophia thought Angela was right behind her and made it out to safety. Once outside she realized Angela wasn't in the crowd. When they found her, she had been knocked unconscious and lay on the floor near the table.

"By the time they got her to the hospital, she was in critical condition. Smoke had filled her lungs, and the blow to her head kept her unconscious. No matter what I...we tried, she wouldn't wake up and start breathing, and finally when I remembered the oxygen treatment that had been used in other cases like hers, it was too late. We never revived her, and I lost her. It should never have happened. If I hadn't been so slow to try the oxygen, we could have forced air into her lungs and got them to working again, but because of my panic I didn't."

Kate said nothing for a moment, but her eyes spoke volumes. She stood and grasped his hands in hers. "I'm so sorry, Elliot. That was a tragic thing for you to bear. But it's time to forgive yourself."

He opened his mouth to speak, but Kate held up her hand. "I'm not finished. You can't change what happened, and you can't bring back Angela. What you can do is lay those memories to rest and build new ones for the future."

A gasp spilled forth from him. "But I never want to forget Angela and the love we had."

"That's not what I meant. Bury the painful memories and keep the good ones. Don't let the bad outweigh the good. You can keep the good ones, but there's a whole wonderful world out there just waiting for you to wake up and start living again. It's time for new memories, Elliot, and this upcoming Christmas season is the best time to make them." She stood and strode to the door. "That's all I have to say. I'll see you here on Monday."

When she closed the door behind her, Elliot slumped into one of the chairs in the waiting room. What she said made sense. Kate had given him much to think about.

CHAPTER
TWENTY-NINE

*E*LLIOT SAT IN his office behind a closed door. His hands shook as he tried to write information on a chart. Finally he dropped the pen and leaned his head on his hands. He massaged his temples with fingers grown weary from a morning filled with patients of one ailment or another.

For two weeks Elliot fought his demons alone, and Kate hadn't spoken about their conversation again. He continued to avoid Abigail, but he watched her comings and goings from the library and about town, and at no time did he see her with Cory. Could it be that there was nothing between them? Hope began to worm its way into his heart.

If he wanted a relationship with Abigail, however, he knew he had to put Angela to rest. He clenched his teeth. It was time to see what God had to say about it. He reached for the Bible he'd placed in his bottom drawer many months ago. He didn't remember why he'd put it there, but he was glad to find it now.

He turned to the passage Doc mentioned time and again and the reverend had mentioned at the wedding, Psalm 139.

Verse 8 caught his eye. "If I ascend up into heaven, thou art there: if I make my bed in hell, behold, thou art there." He'd been in his own private hell for years now, and according to the psalmist, God had been right there with him. A chill ran through his veins as he continued to read.

When he read verses 15 and 16, scales fell from his eyes, and he finally and fully understood what Doc had been trying to tell him. God had known Elliot even in the days before his conception and knew the number of days in his life before he was born. God had known the number of Angela's days too. He had given her to Elliot for those brief days that had been the happiest of his life.

He still didn't quite understand why God chose a short life for Angela. Just thinking about her hurt. The only person he knew who could explain any of it was the same man who had spoken the words from this psalm in church.

Elliot grabbed his hat and hurried from the office. Reverend Winston should be in his office or possibly at home, but Elliot didn't intend to waste any more time before he talked with the young man. That thought brought a brief smile. Never would he have imagined seeking advice about God from a person his own age, but that's exactly what he planned to do.

When he approached the parsonage, Reverend Winston stood on the porch. Elliot's hand went to the breast pocket of his jacket. The Duprees' letter lay hidden in the inside pocket. Without hesitation he headed toward the parson.

"Reverend Winston, may I have a word with you?"

The young minister nodded and waited for Elliot. When he

reached the porch, he spilled forth his request before he could change his mind. "Reverend, may we find a place for privacy?"

"Of course. Come into the parlor. Erin is upstairs resting. We just finished our meal, and she was a little tired."

Elliot nodded. "Being this close to delivery, she needs all the rest she can give her body for what's to come." He followed Seth into the house, where they sat across from each other in the parlor.

He pulled the letter from his pocket and held it in front of him. "I received this several weeks ago. In it two people forgive me for a terrible mistake I made and say they don't blame me for their daughter's death. I must first explain what happened and the reason I haven't been to church."

Elliot then spent the next half hour retelling his story. When he'd finished, Reverend Winston nodded. "I see. That was a tragic event, Elliot, but you've blamed God for every bad thing in your life since then."

"Yes, that's right. I've been reading the Bible today, but I have a hard time trusting a God who allows such horrible things to happen."

"We live in a broken world, Elliot. Sin, suffering, and death still hold sway, and not until Christ returns will they be completely vanquished. In this world we will never understand why God allows suffering, but we have to trust Him that everything that happens has a purpose and meaning, even if we are not allowed to see during our lifetime what that purpose is. You left God and the church, but He's right there waiting for your return. He's never left you for one minute of your life, and He grieves with you for Angela because He understands the pain you've experienced."

Elliot had heard it all before, but somehow, coming from Reverend Winston, it had a different tone. "Do you think God can forgive me for blaming Him for what happened?"

"Oh, yes, Elliot. It's called grace and mercy. He has mercy on us and by His grace forgives our sins."

"I remember giving my heart to the Lord and asking Him to forgive me when I was a boy, but this was just so big and I was so angry with God."

Reverend Winston placed a hand on Elliot's shoulder. "All you have to do is ask, Elliot. Let me pray for you now." And he began, "Father God, my brother Elliot has strayed far from You and lost trust in You. I pray that You will now restore the joy of his salvation and grant him the peace that only You can provide. Help him to understand that You forgive all sins when confessed before You. Guide his feet from this day forward, and lead him into the life that You have planned for him. Amen."

The words from the prayer washed over Elliot like clean, pure water and cleansed his soul of all the hate and bitterness he'd held on to for so long. After the final word, Elliot stood and shook hands. "Thank you, Reverend. I need to do a lot of thinking about what to do next and where to go from here."

The minister grinned and walked with him to the door. "Don't forget to pray along with that thinking."

Once again on the street, Elliot's heart weighed lighter in his chest, but the indecision about what to do about Abigail still plagued him. His guilt over not seeing her remained, but he couldn't do anything until he found out exactly where she stood with Cory.

His growling stomach reminded him that dinnertime

was near. He welcomed the diversion from his thoughts and headed for home.

Aunt Mae came from the kitchen drying her hands on a towel. She stopped at the main dining table with a grin as broad as all outdoors splitting her face. Then she stepped behind Mr. Fuller and placed her hands on his shoulders. "Cyrus and I have an announcement to make."

Abigail wiggled in her chair. She had a suspicion about the announcement, and Mr. Fuller's smile and reaching up to hold Aunt Mae's hand confirmed it.

Mr. Fuller cleared his throat. "Mae Sullivan has consented to become my wife. We are to be married in the early part of the new year."

Cheers went up around the dining room as everyone gathered around to give their best wishes to the couple. Abigail remained at her place and glanced over at Cory. To say he was surprised would be a gross understatement. His mouth hung open, and his hand gripped his napkin like it was a lifeline and he was drowning. Men. They couldn't see the obvious right under their noses.

She leaned toward him with her elbows on the table. "Isn't this just marvelous? Your aunt really deserves to have some happiness with all that she spreads to other people."

Cory's mouth snapped closed and his cheeks flamed red. He looked down. "I can't believe she's getting married. I knew they went to town socials together, but I had no idea this was going on."

Abigail bit her lip with the realization Cory still hurt from her rejection on Thanksgiving. "Just be happy for her."

"I...I will." He shot her an embarrassed glance, then pushed his chair back from the table and approached his aunt. "I'm happy for you, Aunt Mae, and you, Mr. Fuller." He kissed his aunt and shook hands with the beaming banker. "Now if you'll excuse me, I must get back to work." He grabbed up his hat and strode from the room.

Abigail waited until the others had all gone back to their eating or to their own business before she approached the woman who had become like a mother to her.

She reached up to wrap her arms around Aunt Mae's broad shoulders. "I'm so happy for you. You two make a fine-looking couple."

"Thank you, sweetie. We're going to stay here at the boardinghouse. I'll keep running it and Cyrus will keep working at the bank. It'll be the best of both worlds." She stepped back and surveyed the now empty table. "I best be getting these dishes back to the kitchen. Just because I'm getting married doesn't mean everyone will forget about supper."

Abigail stacked a few dishes and headed to the kitchen with them. As happy as she was for Aunt Mae, it served only to make her own situation lonelier.

After Aunt Mae had the dishwater hot and the dishes in soaking, she sat across from Abigail. "All right, sweetie, I can tell something's bothering you. Tell me about it."

Of course she couldn't hide anything from Aunt Mae. May as well tell her the truth and see what she had to say. "You know, when I came to Porterfield, it was to be the librarian. I had no designs on a husband even though I knew the town had plenty of eligible men. I wanted to prove myself as a librarian first."

"Yes, and you've done a fine job of doing just that. But there's something else gnawing at your insides, and I don't think it has anything to do with books."

Abigail expelled her breath in a long sigh. "You're right. I didn't mean for it to happen, but I've grown to care about Doc Elliot a lot." At Aunt Mae's raised eyebrows, she winced. "I know, I know. Cory cares about me, but I had to tell him I don't love him in that way."

Aunt Mae knit her brows together and pursed her lips. "Hmm, so that's why he's been so quiet these past few weeks."

"I didn't want to hurt Cory, but my heart belongs to Elliot. He just doesn't know it yet. I know he used to be a Christian, but he's mad at God for something that happened in his past. I know I shouldn't have these feelings for him until he can get his life straight with the Lord, but I can't help it."

Aunt Mae nodded. "That young doc is hurting in ways we have no way of knowing. We have to pray for him to make things right with God, and then maybe he'll begin to see how much you care."

"Well, it hurts me that he won't even talk to me. He didn't treat me at the infirmary, and ever since my return from that kidnapping ordeal, he's kept as far away from me as possible." His rejection of her as a patient she could tolerate, but not his complete neglect of her as a person. That stung a little too deeply.

"Seems to me like he cares about you. Leastways it does from what I've seen when he's treating you." Aunt Mae tapped her cheek. "Maggie Jensen and I are good friends. Maybe I'll have a visit with her. I want to tell her about me and Cyrus anyway."

"Thank you, but I don't want you to pry into his life since he's made such an issue of keeping it private. Still, I do wish I knew what caused the pain I saw." She stood and leaned over to hug Aunt Mae.

"I have to get back to the library and open up for the afternoon. Thank you for listening, and congratulations again for you and Mr. Fuller."

Once outside, she pulled her coat tighter. Clouds had rolled in to cover the sun and chilled the air. A wind gust threatened to lift her hat from her head, and she grabbed at it with her free hand. Such a dreary afternoon to match her mood. She needed the Lord's guidance as to what to do about Elliot. Praying hadn't done much so far, but she wouldn't give up on him. Somehow, sometime, a breakthrough would come, and whatever haunted him from the past would be forgotten in the promise of what lay ahead.

After the noon meal, Elliot returned to the infirmary with a much lighter heart. A lot of questions had been resolved, but many more were still left to be answered. One of them was exactly what he would say to Abigail or how he could find out her feelings for Cory Muldoon.

He didn't want to spoil her happiness, but now that he was ready to admit his love for her, he longed for her to return it. He shoved his hands into his pockets to warm them because in his haste he'd forgotten his gloves. December usually brought cold weather, but he had known it to be much milder. Today the crisp air supported the new buoyancy of hope in his heart.

"Hey there, Doc Elliot."

Elliot whipped around to find Cory headed his way. He didn't want to talk to or be civil to Cory, but now would be as good a time as ever to find a few answers. "Hello, Cory. What can I do for you?"

"Nothing really. I'm just making my rounds in town to keep people on their toes." His grin accented the twinkle in his eyes.

Elliot only nodded. If Abigail caused that bright look on Cory's face, it would be the end of any hope for a relationship with her. Might as well find out now and not prolong the uncertainty. "Something seems to be making you very happy about now."

Cory laughed and shook his head. "Aunt Mae announced just a bit ago that she and Cyrus Fuller are getting married. Don't that beat all?"

Elliot's mouth dropped open before he grinned as broadly as Cory. "Aunt Mae and Cyrus? But I can't say I'm really surprised after the way she took care of him when he was hurt in that bank robbery."

"Yep, looks like it's been brewing for a while, and I'm happy for her."

"And Abigail? What about her?" From the perplexed look on Cory's face, Elliot's question made no sense, but how else could he raise the subject?

"She's happy for them too," Cory said. "Why do you ask?"

Elliot shrugged but watched Cory's expression with care. Cory's eyebrows bunched and stared right back at Elliot. "You haven't seen Miss Abigail since her ordeal, have you?" Cory asked point-blank.

Heat flooded Elliot, and he looked away from Cory's prying eyes.

Cory pushed the brim of his hat back just a tad and raised his eyebrows. "Well, I think you need to be seeing her soon. She let me know that I wasn't included in her future plans and gave me the impression someone else was."

Elliot gulped and his eyes opened wide. "You're...you two aren't..." He stopped and stared at Cory.

"Nope. She turned me down flat." Then he pointed a finger at Elliot. "Now, if I was you, I'd get myself over to see her pronto. If she doesn't return my feelings, then I hope she does for you." He clapped his hand on Elliot's shoulder. "She may be just what you need to bring some joy into your life. She certainly brought it into mine."

Cory swung up onto his horse and headed for the courthouse while Elliot stood in dumbfounded silence. If Abigail didn't care for the one who had saved her from an awful fate, how could she care about him? Still, almost all the questions rolling through his mind the past half hour had been answered. Now what was he going to do about finding the answers to the rest of them?

CHAPTER
THIRTY

*A*BIGAIL STUDIED THE shelves and shook her head in disbelief. The people of Porterfield had been more than welcoming of the library, and her shelves this week showed it in a big way. More than half of the books were checked out, and another huge stack waited to be shelved. People were filling the long winter nights with the joys of a good story. Could there be anything better?

The bell over the door jangled, and Abigail looked up to see Rachel closing the door behind her. Her friend's cheeks were rosy from the cold temperatures that had finally arrived, and her belly swelled with the baby she carried.

"Hello, and what brings you out in this cold weather today?"

Rachel strolled over to gaze at the shelf of Christmas books. "I thought I'd come in and browse and have a chat with my best friend if she's not too busy."

Heat rose in Abigail's cheeks. "I'm not too busy. Come over here and have a seat." She and Rachel had visited at least once if not twice a week when they lived in Briar Ridge. Since their arrival in Porterfield, those visits had dwindled, and part of it was because of Abigail.

Rachel settled herself on the extra chair and removed her gloves. "It's been awhile since we've had one of our good visits like we did back home. I've missed our times together. When I was in Hartford after Nathan and I married, that's the thing I missed most about home. Then when we moved down here, I missed you even more."

Guilt at her neglect and attention to business rather than friendship rose in her heart. She'd been responsible for that lack of time together. "I'm sorry I haven't been more available, but the library kept me fairly occupied these past months."

"I realize that, but since I was at the church helping to decorate for Christmas week, I thought I'd stop by and chat. Nathan told me how busy you'd been the past few weeks, especially with Christmas so near."

Laughter spilled from Abigail. "I think everyone started dropping in just to see how I was doing, and then they decided to check out a book. It's been quite fun."

"I'm glad for your success. It must give you a great deal of satisfaction." She tapped her gloves against the back of her hand. "One time when we talked, you told me how you were beginning to care about Doc Elliot. Is that still the case?"

Abigail sighed and shrugged her shoulders. "Yes, but he's completely ignored me since the bank robbery. I see him come and go from the infirmary, but he doesn't come over here, and he hides in his office if I stop by to see Kate."

"Reminds me of when Nathan avoided contact with me because he didn't want to court the daughter of a minister."

"Yes, Elliot has something in his past that is eating at him much like Nathan did. I hope it doesn't take a blizzard for Elliot to come back to the Lord because if it does, it may never happen, as I'm told snowstorms like that don't get to this part of Texas."

Rachel laughed. "That's for certain. Here it is December, and we're just now having really cold weather. Back home we would have already had several snowstorms." Rachel reached over and placed her hand over Abigail's. "Don't give up on him. If he's half the man I think he is, it'll be well worth the wait for him to realize what he must do about his past. I waited months for Nathan, and now I'm so thankful that I did."

"Kate and Sophia have said the same thing, and I think both of them know more about his past than they will tell me. They just say to keep praying and wait, but it's wearing on my patience."

Rachel laughed and stood with her hand on the small of her back. "Patience is one thing you had more of than I did. Look at how many directions I was pulled because it was taking Nathan so long to come back, and even then I wasn't sure he ever would."

"I remember." Those days they'd spent together in the spring of 1888 came back with vivid clarity. If Rachel could wait months for Nathan to make peace with his past, she could do no less with Elliot.

Abigail wrapped her arms around Rachel. "Thank you so much for coming by today. I'll keep praying and waiting for Elliot." A grin spread across her face. "If it's to be, the Lord will take care of it."

"Oh, my sweet friend, it's always such a pleasure to talk

with you." She pulled her gloves back on and pushed them down to fit her fingers. "Don't forget the Christmas party at our house next week. You know how much I love the holiday, so I'm really looking forward to our first one here in Porterfield."

Abigail walked with Rachel to the door. "I wouldn't miss it for anything." She stepped out onto the boardwalk to wave good-bye as her friend made her way across to Nathan's law offices. Just as she turned to go back inside to the warmth of the library, she glanced across the street to see Elliot in front of the infirmary.

Their gazes locked, and joy flooded her soul. Her heart kicked up a few beats as they stood with the street between them. For the first time in weeks he didn't immediately turn away from her. Although she couldn't see his eyes, the way he stood so still staring at her told her he actually saw her and perhaps felt what she did.

A gust of wind kicked up dust on the street and ruffled her hair. She should go inside and get out of the cold, but her feet said no. So she stood, paralyzed by his continued staring at her. Then a brief smile flickered before he finally turned and hurried back inside the infirmary.

The spell now broken, Abigail returned to the library and closed the door behind her. Her heart pounded from the brief encounter. Something had changed, and her instincts said whatever it was had to be good. Now to figure out a way to get close enough to have a conversation. Then she'd be able to tell if her instincts were right.

Elliot slumped against the closed door of the infirmary. Abigail had taken his breath right out of his body and sent longings deep into his heart. Ever since Cory's revelation, he had debated how to approach Abigail. He must tell her about Angela, and that was the only thing really holding him back. He remembered the Duprees' letter and how they wished for him to find another love to fill his life. Abigail was that girl, and now he had to figure out a way to make his feelings known.

He made his way to his office and sat at his desk. He needed to work on his patient files, but Abigail filled his mind instead. Twice this week he'd been tempted to march across the street to the library and tell Abigail everything, but each time so many customers had been coming and going, he couldn't do it. He hadn't been able to get up the nerve to stop by the boardinghouse and seek her out there either.

He stared at the papers before him, not really seeing the words. After a minute or two he pushed back his chair and grabbed his coat. The hour had come to quit stalling. God had opened the door, and it was time to take action and step through it. Today was as good a one as any to see Abigail and tell her the truth of why he'd been avoiding her.

With his mind made up, he strode across the street and through the door. The bell jangling overhead caused him to jump and look up. When had she put that thing up there? When he lowered his head, he met Abigail staring at him with her mouth open and her eyes wide. She looked as surprised to see him as he was to hear the bell.

"Doc Elliot, what...what are you doing here?" She stood behind the rail clutching several books to her chest.

"I came to see you. If you're not busy, I need to talk with you."

She laid the books on a table and smoothed her hands down her skirt. "I seem to be in a lull for business, so you're welcome to stay."

If he didn't do this now, he may lose his nerve and walk right out of here. "Thank you." He looked around the room. "Is there a place we can sit?"

Her hand flew to her face. "Oh, of course, yes, right over there at my desk." She nodded her head in the direction of the office in the back.

Once they were seated across from each other, Elliot's throat dried up like the creek in a drought. How should he start, and what should he say? He swallowed hard and began. "I am sorry for not coming to see you sooner. I was deeply thankful that you were returned to us safely and that you suffered no permanent harm." Her expression didn't change, not even her eyes, so he plunged ahead.

"I owe you an explanation of why I've neglected you the past weeks. Some things happened to me in Cleveland, and they've affected my work and relationships here in Porterfield. I thought I could come here and forget it all, but then you arrived, and then Sophia came, and I realized I could never escape the past that has held me prisoner for over two years."

Her brown eyes bored into his, and his first impulse was to jump and run, but he'd been doing that too long. If she didn't understand what he told her now, she never would. He plunged ahead. "I was betrothed to a wonderful woman, but a few weeks before our wedding she died."

Abigail blinked her eyes then leaned forward. "Oh, Elliot, I'm so sorry."

The sympathy and caring in her voice gave him courage to go ahead with all of the story just as he'd told it to Kate. As he neared the end, he added the part about the letter and his talk with the reverend. Tears trickled down Abigail's cheeks, and she bit her lip.

When he finished, Abigail sat silent. Then she jumped from her chair and in a flash knelt beside him. She grasped his hands in hers.

"I can't begin to imagine the grief and pain you experienced with Angela's death. I sensed something was wrong, but I had no idea of such a tragic experience. Seth was right. God never abandoned you, nor did He blame you for your anger. No one could blame you for your emotions."

Elliot nodded. "When I accepted that and truly believed God had forgiven me, I was able to forgive myself."

"It's wonderful that you're seeking God now. He'll never fail you. If I hadn't held on to that when I was taken by those outlaws, I wouldn't have been able to bear it. God protected me, and He'll take care of you."

He hesitated in order to draw strength for what he wanted to say next. *Lord, give me the right words to say to let her know how much I care about her.*

His gaze went to their hands still clasped together. She noticed too and started to pull away, but he held them tight and looked her in the eye. "You know my background, but you don't really know me, and I don't know much about you."

A brief smile flitted across her lips. "Well, you know my medical history better than anyone else around here."

He chuckled at the truth in her statement. "Yes, and I also know that you're a wonderful, caring woman." He shook his head. "What I'm trying to say is, would you be willing for me to call on you so that we can get to know each other?"

At first she said nothing, and his heart raced. Then a genuine smile filled her countenance and her brown eyes danced with excitement.

"Why, Elliot Jensen, I think that's the most marvelous suggestion I've ever heard. I'd be happy to have you come calling."

Elliot's heart soared straight to heaven and back. The happiness he saw in her face gave him energy he didn't realize he could possess. They stood, and it took every ounce of strength he had not to lean down and kiss her. No one would see, and no one would know.

His body moved a step closer and he bent his head toward hers. Then behind him Pete Davis burst through the library door yelling his name. "Doc Elliot, you gotta come quick. The parson sent me. He says the baby's a comin' and Mrs. Winston hurts bad."

He turned. "Tell him I'm on my way." He squeezed Abigail's hands. "We'll finish this later."

He sped out the door and across the street to get his bag.

CHAPTER
THIRTY-ONE

*A*BIGAIL BLEW OUT her breath and slumped into her desk chair, arms dangling to her sides, her mouth open. What had just happened here? Had it been real? Had Elliot been about to kiss her? Questions rolled through her mind like colored glass fragments in a kaleidoscope. Each fragment overlapped the other until they became a jumbled mass in her thoughts.

She sat still, savoring the time just past. Never had she been as close to Elliot as she had been in those moments when he opened his heart and soul to her. It must have all been a dream. No, Elliot sat right there in the chair across from her and told the story of what had happened in Cleveland. Her heart ached with the story of the death of Angela. No wonder his eyes had carried such sadness. While it ached with grief, her heart also soared with joy at the words he'd spoken. He did care about her, and he wanted to call on her.

Her fingers touched her lips. He'd bent his head and leaned down to her. She could almost feel his lips touching hers, but then Pete had run in.

What terrible timing, but of course babies had no sense of time. Erin's baby! Gracious, she had to check on that. After all, Erin was the sister of Daniel's wife, and that made her family.

Kate was probably already there to assist Elliot. They didn't need Abigail, but she wanted to be there anyway. She grabbed the "CLOSED" sign from the drawer and hung it in the window. Then she gathered up her coat, hat, and gloves to ward off the cold air and hurried outdoors. On the boardwalk she almost collided with Henry Wilder, who steadied her with his hands.

"Whoa, there, Miss Monroe. Where are you off to in such a hurry?"

"Erin Winston is having her baby, and I'm going to see how it is progressing." She strode off across the street.

Henry caught up to her. "My buggy is right there, so let me take you to the parsonage. It'll be quicker."

Abigail didn't have to think twice about that offer. She nodded and ran over to his rig and climbed in. "Thank you. I do want to get there as soon as I can."

He climbed up beside her and flicked the reins. As they were about to pass the boardinghouse, she grabbed his arm. "Wait just a minute. I want to see if Aunt Mae knows. She can come with us."

She raced through the back door to find it empty. After calling her name a few times, Abigail turned to leave when Aunt Mae rushed through the door from the dining room. "What is it, dear child? You sound frantic."

"Erin's baby is coming. I thought you would want to know. Henry has his buggy waiting out front. He'll take us there."

"Oh, mercy me. Let's go." She pulled off her apron and threw it on the table then grabbed her coat and hat to follow Abigail.

They squeezed onto the buggy seat, and for once Abigail blessed her small frame. The trip to the parsonage took only minutes with the horse leading the way. When they arrived, she jumped down and left Henry to help Aunt Mae.

Abigail burst through the door to find Seth alone in the parlor. "Where is she? What's going on? Is Elliot here?"

Seth's hands grasped her arms. "Slow down. She's in the bedroom, she's having the baby, and yes, Elliot is with her. So is Ada. Doc says it might be awhile since first babies usually take their time."

Aunt Mae marched through the door. "Where's that niece of mine? Is everything all right?"

Seth hugged his aunt. "Doc Elliot, Kate, and Ada are all with her, so she'll be fine."

Aunt Mae shrugged off her coat and then her hat. "I'll get some water to boiling and find some extra towels and such."

"Hot water will be good since that's what I was about to do."

A cry echoed from behind the closed door to the bedroom, and all color drained from Seth's face. "Something must be wrong."

Aunt Mae patted his arm. "No, no, that's normal. Why don't you see to doing something else for a while? She'll do just fine with Kate and Doc in there." She glanced at Henry, who had entered the parlor. "Why don't you take this father-to-be for a little ride to calm his nerves?"

"No, I don't want to leave. I have to be here."

Henry stepped up. "Of course he does. Why don't we just

sit down over here in the corner and let the ladies do their work?"

Seth nodded and let Henry guide him to a chair by the window. Abigail heard Henry's voice as he began talking to Seth, but she couldn't make out the words. Not wanting to appear to be eavesdropping, she hurried to the kitchen where Aunt Mae filled pots with water from the pump on the sink.

Despite the chill in the room, drops of perspiration dotted Elliot's brow. The birth of a baby always gave him a sense of inadequacy in God's big scheme of things. Childbirth was a natural part of life, but it never ceased to amaze him at how God put together human life. That was one thing he'd forgotten the past two years. Although he hadn't considered it at the time, taking Erin Winston and Rachel Monroe as patients had been the beginning of God pulling him back into the fold.

He'd done a fair job of resisting that pull until now, but the few minutes he'd spent with Abigail earlier broke the last bonds of restraint. That moment had been so right, and the peace that had abandoned him began its slow return to his soul.

He jerked back to attention when Erin screamed again. Her face turned red, and she grimaced as she moaned. Kate and Ada grabbed her hands and spoke words of comfort. Elliot checked her again then frowned. First babies took their own time in coming, but he hoped this one wouldn't delay. He washed his hands again using the antiseptic Doc made him carry in his bag. This was his first birth since he'd come to Porterfield, although he had assisted Doc once. Erin was Elliot's patient, so he would take care of this one.

Elliot searched his mind for all the information he'd read in journals about delivering babies. Some methods seemed a bit harsh, but others made complete sense, like helping the mother breathe correctly.

When Erin calmed down again, he told her to breathe slowly and evenly, then he began a closer exam. Everything appeared normal, and the baby's head hadn't yet showed itself. That wasn't unusual but would prolong the agony for Erin.

Aunt Mae tiptoed into the room. "I've brought some extra clean towels and have hot water ready when you need it. How's she doing?"

"No need to be quiet right now. You can talk to her if you like." He watched Aunt Mae lean over and kiss Erin's glistening forehead. After Aunt Mae deposited the towels on the dressing table against the wall, she left the room once again on tip-toe. "I'll be back with the water."

Elliot moved to stand beside Erin. "It's going to be a little while yet. I want you to relax as much as possible between contractions. When the contractions get really close together, we'll know the baby is really on its way. When contractions come, I want you to breathe in short spurts. Don't push or strain until I tell you to." He glanced across the bed at Mrs. Muldoon. "If you'll help her do that, I think the contractions will go better."

She nodded and bent down to wipe the perspiration from Erin's brow. "Relax and do like the doctor says. When that little one comes, all the pain will be worth it."

Erin smiled and did appear to relax under her mother's care.

Elliot remembered reading about how Indian squaws sat in a squatting position to have babies and that they came faster that way. That may work out on the prairie, but he wasn't sure the ladies here would appreciate such a position. Perhaps if he could get her to sit up so she wasn't flat on her back, she would feel better.

He made the suggestion, and Kate and Mrs. Muldoon helped Erin sit up with a extra pillows behind her.

"Just do whatever it takes to stay comfortable," he told her. "If you need to get up and move around a bit, that's fine too."

He stood and said, "I'm going to see Seth and give him a little reassurance. I'm sure he's very anxious about now."

When he entered the parlor, Mrs. Newton, Seth's aunt, had arrived, and Seth and Abigail were telling her what was happening. Mrs. Newton spotted Elliot and hurried to his side. "May I go in to see her?"

Elliot grinned and nodded to Abigail. "Yes, of course, and you too, Miss Monroe."

Her head jerked back and her eyebrows lifted. Whether it was because he'd called her by Miss or if she was surprised he'd let her see Erin, he didn't know, but she didn't hesitate to join Mrs. Newton.

Seth grabbed his arm. "What's going on? Why is she yelling out like she does?"

"That's normal during childbirth. The contractions that help the baby move do hurt, but it's very necessary for the baby to move down and out of her body. Most likely she won't remember the pain long after she holds the new baby in her arms. At least that's what I've heard." Distraction was in order for this young man. "Tell me what you plan to name the baby."

Seth blinked his eyes and shook his head. "Uh, it's Felicity Ada for our mothers if it's a girl. A boy will be Connor Allen for our mothers' names before they married."

"Those are fine names for a baby." He placed a hand on Seth's shoulder. "The best thing you can do is stay calm yourself and do whatever you would normally do on a Thursday afternoon. Think about how good it will be to hold little Connor or Felicity in your arms."

Seth's look of worry turned to one of calm assurance. "Usually I'm at the church, but I'm not going anywhere until that baby gets here. God is here with us."

"Yes, He is, but remember, you'll hear her yell a number of times more before little Felicity or Connor makes an appearance."

Seth nodded and returned to his chair in the corner by Henry Wilder. Elliot stared at the reporter. He'd wanted a story from Elliot, and when this was over, a story he'd get. Now that Elliot's guilt had drained away, the townspeople deserved to know more about the man who treated their ailments.

When he returned to the room, Abigail left as was only fitting for a single woman to do under the circumstances. The skies outside the room gradually became darker as evening set in. Elliot's stomach rumbled with hunger, but he ignored the pangs to concentrate on the young woman on the bed. More hours than he liked to count had passed since Erin had begun contractions. After the next contraction, he'd check again and try to figure out what was taking so long.

He studied the women sitting around the bed, each quiet and filled with her own thoughts. Kate's contemplative expression most likely meant she was thinking about the medical aspect of this delivery.

Erin pushed herself off the pillow and cried out again. Elliot rushed to her and checked for signs of eminent birth. He could now see the baby's head. "OK, Erin, it's time. Mrs. Muldoon, hold her up and scoot her farther down on the bed."

Once he had Erin positioned, he said, "OK, now you start pushing. Every time you feel a contraction, push hard."

For the next few minutes both he and Erin worked their hardest for the baby to be born. "Here it comes, Erin. You're doing great. One last push." The baby slipped right out into his waiting hands. "It's a boy."

He wiped the fluid and tissue from around the baby's mouth, but he hadn't started breathing, and a blue tinge circled his mouth. Elliot removed more fluid from the baby's throat. He had to start breathing…now. Don't panic. *You know what to do. God, make this work.*

Elliot had seen a doctor in Cleveland do something very different for a newborn baby who had trouble breathing. Acting quickly, he held the baby by the ankles and gave one good slap to the baby's bottom. The shocked voices of the women almost drowned out the joyful sound of the baby's first breath and cry. "Welcome to the world, Connor Allen Winston." Never had he been so relieved to hear a baby crying.

Kate scowled at him and grabbed the baby from him to wrap it in a tiny flannel blanket. Ada set a pan of warm water on the table and dipped a cloth in it to wash the baby's face. Kate then laid the bundle in Erin's arms before rushing out to tell Seth.

In a flash Seth was through the door to kneel at Erin's bedside. "He's beautiful, and so are you."

Elliot left the room to give them a moment of privacy. In the hallway, Kate grabbed Elliot and hugged him. "I almost died when you slapped that baby's bottom, but then I heard him cry and knew you had saved his life. You're a good man and a smart doctor, Elliot Jensen."

Seth stepped through the doorway holding his son in his arms. "Kate said that if you hadn't known what to do, we would have lost him. Thank you, Doc Elliot. I for one am deeply grateful that God brought you to Porterfield."

A new awareness rose in Elliot. God did have a purpose and a time for everything in His world, and now He had given back Elliot's future, one that he prayed would include a sweet, accident-prone librarian.

CHAPTER
THIRTY-TWO

*E*LLIOT SAT BESIDE Abigail at the Christmas Eve service. Green garlands dressed up with bright red bows decorated the church. Candle stands with more red bows sat at the end of each pew row and lent a special glow to the room.

He spotted Henry Wilder and nodded to the man Elliot had thought would ruin his life. Instead, the article that appeared in the paper this week spoke of Elliot's successes as a doctor and only mentioned the Cleveland incident as the tragic accident that took the life of a girl he was to marry. He'd never seen such love and empathy from people as he had the good people of Porterfield. He should have...no, he wouldn't go down that path. He had Abigail now.

Two rows ahead, Erin sat holding baby Connor wrapped in a bright blue blanket knitted by his grandmother. Proud papa, Reverend Seth Winston, stood behind the pulpit and read from the Scriptures.

As the reverend's rich baritone voice quoted the verses describing that night in Bethlehem, awe and wonder filled

Elliot to overflowing. For the past week he and Abigail had been together almost constantly. He'd found a dozen excuses to pop in at the library, and she'd been to dinner at the Jensen home twice. Each time he saw her, his love grew, and tonight he planned to ask her to make that love permanent.

When the preacher reached the part with the shepherds, Kate Monroe, along with her brothers' wives dressed all in white, stood up in the choir section behind the pulpit. Kate began singing "Gloria" with the other three women joining in. Chills coursed through his veins at the ethereal sound of their voices that seemed to come straight from heaven.

He reached over and grasped Abigail's hand. He closed his eyes and saw the image of the shepherds on a star-filled night beholding a host of angels proclaiming Christ's birth. What joy must have filled them as they heard the message and then hastened to find their Messiah in a manger in a hillside cave in Bethlehem.

After two years of avoiding God and church, Elliot had never felt more at home than he did in this place as he listened to the ancient story of the miraculous birth. Reverend Winston spoke the words, and Elliot's mind jumped forward to the sacrifice of the cross years later. All he could do was thank the Lord for never abandoning him and for taking care of him during a desolate time in his life.

As the reverend finished the story, he stretched out his hands toward the congregation and invited them to light their candles and sing one last song before going out into the night. A person at the end of each row lit a candle then passed the flame down the row. Soon the entire church was aglow with candlelight. The organist played the first strains of "Silent

Night," and then the congregation lifted the words heavenward with one voice.

He glanced down at Abigail, and she gazed up at him. He prayed the glow in her eyes came more from him than the candle flame shining in her hand.

When the song ended, a brief prayer sent them out into the darkness with their candles still glowing.

Aunt Maggie stopped them outside. "I know you're staying with Kate and Daniel tonight, Abigail, but please stop by for a few minutes and share some wassail with us. This is a special Christmas for us with Elliot returning to his faith."

"I'd like that, Mrs. Jensen. Thank you. Kate and Daniel are at Seth and Erin's to visit with them and little Connor. He's such a beautiful baby, and if it hadn't been for Elliot's quick thinking and rather alarming action, he might not be here."

She squeezed his hand, and he wanted to hug her right there, but too many people would see, and he would do nothing to mar her reputation. Even if the rules of courting were all but gone in these more modern times, he'd rather follow the old ones and be safe.

They walked away from the crowd, and Abigail continued to hold his hand. "Do you want to stop by and see Erin and Seth before we go to your house? I know how thankful they are for you and what you did."

He had a hard time hearing her call the reverend by his given name, but then she'd grown up with him, and his sister was her best friend. He'd have to get used to it if Abigail became his bride. He'd know if that was to happen soon enough. "They've all expressed their gratitude in one way or the other. I have something else in mind. Let's walk a little ways... unless you're too cold."

"Not a bit, and I'd love to walk with you." She snuggled against his arm, her head barely reaching his shoulder.

The words he'd written down and rehearsed flew out of his mind. What did they matter anyway? He'd just say what was on his heart, and that heart was so full the right words would be in there somewhere.

Along the sidewalk that stretched in front of the boarding-house, gas lights gave off a soft glow that tinged all around it in rays of gold. He raised his eyes to the sky, a dark expanse of blue black shimmering with stars that winked in a haphazard pattern among the clouds. As they moved across the sky, an opening in the clouds revealed the nearly full moon. A perfect night for declaring his love.

Abigail felt she might burst with happiness. She prayed Elliot felt it too. She followed his gaze to the sky and sighed. "Christmas Eve is always a special time. Tomorrow will be busy with gifts, food, and family fun, but tonight in the silence we can marvel at what the shepherds experienced well over a thousand years ago."

He squeezed her hand now tucked under his arm. "I felt that tonight when Kate and the others sang. I'd been told Kate had a good voice, but I'd never heard her sing much of anything except some ditties around the clinic to distract our youngest patients."

"Daniel told me that it was her singing "Amazing Grace"

that opened his eyes to how much he loved her. Isn't that romantic?"

"Hmm, I suppose, if you say so."

Elliot must not have a romantic bone in his body. In the days since his declaration in the library, he'd done nothing to show whether he loved her like she loved him. Oh, he cared about her, but he never really said anything that promised of more. She hadn't come to Porterfield in search of a husband, but God had put Elliot squarely in the middle of her life, and she wanted more than anything to marry him. She'd have to come up with something to hurry things along.

"You're quiet. What's going on in that pretty little brain of yours?"

If only she could tell him the truth. Why did women always have to wait for men to make the first move toward talking about love and marriage? It just didn't seem fair.

They stopped in front of the boardinghouse. The house was quiet and dark. Everyone living there had somewhere else to be tonight.

"I suppose we should start back toward your aunt and uncle's, but it's such a beautiful night, I hate to go in." With Elliot beside her, she had all the warmth she needed for the cold evening.

They walked a few more steps, then Elliot stopped and turned her around to face him. He held both her hands in his. The moon gave off just enough light to illuminate his face and the serious expression there.

Her heart skipped a beat. Was this the end instead of a beginning? Her throat tightened so she could barely swallow waiting for him to speak.

She watched as he pulled his shoulders up and stood to his full height at least a foot above hers. Then his hands squeezed hers in almost a grip of death. A shiver coursed through her veins.

"Abigail, you are the most wonderful girl."

He hesitated, and she waited for the "but" to follow. It didn't.

"I know I said we should learn more about each other, but I know everything I need to about you. You're fun, you're kind, you're hardworking, and you're brave."

He stopped again as though searching for words. Abigail's patience wore thin. She narrowed her eyes and looked up at him. "Elliot Jensen, do you love me?"

His head jerked back and his eyes opened wide. "Uh...yes...yes, I do love you. That's what I was trying to say."

At last. Excitement grew within her. Who said it was better to wait for him to speak? "And do you want to marry me?"

He laughed aloud. "Yes...yes...I want to marry you."

"And I want to marry you. Now was that so hard?" She lifted her chin and smiled. His eyes glimmered in the light.

"No, it was as easy as what I'm going to do now."

He bent his head and his lips brushed across hers, light as a feather then back again, a little more firmly this time. His grip on her hands loosened, and his arms came around her back to pull her against his chest. This time his lips met hers with such force that she flinched, but then she relaxed into the kiss that rocked her to her shoes and back again.

His heart beat in rhythm with hers as they savored the moment. Finally they parted, his breathing as labored as hers.

"Abigail Monroe, you are the most independent, forward woman I know, and I love you for it."

There, he'd spoken of love on his own this time. If she had any more happiness in her, she would absolutely burst.

His lips met hers again, and tears of pure joy stung her eyelids. Truly God had brought her to this place and to this man. And as she reveled in his kiss, she knew that this was a true beginning, a winter promise to carry her forward into the days and years to come.

Coming from Martha Rogers in May 2012,
book four of Seasons of the Heart—
Spring Hope

CHAPTER ONE

Porterfield, Texas, February 13, 1891

*T*HE COLDEST NIGHT of winter thus far chilled Deputy Sheriff Cory Muldoon to the bone as he made his rounds in the alleyways of Porterfield. Cold wind howled around the corners of the buildings now closed up for the night. Most everyone in Porterfield had gone home to their families and warm homes. This was all the winter he cared to experience, and even this would be only a few days as the weather in Texas could change in a heartbeat, summer or winter.

Lights and music from the saloon rang out and mocked the dark silence of its neighboring buildings. Friday nights found cowboys and lumberjacks both squandering their hard-earned money on liquor and women. Tonight would be no different despite the cold, near freezing temperatures. Most likely at least one or two of them would end up in the jail for a spell.

Cory turned up the collar of his sheepskin-lined jacket and shoved his hat farther down on his head. When he rounded the corner of the livery, the gentle nickering and snorts of the horses boarded there broke the quietness of the night.

A cat skittered out from behind the general store, and a dog barked in the distance. Ever since the bank robbery last fall, he or the sheriff had roamed the alleys behind the main businesses every night to make sure everything remained locked tight and secure. So far he'd seen only a typical Friday night with everything as routine as Aunt Mae's boardinghouse meal schedule. Of course, being Friday the thirteenth, anything could happen.

They already had two men put up for the night back at the jail. Sheriff Rutherford took the night duty to keep the jail cells warm so Cory could have Saturday off for his Aunt Mae's wedding. Ole Cooter probably got drunk and disorderly just so he'd have a warm place to sleep tonight and not have to go out to his shack. Cory held no blame on the man for that. Durand, the saloon owner, caught the other man cheating at cards and had him arrested. Maybe the card shark would move his game on to some other town.

Cory shivered despite the warm coat and hoped Abigail and Rachel would have dinner waiting for him back at the boardinghouse. What with Aunt Mae's wedding tomorrow, those two women had taken over mealtimes until his aunt returned from her wedding trip.

What appeared to be a pile of trash sat outside the back door of Grayson's mercantile. Ordinarily the store owner wouldn't leave a heap in the open like that. Cory hesitated in making an investigation, but the snuffling and nickering of a horse grabbed his attention. His hand caressed the handle of his gun. No one and no animal should be here this time of night.

The horse, a palomino, stood off to one side. He wore a saddle, but the reins dangled to the ground. Cory went on alert, his eyes darting about the alley in search of a rider. He reached for the reins and patted the horse's mane then ran his hand down its flank. "Whoa, boy, what are you doing out wandering around?" No brand on his hind quarters meant he didn't belong to a ranch around here, and Cory didn't recognize the horse as belonging to any of the townspeople.

The pile by the back door moved, and along with the movement, a moan sounded under it. With his hand on his gun, Cory approached the mound. An arm flung out from the heap, and another cry. This was no animal, and he knelt down to pull back what looked like an old quilt.

When the form of a young woman appeared, Cory jumped as though he'd been shot. Every nerve in his body stood at attention as he reached out to remove more of the cover. A woman lay huddled under the quilt, and her body shook from the cold while a cough wracked through her chest, followed by another cry.

On closer inspection he realized she was younger than he first thought. Her smooth, unlined face and tangled hair were that of a young woman. She couldn't be more than twenty, the same age as his sister Erin.

He bent over her to pick her up, and she started to scream, but another coughing spell prevented it. When her blue eyes peered up at him, they were so full of fear that they sent daggers of alarm straight to his soul. This girl was in trouble.

"Don't be afraid. I'm the deputy sheriff. I won't hurt you, but tell me your name and let me take you to the doctor." He pointed to his badge in hope of reassuring her.

Instead, her gaze darted back and forth as she pulled the blanket up under her chin. Her ungloved hands trembled with the cold. He removed his glove and reached out a hand to touch her forehead then yanked it back. She burned with fever.

"You're sick. We need you to get you to Doc Jensen's right away." He slid his hands beneath her to scoop her up into his arms. He almost lost his footing as he rose, thinking she'd be a heavier burden than she was. Light as a feather meant she was probably malnourished too.

She moaned against his chest. "I'm so cold."

Her voice, weak and hesitant, touched a nerve in him. He had to get her warm. Cory made sure the blanket covered her then grasped the horse's reins. A low whistle brought his own horse closer. "Follow us, Blaze. We're going to the infirmary.

He held the girl tight to his chest to transfer some of his warmth to her. The quicker he could get her to Doc, the quicker he could warm her up and treat that cough.

No time to worry about drunken cowboys or lumberjacks tonight.

The man who called himself a deputy carried her in his arms. With his gentle touch and voice, this man wasn't like others she had known. Her body burned with heat then turned ice cold with shivers. So much pain raked her body that she didn't have the strength to resist him anyway.

The man cradled her to his chest. "We'll be at Doc Jensen's in just a few minutes. Hang on, little lady."

Little lady? Little, maybe, but certainly no lady by his standards. Another cough wracked her chest and set her throat afire with pain. Her thin jacket and the quilt had been no match for the cold, especially after she'd crossed the river. There hadn't been enough heat in the day to dry her clothes before chilling her to the bone and causing this cough. She'd lost count of the days since she left home and had no idea how far she'd come. She'd avoided towns as much as possible, only entering long enough to pick up food at a mercantile.

Pa had to be on her trail by now, or he'd have others searching for her. Either way, she didn't plan to get caught and be dragged back to Louisiana. Even now the memory of all that she had endured because of Pa made her stomach wretch. She'd die before she let anyone take her back to that.

The man called for someone named Clem to go get the doc and he'd meet him at the infirmary. Maybe he was a sheriff after all since he was sending for help. She didn't dare open her eyes lest he see her fears again. Until she could be absolutely certain he meant her no harm, she'd stay still and quiet.

She inhaled the masculine scent of horses, sweat, and leather. He smelled like hard work and not a trace of alcohol. Unusual for a man, even a lawman. In the background raucous music came from a saloon. She'd recognize the tinny sound of saloon piano anywhere. It disappeared in the distance, and they proceeded down the street and up what felt like stairs or steps onto what must be boardwalk or porch.

He set her on her feet, and she peeped with one eye while he fumbled in his pocket then pulled out a ring of keys. In the next minute he had the door open and strode through it carrying her once again.

Antiseptics, alcohol, and carbolic acid greeted her nose. This must be the doctor's office. Not until he laid her on a hard surface did she open her eyes, half expecting him to be leering over her. Instead, he had walked away to light a lamp, which filled the room with flickering shadows dancing on the walls. A glass door cabinet stood against the wall, and another bed sat a few feet away from where she lay.

He returned to stand beside her, and she almost shrank in fear at his size. Well over six feet tall, he'd removed his hat to reveal a mass of dark red hair curling about his forehead. His hand caressed her forehead, but she did not flinch even though every inch of her wanted to. No need for him to know her fears.

"I see you're awake. The doc will be here in a minute. He'll fix you right up."

Instead of resisting, her body relaxed at the gentle tone of his voice. He certainly didn't fit her idea of a lawman or a cowboy. No one but her ma had ever treated her so kindly. Most people treated her like trash under their feet and didn't care whether she was well or sick. Still, he was a man. She had to be careful.

A woman's voice sounded, along with another man's. She turned her head to find a beautiful red-haired woman and an older man entering the room.

The one who must be the doctor stepped to her side. "Well, Cory, what have we here?" His eyes held only concern and kindness behind his wire-rimmed glasses.

"I found her in the alley behind the general store. She must have come in on horseback and fallen there."

The woman brushed hair from her face. "Can you tell us your name?"

Her heart thumped. What if Pa came looking for her? But if she lied and stayed here, she'd have to keep lying. Another fit of coughing had the woman holding her upright and rubbing her back. When the spell ended, she whispered her name. "Elizabeth Bradley."

The woman helped her lie back down. "Hello, Elizabeth. I'm Kate Monroe, the doc's nurse, and this fellow who brought you in is my brother Cory. He's deputy sheriff in town."

Just having her there gave Libby a sense of safety she needed with two men in the room. Her kind eyes, a green color that reminded Libby of the fake emeralds some of the saloon girls wore, had a tender look to them.

The doctor listened to her chest with a funny-looking bell on something hanging from his ears. He frowned then pulled the contraption down around his neck. "I hear a lot of congestion in your lungs, young lady. How long have you been in the cold?"

"I don't know. I think it's been several days. I left home in the middle of the night on Tuesday." The days and nights had run together as she lost all track of time.

The doctor shook his head. "This is Friday night, so you've been out at least three days. No wonder your lungs are so congested." He turned to the one called Kate. "Get a bed ready for her. She's staying the night, and maybe longer."

Libby tried to sit up but began coughing again. She couldn't stay here. Pa would find her. Her destination had been to head west then south where the winter temperatures were not as severe. She'd lost all sense of direction after the first night and had no idea which way she'd come.

Kate's warm hands pushed her back down, gently but firmly. "Lie still, Elizabeth. The doctor is right; you have to stay here."

Tears welled in Libby's eyes, and she squeezed them tight to keep them from falling. Though hard, this bed was so much better than the ground where she'd slept the past nights. Hospitals and doctors cost money. That's why Pa wouldn't go for the doctor until Ma was too sick to recover.

The doctor gave her something that tasted bitter, but she swallowed it and then lay back against the pillow Kate had placed beneath her head. The low murmur of voices ran together in a blur. One of the men said he'd stay, but the other one said something about a wedding. Who was getting married? Maybe they'd forget about her.

The tension ebbed from her body as the medication took over. Someone, most likely Cory since the doctor was an old man, picked her up and took her into another room where he laid her on the bed. She almost sighed at the cotton softness of the mattress beneath her. So much better than pine straw and hard-packed dirt.

Kate's voice followed behind then shooed the man from the room. "I'm going to help her get settled for the night, so she doesn't need you. Go on back to the boardinghouse. I'm sure you'll find Abigail has something for you to eat."

A few minutes later Kate had removed Libby's still damp and dirty clothes and slipped a warm gown over her head.

When Libby slid her arms into the sleeves, she realized it was her own gown. "How did you get this? It's mine."

"Cory brought in the satchel you carried on your horse, and I found the gown in it. I warmed it by the wood stove in the other room."

That warmth along with the medication earlier eased away the pain, and Libby let her eyes drift closed. Perhaps this was the place she should stay after all. She pulled up the covers and turned on her side. She'd think about that tomorrow. Tonight she'd sleep warm and dry for the first time in too many days to count.

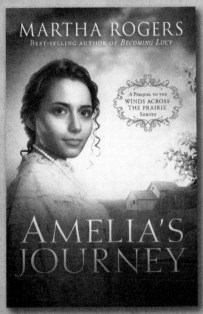

FREE NEWSLETTERS
TO HELP EMPOWER YOUR LIFE

Why subscribe today?

❑ **DELIVERED DIRECTLY TO YOU.** All you have to do is open your inbox and read.

❑ **EXCLUSIVE CONTENT.** We cover the news overlooked by the mainstream press.

❑ **STAY CURRENT.** Find the latest court rulings, revivals, and cultural trends.

❑ **UPDATE OTHERS.** Easy to forward to friends and family with the click of your mouse.

CHOOSE THE E-NEWSLETTER THAT INTERESTS YOU MOST:

- Christian news
- Daily devotionals
- Spiritual empowerment
- And much, much more

SIGN UP AT: **http://freenewsletters.charismamag.com**

8178